MW00413725

PICTURES OF A DYING MAN

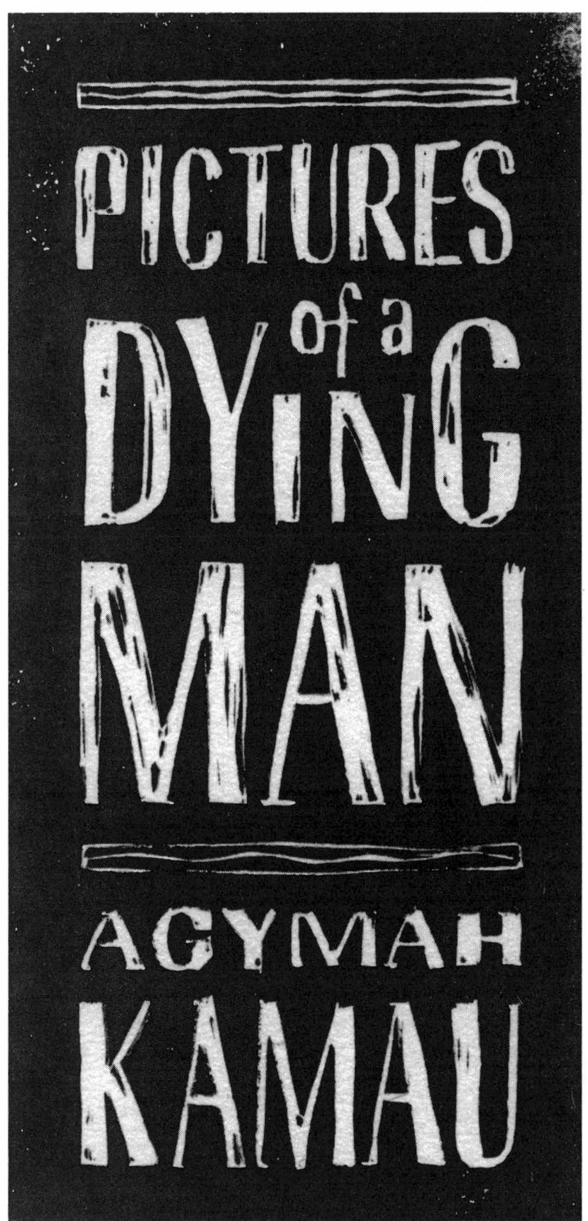

COFFEE HOUSE PRESS :: MINNEAPOLIS

COVER DESIGN & ART: Kelly N. Kofron
BOOK DESIGN: Kelly N. Kofron
AUTHOR PHOTOGRAPH: Sandra Sellars

AUTHOR'S NOTE: Deepest appreciation to everyone at Centrum and Ucross for your hospitality and gift of solitude that were immeasurable aids in the process of writing this account of the life of Gladstone Augustus Belle. The spirit of Mr. Belle thanks you and I thank you. Thanks also to the Virginia Commission for the Arts for financial support given when most needed.

Coffee House Press is an independent nonprofit literary publisher supported in part by a grant provided by the Minnesota State Arts Board, through an appropriation by the Minnesota State Legislature, and in part by a grant from the National Endowment for the Arts. Significant support has also been provided by The McKnight Foundation; Lannan Foundation; The Lila Wallace Readers Digest Fund; Jerome Foundation; Target Stores, Dayton's, and Mervyn's by the Dayton Hudson Foundation; General Mills Foundation; St. Paul Companies; Butler Family Foundation; Honeywell Foundation; Star Tribune Foundation; James R. Thorpe Foundation; the Bush Foundation.; the law firm of Schwegman, Lundberg, Woessner & Kluth, P.A.; and many individual donors. To you and our many readers across the country, we send our thanks for your continuing support.

Coffee House Press books are available to the trade through our primary distributor, Consortium Book Sales & Distribution, 1045 Westgate Drive, Saint Paul, MN 55114. For personal orders, catalogs, or other information, write to: Coffee House Press, 27 North Fourth Street, Suite 400, Minneapolis, MN 55401.

Good books are brewing at coffeehousepress.org.

LIBRARY OF CONGRESS CIP INFORMATION
Kamau, Kwadwo Agymah,
Pictures of a dying man:novel / by Kamau, Agymah.
p. cm.
ISBN 1-56689-087-X (alk. paper)
1. West Indian Americans—New York (State)—New York Fiction.
I. Title.
PR9230.0K36P5 1999
813—dc21 99-35461
CIP

10 9 8 7 6 5 4 3 2 1
first printing / first edition

Dedicated to Earnest C. Turner,
friend, neighbor, and true gentleman,
who departed on May 30, 1999,
and to all those who have passed on
but whose lives are beacons for us all to follow.

Following is the story of Gladstone Augustus Belle quilted from excerpts extracted from his journals, which he kept religiously until the day he died, as well as from the accounts of those who knew him, some of whom have since died while others to this day bear me deep resentment, even enmity.

My mother would've said, I told you so, because over the years we'd become accustomed to this reaction from neighbors who, because of my evident gift of empathy, unburden into my ears their most intimate secrets and deepest troubles. Always she would say she don't know why I don't put the gift I have to good use and write a column like Dear Suzy. Charge people she'd say.

Now I've taken her advice.

But two months almost to the day of Gladstone's death my mother passed away. Now it's months later, and her absence still pervades the house, so much so that often a sound, a movement of the air, an intuition, causes me to turn expecting to see her as she appears in my dreams at night—vivid, vital, no longer the annoyance I often thought she was.

But she is gone. And with each false intuition of her presence comes growing consciousness of love I always must have felt but which surfaces now with awareness as bitter as aloes and useless as a cripple's limbs, awareness of love mutually uncultivated and obscured by quarrels, adolescent tug-of-wars that extended into adulthood, and discord that seems trivial now but which flourished with the virulence of wild and choking weeds.

Mumah is dead. And only now have I begun to appreciate that surely there were reasons why it seemed not to be in her nature to coo and cuddle, reasons that I may have come in time to understand. Now it's too late.

So now I miss her with the frustrating impotence of love discovered after death.

It is partly for this reason that I resolved to find an answer to the question: who was my childhood friend Gladstone Augustus Belle?

One final note. Occasionally in the interest of continuity I did take dramatic license, as they say, and embellish to round out and add flavor to the tale. But these embellishments are minuscule and few and in no way detract from the veracity of the story.

So to you Mumah, wherever you are, I hope that you approve.

I

Opinions are like genitals—everyone has them. So, though no one knew why Gladstone Augustus Belle slung a rope around a ceiling joist in his bedroom and hanged himself, everyone had an opinion on the matter.

No one knows the reasons or the circumstances, but there is one point on which everyone agrees: it was a beautiful day, certainly not a day one would ordinarily choose for death.

Midmorning. School childrens' singsong voices drifting through the windows of the schoolhouse on cool breezes that rustled the tree leaves, caressed women's thighs, rippled their frocks and brought sighs to everyone's lips—everyone except Gladstone Augustus Belle. Midmorning, when Isamina Belle, wearing a thin-strapped, black-and-white polka-dot dress and high-heel shoes, left home, headed toward the main road where the hawkers had already set up their trays along the roadside ever since disembarking from the country lorries at sunup; Isamina on her way to purchase provisions to prepare her last meal for her and her husband, she said later.

Yes, it was midmorning with the fragrant steam of hot cocoa bathing my face as I sipped from my enamel cup as through my front window I enjoyed the rhythm of Isamina Belle's buttocks undulating as she passed by.

Midmorning when after returning from a short stroll taken to inhale the freshness of the air I noticed my mother standing still and holding her dust rag motionless on the back of the mahogany rocking chair listening to some distant sound audible only to her ears and instantly I knew that as sure as steam rises from a hot, tar road after a sudden tropical shower I was about to hear one of her dramatic, prescient pronouncements: somebody sick, somebody dead, an accident just happened or is about to occur, a tragedy has struck, a cataclysm about to erupt. A regular psychic, my mother is.

And no sooner do these thoughts enter my head than, "Gladstone just dead," she says, all the while fixing me with one of her accusing stares.

Inwardly I'm saying, Oh Lord, but aloud my only response is, "Yeah?"

Because how else can one respond to a woman standing in the middle of her house staring into space then announcing that somebody somewhere else just died?

I'm a schoolteacher, perhaps not the best educated of persons. But one thing education has given me is a fair dose of skepticism. Which often tends to put me at odds with friends, neighbors, and of course Mumah who is giving me this look as though I've just bashed in the head of a crippled infant—because of the skepticism she has read in my face, I surmise.

But surmising can lead you down the wrong track sometimes, because instead of commenting on my disbelief she's asking me, "What that boy ever do you, eh? What Gladstone ever do you?"

I'm puzzled.

And she continues, "Why you so bad-minded?" A rhetorical question, I assume; because she's going on about how grudgeful-minded I am. "Since you was small," she's saying, talking about how she carried me nine months inside her belly but she got to say it: "You hate to see people do better than you." (Which, I must tell you, isn't true.) And she's pausing and then asking as if it's one of the great puzzles in the universe, "Why you so, eh? Why you like that?" and shaking her head in deep befuddlement. "You en get it from me," she's saying. "And your father, God rest him in his grave, wasn't like that. Here it is I tell you a man dead and all you can say is 'yeah'?"

Gradually I'm beginning to get my bearings. Mumah—always able to find something good to say about even the most evil of persons, her motto being, "If you can't say something good about somebody, don't say nothing at all," a philosophy that I'd come to realize excluded both me and my father. I always believed that it was her constant nagging that killed him. Natural causes? She was the natural cause, or so I used to think.

So there she is saying in one breath that Gabby just died and in the same breath accusing me of . . . what? Indifference perhaps? Indifference to an event that, as far as I knew, had occurred only in her mind? I shrugged figuring, What's the use?

"I think we should go and see what happening," she says.

And instantly dread is a leaden weight settling in my stomach; because superstition, no matter how firmly dispatched, no matter how deeply buried, is like a restless spirit that often will arise and cause even confirmed atheists to appeal to nonexistent deities ("Oh Jesus Christ!" they will yell, or "Lord have mercy!" they will bawl) when staring eyeball-to-eyeball with death.

Such was my predicament that morning.

Because, you see, it is one thing to entice a woman's fidelity away from her man, especially if that man is someone you disliked since childhood. But to hear your mother say that this same man is dead? Well, that's another matter entirely. Because what if by the most extraordinary coincidence she was right? What if he had committed suicide and his wife's infidelity with me was the cause? That's a heavy burden for anyone to bear.

So I'm trying to hold on to skepticism that is as fragile as the bravado of a terrified man in a cemetery at midnight, because I cannot deny that there were times my mother talked about things before they happened, like the day she turned to Pa and said, "Sheila dying," whereupon she put on her shoes and walked over to her best friend's house only to see Sheila lying dead on her bed when she opened the front door and went in.

According to her, Sheila appeared before her while she was sitting at the table picking rice and said, "I gone, Esther." Clear as day.

Now I know what you're saying and what I probably would say were I in your place. Shit or get off the pot; believe or don't believe. But you think it's easy, eh? You think it's easy?

I don't know what expression my face wore that morning, what caused my mother to stare at me, suck her teeth, shake her head, and say under her breath, "You young generation" before ordering me to "Come along. Let we go over there and see what happening."

"Come! Hurry up!" she said. "God forbid you might learn something with your unbelieving self."

And with that she slipped on a pair of my father's old shoes that she'd turned into slipslots by mashing down the heels, and strode to the door.

As soon as we got outside and I looked down the road toward Gladstone's bungalow and saw Gladstone stepping from his front door I relaxed.

"Well, look like you were wrong . . . ," I begin to say but am interrupted by a sharp "Shhh!" from Mumah at the same moment that a gray-haired lady whom I could have sworn was Gabby's grandmother comes out of the house behind him—old Miss Mimi who'd died and left her property for Gabby. Except that number one, Miss Mimi is long dead and buried and two, this old lady is walking upright and not bent over walking with a cane like Miss Mimi used to do.

As warm as the sun was that morning a shiver shook my body as it suddenly occurred to me that I'd just seen both Gladstone and Miss Mimi walk through the front door. Not the doorway, the *door.* A *closed* door. And Miss Mimi is descending the front steps holding Gabby's hand and walking down the gap toward us with Gabby staring straight ahead with his eyes focused on some spot in the distance while Miss Mimi is contemplating my mother eyeball-to-eyeball with a slightly smiling expression as though it's the most natural thing in the world for a jumbie to be walking in broad daylight and greeting living human beings. And I'm so wrapped in the surrealism of the moment that as they're getting close I raise my arm and open my mouth but can only manage to say, "Ga . . ." before my mother snatches down my arm and snaps, "Don't touch him," wrenching me back to reality and making a U-turn still holding my arm and pivoting me with her so that we're headed back in the direction of our house. I can sense Gabby and Miss Mimi right behind us.

"Don't look back!" Mumah's voice is a hiss.

One day a few weeks later as we are recollecting the event I chuckle and say, "What would've happened if I'd turned around and looked back, eh? Think I would've turned into a pillar of salt? Heh heh heh." My mother just stares at me and says, *"Now* you bad, eh? *Now* you got a lot of mouth, eh? Why you didn't say that *then?"*

Touché. Because on the morning of the event I couldn't have uttered a word even if the thought had occurred to me.

My mother's firm grip on my arm kept me moving.

After a while I felt her release my arm. "Go on," she said. "You can look back now if you want."

I turned and looked over my shoulder.The road was as empty as a virgin's womb.

I stopped, my belly a yawning void, my mouth as dry as chalk.

And the day suddenly had a different feel to it as if everything had stopped moving and every sound was coming to me as through a funnel: a barking dog, a crying infant, the *fwap fwap fwap* of clothes on a clothesline whipped by the breeze, the *hooot hooot* of a train whistle far away.

"He dead," my mother said, and her voice came to my ears as from a distance like the hooting of the train whistle.

When we reached our house and my mother turned to go inside I kept walking. To calm the turmoil in my head.

"Where you going?" she asked me.

"To the beach," I said.

Right away she says, "Wait. Let me go with you."

"I'll be all right, Mumah," I told her. She could be so protective sometimes. I kept walking.

The surface of the sea was as smooth as glistening glass. Breezes rustled the coconut tree limbs overhead and I watched sea bathers submerged shoulder-high and chatting, some swimming in solitary early-morning exercise as I wondered whether Gabby had discovered that his wife had been two-timing him and the person she'd been doing it with was me.

Just then in the freshness of morning came Gladstone strolling up the beach, hands in his pants pockets, head down. And if I was at all hesitant to acknowledge it before I knew for certain then that Gabby was dead as I watched him vanish as if entering an invisible door there in broad daylight, looking over his shoulder at me with a gaze that continues to be the last image before my eyes at night, a gaze that haunts my nightmares, a gaze of accusation.

But that morning, sitting at the foot of a coconut tree, I found myself thinking of the last day Gladstone and I spent at that same beach as childhood friends umpteen years ago.

We had the day off from school—the Queen was visiting the country—and Gabby and I were just about to leave his mother's house for the beach. But before we could reach the door Miss Esther stopped him with, "Gladstone, where you going?"

"To the beach, Ma," he said.

"Look, go and change them pants," she's telling him. "You expect to traipse all the way to the beach with that old pants that frizzling out in the seat? You just pass for secondary school. You got to start holding up your head."

"But Ma, this is the pants that I always does bathe in," Gabby says. "What wrong with it? Look at Vic pants."

Actually they were my brother's pants.

Miss Esther is glancing at me and cutting her eyes in an expression that clearly says that mine is not exactly the kind of example she wants Gabby to follow, for more reasons than one, and she tells Gabby, "Look, go and change your pants. You en got no pride?"

Funny how details can survive in memory: the village quiet as a ghost town with almost everyone on the main road waiting for the Queen's motorcade to pass on the way to Government House; the searing heat of the overhead sun; the only sounds in the air—a cock crowing somewhere in somebody's yard, water gushing into a bucket under the standpipe down the gap, the *paks!* of dominoes slamming on a table under the umbrella shade of the evergreen tree next to the rumshop; Gabby and I approaching the standpipe with the sound of water gushing into Miss Crawford's bucket almost drowning out her voice and Miss Taylor standing next to her with her face sour as usual and with her bucket dangling from an arm so fat it filled the sleeve of her blouse.

Gabby and I said Good day.

Miss Crawford returned the greeting and asked us where we going in this hot sun.

Miss Crawford—she's dead now, God rest her in her grave—a woman who always had a smile and a pleasant thing to say. Didn't mind the children coming into her yard and picking the gooseberries off her tree, "As long as you don't leave my yard dirty," she would always say.

But Miss Taylor? A different story. Bad-minded. That day staring at Gabby and me as if we'd committed some grave offense simply by being children, dropping remarks about little vagabonds always running about with their backside at the door like their ass is a movie picture or some kind of entertainment people want to see. Some people don't know how to dress their children right, she's saying. Encouraging all kind of iniquity. Sodom and Gomorrah, is what the world coming to. Sodom and Gomorrah.

And I'm itching to give her a piece of my mind. Why don't you mind your big, fat business? I want to say, knowing the remarks she's dropping are aimed at me. But I remain silent, restrained by the cut-ass I knew would be waiting for me when I returned home, no matter how wrong she was. That's the way it was then; not like now when children talk back to grown-ups as if they are equals.

When we reached the main road Gabby asked me if I had my uniform and books yet.

I remember taking a little time before answering, "I en going to high school."

Gabby stopped. "What you mean you en going?"

I couldn't tell him that from the minute we got the news that I'd passed, my father tried everything to come up with the money to buy uniform and textbooks and pay school fees but everybody had a hard-luck story—even Pa's rum-drinking friends. *Especially* his rum-drinking friends, according to my mother. Everybody kept saying they wished they could lend him the money but they didn't have it. Even Uncle Fitz, my father's brother, saying how he catching hell too but giving my father a whole bag of sweet potatoes and yams to bring home, which made my mother grumble, wanting to know what we going do with a whole bag of ground provisions, eh? Sell it and pay school fees? And Pa defending his brother, telling my mother don't be ungrateful, Uncle Fitz give them what he can afford. And my mother beginning to answer back that she en know what that cheap old billy goat saving up his money for because he en got chick nor child and somebody going wait till he get pissy and dotish in his old age and rob every cent from him and it going serve him right. . . . But Pa butting in right there and saying, All right! All right! He en want to hear no more bad talk about his family. And my mother mumbling under her breath, What kind of family it is that so stingy? And Pa bawling how he en see her family helping, eh! He en see them helping!

Even Mr. Bailey that owned the cement warehouse Pa used to work at refused to lend him the money, saying, "How you going pay me back, eh? And what going happen next term? Borrow again? Besides," he said, "business tight."

For as long as I could remember, Gabby and I always talked about going to secondary school. We went to private lessons at Mr. Gittens on evenings after school; took the eleven-plus exam together, and the postman delivered the letters from the Ministry of Education the same day, causing Miss Esther to run over to our house and she and my mother jumping up and down saying, "They pass! They pass!"

But gradually two things began to eat away at the happiness in our house. Number one, I didn't pass for Wilberforce, the premier high school; I passed for Drakes Secondary, which is for those who passed the exam but not with top marks. Secondly, it appeared that without a scholarship even Drakes was out of the question.

Of course, I didn't tell all of this to Gabby when he asked me what I meant by I'm not going to high school. Instead I snapped "Everybody en pass for Wilberforce with a scholarship, you know. Everybody en lucky like you!"

Later I learned about the letter Gabby's parents got at the last minute informing them that Gabby hadn't received a scholarship after all. A mistake had been made. But that happened a few weeks later.

We reached the beach curving like a half-moon toward the lighthouse at Bingham's Point. Children were off from school because of the Queen's visit, splashing in the water, lying on the sand, poking into crab holes, tumbling and shrieking in the waves; I remember two men jogging toward the lighthouse (I remember thinking that they were tourists because back then jogging wasn't fashionable as it is now, and people used to think it was a big joke to see foreigners running, puffing and blowing, with no place to go); I could see heads far out between the yachts at anchor, floating and bobbing like buoys.

To the right, behind the barbed wire fence, oily-skinned whitepeople lay with their skins glistening in the sun; waiters weaved between beach chairs and blankets balancing trays on their palms; a whitechild tumbled after a red-and-blue beachball that was nearly as big as he was; two boys about the same age as Gabby and me, one a backra with sand-colored hair, the other brown-skinned with dark-brown curls were patting the sand into a sand castle; on the patio of the yacht club, grown-ups, some in pants-and-shirt, suits, dresses, others in bathing suits, some black, some white, a couple of Indian-looking ones, were chatting and drinking just like the people in the rum advertisements that come on the screen before the movie pictures at the Royale Theatre.

Gabby and I waded around the fence and the sign that read,

KEEP OFF THE BEACH
PROPERTY OF THE YACHT CLUB
TRESPASSERS WILL BE PROSECUTED

But as we splashed through the waves to keep away from the beach, keeping our eyes out for the watchman and his stick, I heard, "Hey you!" The backra boy with the sand-colored hair. "What you doing here?" he wanted to know.

I stopped. "You want to do something about it?" I asked him.

Gabby squared his shoulders and said, "Yeah! You want to fight? Come out here if you bad!"

The backra boy looked at his brown-skinned friend, stood up and began running toward the club, leaving the brown-skinned boy kneeling and dribbling wet sand through his fingers and staring at Gabby and me like a watchdog guarding us from running away till the whiteboy came back.

"I think he gone for the watchman," Gabby said and took off bird-speed, splashing onto the beach and running toward the other fence that boxed off the yacht club beach, kicking up sand behind him as he's running.

At the same time the watchman comes rushing from the side of the yacht club with a big stick raised in the air and hollering, "Get off! Get off this beach!" Like it was his beach.

What an ass. Some of those whitepeople probably were tourists and we always were told to "Keep away from tourists. Them tourists have diseases." We wouldn't have stayed on that beach anyway.

Years later when the barbed wire fence came down (by then Gladstone was minister of tourism and culture and first thing he did was to issue a ministerial order outlawing private beaches and requiring public access), I lay on that same beach and saw the same watchman with his back bent, hair now gray, picking up trash—sweet-drink bottles, paper, used condoms—an old man with a shame-faced look, eyes downcast and not looking into my face, the same man who always used to chase us with his stick.

And that day years later as I'm lying there watching him, a group of young boys stopped and a little runty one in the group hollered, "Hey! Watchy!" while the other boys flung a hail of pebbles at the old man, with one of them shouting, "Where your stick now, Watchy?"

And the old man raised his arm to shield his face, then lunged as if to chase them. But he didn't. His authority had been stripped away.

And sitting there on the beach that day it occurred to me that for this bare-headed old man wearing khaki short pants and canvas-and-rubber-tire zapats on his feet, independence was a windy storm that whipped his authority away and left him naked to the jeers and stones of little boys. But I couldn't feel sorry for him for long, the son of a bitch. He got what he deserved, because here was a man who took out his dick to piss on people and the wind changed, blowing the piss right back in his face.

Anyway, on the day when the Queen was visiting and the watchman chased us, Gabby and I didn't stop running till we reached about halfway between the yacht club and the fish market. We dropped our shirts under a manchineel tree and bent over, catching our breath.

The sunlight was like sparkling jewels on the surface of the sea.

Out in the harbor, huge cargo ships sat like dark sea monsters.

A motorboat roared past not far offshore, trailing a woman on skis and a plume of spray and spreading swells that rocked the fishing boats at anchor.

That day Gabby and I swam out to the fishing boats, dove for sea eggs and ate them raw, built a sand castle, climbed one of the coconut trees for coconuts. It was a good day. And while we lay on the sand we noticed some boys playing cricket down near the fish market.

Gabby said, "Leh we go for a play."

But I said no. I didn't feel like playing cricket. As usual I was feeling good just lying on the sand with the sun turning the water on my skin to salt.

I watched the fellas taking turns batting, bowling, and fielding. I couldn't help but laugh when Gabby dropped the bat and flung his arms in the air disgusted after he got bowled out, the ball whizzing between the two upright wicket sticks behind him.

I smiled when Gabby dove like a professional cricketer to catch a ball then threw it up in the air hollering, "You out! You out!" and grinned at me excited because he'd caught the ball and out the boy that hit it (Gabby was one of the clumsiest boys in the village, always dropping the ball, so this was a special achievement for him that day).

I waved back and smiled but he'd already turned back to the game. My friend. I'd known him all my life, it seemed. We were even born in the same month. But until that day I'd never really thought of him as my friend before—he just was.

But as I was soon to discover, friendships are as impermanent as shifting sand.

As I sat on the beach on the morning of Gladstone's death mourning the long-ago loss of a childhood friendship, Isamina Belle too was making a discovery.

ISAMINA BELLE

As Isamina Belle confided later, when she stepped in her front door and saw her husband hanging from a rope tied to a joist, with his head bowed as if in prayer and his feet dangling inches from the floor, the first thing she did was to hasten and fling open all of the windows in the house.

And with the cleansing breeze whipping the window curtains and riffling the pages of a magazine on the center table, she held a handkerchief to her nose and stared at her husband dangling by a rope and thought, what a trickster life is, eh—always springing surprises on you. Because here was Gladstone, a fussy man, compulsively clean, showering twice, sometimes three times a day and with the whiff of cologne surrounding him like an ever-present shield, yet here he was stinking up the house with the shit that stained the seat of his pants and dripped from his heel.

A meticulous man who planned every detail of this house years ago, so that on the final day after the workmen packed their tools and were walking out the door and she asked the foreman if he was finished and he said yes, she looked up at the exposed rafters. What about these? she asked him. The bossman say leave them like that, he said. That evening when Gladstone came home he looked up at the exposed rafters and joists with his hands in his pockets and told her yes, the foreman was right; he didn't want any ceiling. A fleeting frown of puzzlement wrinkled her brow but she let the subject flutter to the ground, not wanting to start an argument. They were newly married then.

These thoughts are streaming through her head as she fixes her gaze on Gladstone swinging from the rafters that the painter had stained and varnished a gleaming mahogany brown thereby causing her to see the beauty in what she'd at first considered an eccentric idea. And over the years she'd come to enjoy the unmuffled symphony of raindrops pattering on the galvanized zinc roof and the coziness the sound brought to the house, particularly on rainy nights.

She even found herself defending this feature of her home against critics like her father who, in that redleg, country way of his that would surface every now and then, wanted to know if Gladstone "run out of money before the house finish." She said no, they liked it like that. But he stared at her with an expression that told her he didn't believe her and later when she was leaving he offered to lend her some money if she and Gladstone were having a hard time. Don't be too proud to ask, you know, he told her. That is what fathers are for.

Most of their guests would glance at the unceilinged roof but would usually keep their mouths politely shut, although once at a party Courtney Walcott, then minister of labor, had too much to drink and flung his arm around Gladstone's shoulder and drawled out loud, "Wha happen here, boy? Plan to HANG YOURSELF? Haw haw haw haw hawwww!"

And another time, Susan Baptiste who was a radio announcer at the time (before she got the job as public relations officer for the prime minister), just fresh back from Canada, looked up at the varnished rafters with a rum-and-coke glass in hand and said in the loud, freshwater-Yankee voice she brought back with her from Canada (after only four years in the place, mind you), "I *love* this! Chic! Trés chic!" and Isamina is thinking, What a stupid bitch, while Susan Baptiste is going on with, "Was this your idea, Gladstone?"

But before Isamina could snap an answer back at the short, pretentious little bitch with her tight, knee-length dress and round, metal-framed glasses who Isamina could see had an eye on her husband, Gladstone walked over and rested his hand on Isamina's shoulder and said, "No. It was *our* idea," which wasn't true but it shut the little bitch up.

But those were the early days.

Now here he was dangling from a rope lashed around one of the same joists he was so proud of.

———

As the old people say, who feels it knows. Nobody can understand, unless they travel that road, how it feels to step through the front door of your house on an ordinary day, out of the morning sun and a cool breeze, into a silent house stinking of shit and before your eyes is the man you've lived with for twenty-odd years hanging from the roof with the seat of his pants stained and damp, a chair lying on the floor with its legs in the air like a dead fowl-cock, and a pile of soft shit spread like a pancake on the floor below his feet.

To this day, all Isamina remembers is a voice in her head saying, Call the police. She remembers turning and walking out of the house, through the village, down to the police station on the main road with the sunlight warm on her face.

She can't tell you who she passed on the road or who was in the police station besides Sergeant Straker hunched over at the desk writing in a notebook.

She remembers the rasp of his pen scratching the page, him dampening his fingertip with his tongue and flipping the page then looking up at her with his glasses scotched near the end of his nostrils and saying, "Yes?"

"My husband messed himself," she remembers saying.

Perhaps the constable came into the room then; perhaps he was there all along—she can't recall. But she heard a snicker and saw standing in the doorway behind the sergeant a tall, dark-skinned young policeman wearing a dazzling white, starched tunic with no belt, smiling with his eyes shifted to the ground, not meeting hers, as is often the case with these common-class people around here.

"Okay," Sergeant Straker said. "Start again. Why Mr. Belle mess himself?"

"He kicked over the chair," she said.

"He kick over the chair." Sergeant Straker's face had the blank expression you see on the faces of people who're trying hard not to laugh. "All right," he said after a while.

The constable blew his nose.

"Why he kick over the chair?" the sergeant asked her.

"To hang himself."

It was only after the mortuary van drove away with her husband's body that it occurred to Isamina that she could've called the police from at home on the telephone.

All of a sudden the very air in the house felt heavy with the emptiness of her husband's absence.

But her eyes remained dry. Because, though pain can be vented with the warm flow of your tears, very often grief can remain a frozen lump in the far reaches of your soul.

So from the day Gabby hanged himself to the day of the funeral two days later, Isamina went about her duties cleaning the house, sweeping the yard, washing her clothes and Gladstone's things and hanging them on the line and, after the postmortem, making arrangements for the funeral with the undertaker, the minister, the cemetery.

All of this helped to calm her and keep her eyes dry, so much so that the neighbors began to gossip, saying things like:

—*How she can act so like nothing en happen?*

—*Is like she couldn't wait for him to dead, yes.*

—*She could at least* ACT *like she grieving, eh?*

But gossip is like a bee flitting from flower to flower in search of nectar.

SONNY-BOY

So it was that the day after Gladstone Belle died, when a taxi stopped in front of the house where he'd grown up, the wooden house where his mother still lived, gossip shifted from the deceased former deputy prime minister and his widow and lit on the man who got out of the backseat of a taxi and stood waiting while the driver hefted a suitcase from the trunk of the car, an elderly man dressed in shiny black pants, a short-sleeved plaid shirt with a buttoned-down collar and a brown felt hat.

—*Who that?*

—*Well, well, well, look my crosses. It is Sonny-Boy!*

—*Sonny who?*

—*Sonny-Boy. Gladstone father.*

—*Sonny-Boy? Sonny-Boy that living in Away all these donkey years? Look like Away en do a thing for him. Looka him. In shirt-and-pants like if he just went down the road for a walk. And one stinking suitcase.*

And so on it went, with one person saying how he musta ship a barrel separate and another voice chiming in wanting to know what barrel? Sonny-Boy was always cheap and stingy from since he was small, so it shouldn't surprise nobody that he would come back after all these donkey years and not bring back even a kerchief for nobody.

Sonny-Boy took his suitcase and walked toward the house he left so many years before, wondering if this really was the house he, Esther, and Gladstone used to live in. The gad daim thing was smaller than his garage back in Florida. The whole gad daim country had shrunk while he was away.

Driving from the airport, roads that he could swear used to be major highways now were so gad daim narrow and winding that he sat in the backseat of the car gripping the armrest on the door and expecting a gad daim head-on collision any blinking minute fuh Christ sake. When the taxi driver had to pull into the gutter so that the bus coming toward them could squeeze by, he asked the taxi driver, "They using bigger buses over here now, eh pardner?"

To which the taxi driver sucked his teeth and Sonny-Boy could see the scorn in the man's eyes in the rearview mirror and he imagined the taxi driver calling him all kind of chigger-foot country buck who come back acting as if he is a tourist.

But he, Sonny-Boy, wasn't pretending, not like his friend Clement sister (Joan, her name was) who went away for a fourteen-day vacation years back and came home asking in a Yankee accent, "Where is the feesh mawket?" The fish wha? people asking. And even Clement laughing at his own sister to see how stupid she behaving. And Sonny-Boy chuckling now at that long-ago memory. No. He wasn't like that. The place really looked small.

The taxi turned off the highway and for a moment he thought the driver had the wrong address, because before his eyes was a collection of small houses huddled higgledy-piggledy and separated by alleyways where half-naked children ran around yelling and playing, fowls scratched in the dirt, and mangy dogs and hungry-looking cats looked as if the hot sun had drained all the energy from their scrawny bodies. This wasn't the village he left twenty-odd years ago. Couldn't be.

Because this village main road that was a good-sized highway in his memory now had shrunk to the size of the alley behind his house in Florida, an alley barely wide enough for the garbage trucks that came every Friday.

He looked through the car window up at the Springers' house on the hill high above the village and remembered leaving nearly thirty years ago intending to save some money and come back and build a similar (but bigger) mansion nearby on the same hill (so the Springers could see is not only them could live in big house, yes), where he would come out on his balcony in his robe just like a movie star and look down on the village where he used to live, and enjoy a life of tropical retirement with Esther.

But now it's not the wonderment of old that he's feeling but shock as he stares at the pitiful little cream-colored bungalow perched on the hill with its open carport (shit, even *he* had an enclosed garage . . . and he didn't have no gad daim car), probably no more than three small bedrooms, living room, and kitchen, and he's realizing that his house in the States is bigger than this gad daim mansion he'd carried around in his memory all these gad daim years.

As you can tell, "gad daim" were the favorite words Sonny-Boy brought back with him and became the legacy he left behind, with little children running around saying gad daim this and gad daim that for weeks after he left.

In that moment looking up at the Springers' house on the hill, Sonny-Boy's mind was not on legacies as he felt behind his eyes and in his chest such a deep sense of loss that if he wasn't a man he would've allowed the tears to pour from his eyes right there.

All these years while he was away this was the place he knew he would be coming back to some day. Home. All these years he refused to apply for American citizenship, hanging on to his identity, his memory of home. I ain't no minority, he would always insist. He noticed that sometimes this would piss off people, especially when he added half-jokingly, I have a country. But he didn't care. He rejected the inferiority the word minority implied. And he did have a country.

But now here he was, back for his son's funeral, and it was like visiting a foreign land. It would've been better if he hadn't come back at all. Then at least his village would have been preserved in his memory, remaining as it was when he left. But here he was looking around at a strange, small place that wasn't home. This wasn't the country he left years ago and stored in his memory all this time.

With suitcase still in hand, he walked around the house to the backyard and gazed at the lush green of the fruit trees on the slope of the hill behind the house he'd helped build, and at the cultivated plot at the bottom of the valley that Esther farmed and which he helped her with a little bit until he left for America (Miss Esther will tell you different), but which Esther now tended by herself (she will tell you that was always the case).

At least, everything down in this small ravine that in his memory had been a vast verdant valley looked the same as he had left it, only smaller. Much, much smaller. And he remembered that working this fertile land had been hard work and wondered how Esther'd managed alone all these years (same way she managed when he was there, Miss Esther told me later).

And for the first time Sonny-Boy felt guilty knowing that it took the death of his son to bring him back. Looking down at the plot of land that Esther worked, he could no longer salve his conscience with the thought of the few dollars he sent her every month and the barrel of clothes and food he shipped down every December. He tried to recall why, when he got too sick to stay in New York, he decided to move to Florida instead of coming back home, but he couldn't remember his reasons.

This plot down in the valley was supposed to go to Gladstone when both he and Esther were gone. But standing there, Sonny-Boy wondered how Esther must have felt knowing that she would be the last one in the family tending this land, wondering what would become of it. Because Gladstone never had any interest in farming even as a boy. And after so many years had passed she must have come to the conclusion that Sonny-Boy wasn't coming back to live.

Now Gladstone was dead. And standing there he knew that he definitely wouldn't be coming back here to live. This wasn't home anymore. Funny thing was, America wasn't home either. Even with his big house in Florida he was as homeless as Gladstone had been after he had been evicted from his apartment all those years ago in New York.

Gladstone. Now lying in a coffin down at the funeral home.

Children aren't supposed to die before their parents. It is the duty of your boychild to take care of the responsibilities of your funeral and be the chief bearer of your coffin, bearing you to your final resting place.

You don't expect to be called to the phone at work and hear the voice of the woman you lived with, the mother of your son, saying in your ear from thousands of miles away, "Gladstone gone." And he's asking her what she mean and she only repeating, "Gladstone gone."

"You mean . . . he dead?" And she's saying, "Yes. He kill himself." And in the silence that follows, you not sure if the distance or the phone lines somehow jumbled her words and caused you not to hear right until you hear her voice saying, ". . . tie a rope around his neck and jumped off a chair."

He can't remember asking the supervisor for the rest of the day off like he did when he met Gladstone at the airport twenty-odd years ago. Everything is a blank between him getting the call from Esther and locking his house to leave for the airport. What did he tell the supervisor? My son is dead? My only son just got up on a chair and jumped off and killed himself? Did he say that?

He can vaguely recall, as in a dream, the sympathy in the supervisor's voice as he said, "Hey, go home. We can take care of things here." Of course they bleddy well could. If he was gad daim dead instead of his son everything would bleddy well go on, wouldn't it? Did the words flare up in him as they are now? Well if they did, the hell with it. It was just a part-time janitorial job anyway, something to keep his mind occupied in his retirement and help him pay his bills.

So here he was now, staring down at a mango tree heavy with big, green mangoes, the first tree he planted down there, and wondering aloud, "Why? Why the boy do it? Why he gone and kill himself?"

Just then he heard Esther's voice behind him coming from the house saying, "That you Harold?"

He turned expecting to see the young woman he left long ago promising to return, but saw instead an old woman with gray hair plaited in thick braids and wearing a dress he remembered sending her many years ago now faded with washing and bleached by the sun. But her face. Her face didn't have a single wrinkle, as though it had made a decision to preserve itself, waiting for him to return.

"Esther?" he said.

Later after they ate dinner and the evening was mellow, with the two of them sitting on two benches in the yard and the stars filling the sky, not like in America where the brightness of the streetlights overpower the stars and cause you to scarcely even remember there is a moon and most of the time you don't know east from west (Sonny-Boy couldn't remember when last he see so many stars), he asked her, "Why he do it, Esther? You know why he do it?"

She didn't answer. Instead she said, "Remember when Gladstone play truant from Mr. Gittens private lessons and you tar his behind and march him to Mr. Gittens, then Mr. Gittens beat him again in front the whole class till he pee himself?"

"He never play truant no more," Sonny-Boy said. "And he win a scholarship . . . till them brutes take it away."

They spent the rest of the night recalling memories of their dead son's childhood, two figures illuminated in the yard by the light of the full moon and serenaded by crickets and frogs.

Later in the middle of the night Sonny-Boy woke up and put his feet on the floor to get up to go in the yard to pee. But he never got off the bed. Because there in the bedroom lit only by the flickering lowered light of the oil lamp the fragrance of flowers filled his nostrils.

And Sonny-Boy swung his feet back onto the bed and snuggled up to Esther's back. He could hold his pee till morning.

Esther brushed off his arm. "Hey. What you doing?" Her voice was surprisingly alert for somebody who should have been deep in sleep. "None of that," she told him. "Keep your hands to yourself."

"Look, hush, woman," Sonny-Boy said. "Just trying to keep you warm, is all."

Esther smiled to herself. She had smelled the flowers. Men. Never can admit when they frightened. But the smile faded from her face because a father shouldn't be frightened of the spirit of his own son, his own flesh and blood.

Meanwhile Sonny-Boy lay curled up with his hands between his knees, staring in the darkness at the back of Esther's head and wondering how a son of his could kill himself to escape whatever problems in life he was facing. He, Sonny-Boy, couldn't even *imagine* killing himself. Yes he believed in heaven and all that, more so now than when he was young and strong—the older he get, the more he find himself going to church and reading the Bible, like taking out an insurance policy just in case (he hope God didn't hear that). But the only life he knew about for certain was the one he was living. He couldn't see anything that could be so terrible in his life to cause him to end it. And Gladstone was his son so you would figure like father like son. He couldn't understand it.

And there in the darkness and silence as he tried to remember what kind of father he had been before he left for America, what legacy he'd passed on to his boy, brief images came to mind, some hazy, some sharp, pieced together like bits of broken film: he, Gladstone, and Esther in the park one Christmas morning with Gladstone on his shoulders, Esther walking next to him in a new dress, he in his one gray suit, strolling, mixing with the crowd of people that come to listen to the police band play early Christmas morning; he and Gladstone coming from the beach one early morning with scarcely any traffic on the road and the two of them stopping at a shop to get something to eat; little Gladstone running pell-mell down the gap to meet him coming home from work on evenings shouting, "Daddy! Daddy!" with joy in his eyes.

This last image brings a smile to his face, a smile that fades when he realizes that as hard as he tries all he can recall are more of these kinds of general recollections such as Gladstone around the house wearing khaki short pants; him thumping Gladstone across his head for something he'd done wrong; the one time he really whip the boy's behind (for playing truant from school and going with his friends to the beach to climb the trees and pick coconuts); Gladstone studious after that cut-ass, studying his homework with his head so close to the kerosene lamp on the table and Sonny-Boy teasing him, telling him "Boy you go fry your brains leaning so close to that lamp."

He tries to recall close, shoulder-to-shoulder, father-son moments like him sitting down and talking to the boy man-to-man, teaching him things, even simple things. But what could an uneducated man like him teach a boy as bright as Gladstone, eh?

One time after watching Gladstone playing cricket and seeing how awkward his son was, he get the idea to take the boy with him on Saturday afternoons to watch first-division cricket so he could develop an appreciation for the game and really learn it.

So the next few Saturdays he and Gladstone walking together in the quiet afternoon hot sun, heading toward the elementary school playing field and the two of them sitting on the ground under the shade of a tree while out on the field the players are human chess pieces dressed in sparkling white and the shouts, the crack of ball against bat, the heckling, the applause, red ball skimming on green grass, blue sky, cool breezes on a warm Saturday afternoon, his son by his side, all come together in a sweet feeling of contentment. But good things don't last long. One weekday he's coming in from work and overhear Gladstone telling one of his friends he prefer stay home and play cricket than go to the park and watch it, and even though disappointment is a lump in his chest he got sense enough to know not to force the boy to do something he don't want to do.

Perhaps fathers and sons weren't meant to be buddies. He did the important things: working hard to put food in Gladstone's belly, clothes on his back, a roof over his head; leaving home and family to go to that gad daim, godforsaken place so his son could stay in secondary school; nearly killing himself working to keep the boy in college in New York.

"What?" Esther said.

"Nothing," Sonny-Boy murmured. "Nothing," not aware that he had begun talking aloud.

Soon after that he fell asleep.

And as he began to snore Miss Esther felt a cold draft whistle through the bedroom jalousie window and flutter the curtains, and she heard footsteps padding on the other side of the partition, which caused her to whisper in the darkness, "Gladstone?"

The footsteps paused by the bedroom door but no one answered.

She whispered again, "That you, Gladstone?"

And the footsteps entered the bedroom, paused by the foot of the bed, then slowly padded away, sounding as though whoever it was just walked right out through the side of the house and into the night, leaving Miss Esther lying in the darkness whispering to herself, "Gladstone?" and speculating that what she just witnessed is the punishment Gladstone suffering in the spirit life for killing himself. This is an added burden on top of her grief. Is bad enough to carry your child in your belly for nine months, watch him grow and reach manhood, then have to watch him being lowered six feet under. No mother should have to bear that burden. On the other hand she have to admit that whatever punishment Gladstone receiving now he bring on his own self. Life is precious. You en make life, you en got the right to end it—not even your own.

Next day when Miss Esther expressed this opinion to Sonny-Boy, Sonny-Boy had less philosophical matters to worry about.

"If he restless," Sonny-Boy say, "then he should take his restlessness some place else, because son or no son and as much as I love him, duppy is duppy. And I for one don't want to see no gad daim duppy in the middle of the night."

Miss Esther was so stunned at this, all she could do was stare at Sonny-Boy with an appalled expression on her face.

[Excerpted with the permission of Yvette Belle from one of several journals containing the inscription: To my daughter Yvette. Perhaps some day you'll understand.]

Dear diary,

Life is a brief and futile journey. I peer down the tunnel of remembrance and recall years of boyhood, youth, and young manhood as fleeting as the trajectory of a pitching star (even though then the future seemed endless as the universe).

But memory is a mirage, the future is a fast approaching end, and the present is seasoned with regrets about mistakes made, opportunities missed—like man-to-man talks with my father yearned for, but unrealized. But what would we talk about? Shared memories? A relationship stillborn and undeveloped? And what would be the point of such an exchange when the past is a road that can be traveled only in memory?

One such memory I have is the recurring recollection of a hand shaking my shoulder one boyhood morning long ago and my father's voice saying close to my ears, "Brute . . . Brute . . . Get up."

And I recall rubbing my eyes and stretching and the yellow lamplight telling me that the sun hasn't yet chased away the darkness outside, while my old man is standing over me in his swim trunks and asking if I want to go for a sea bath.

"Well, you want to go or not?" he's saying.

And I have five minds to answer back with, "What you think?" But such impudence was not tolerated then from the young.

But he ought to have remembered that the last time he took me to the beach was years ago (I couldn't have been any more than about four or five) and the sea was a vast growling monster going *pshoom!* and rushing up on the beach frothing at my ankles, pulling sand from under my feet and retreating as he gripped my hand thereby preventing the sea monster from swallowing me altogether.

That morning my father walked with me hand-in-hand into the water then held me up with my feet dangling above the swells, above waves that were like lizards' tongues reaching above his waist and buffeting him as they rolled in, trying to knock him over to get to me.

I bawled with fright while my father laughed with his gold tooth glistening in the foreday morning light saying, "You got to learn to swim, Brute. You's a man."

But I wasn't a man. And as my mother always used to say, The sea en got no back door. So I remember screaming and hollering, begging him to put me down! Put me down! I want to go back on the beach!

The men laughed and one of them said, "Harold, your boy fraid the sea."

Whereupon my father's hands roughened and his gold tooth vanished behind an angry frown as he marched from the sea and set me down on the sand telling me, "Don't move from there!"

And I watched him hit a header in the blue-green ocean and swim out to the yachts anchored so far out in the bay that he and the men swimming with him became dots bobbing in the waves.

That was the first and last time my father took me to the beach until this particular morning four or five years later when he's asking me if I want to go for a sea bath and is waiting for me to answer right away as if he forgot about the first time years ago and all the mornings after when he would mount his bicycle and ride off by himself leaving me lying on my bedding on the floor listening to the diminishing *tickticktick* of his bicycle.

I sprang up and began folding my bedding so fast he laughed. "Take your time, Brute," he's saying. "Take your time." And he's chuckling.

The roads were empty, house windows shuttered tight, the sun a faint glow lighting up the sky in the east, a foreday morning breeze blowing cool and sweet on my skin while behind my head is the inhale and exhale of my father's breathing as he's pedaling the bicycle with me sitting in front of him on the bar.

When we reached the beach we folded our clothes and laid them on the bicycle leaned up against a grape tree. I trotted to the water and waded out bracing against the frigid seawater but continuing till it reached chest-high.

I looked over at Pa hoping to catch him noticing that I was now a big boy, no more crybaby, and perhaps even saying to his friends, See? That is my boy. Gladstone. But Pa was talking and laughing that deep, Haha, man-laugh with the rest of the men standing in a circle in the water.

I ducked my head a few times then pinched my nostrils and sat in the water and sank till my behind hit the sand and when I sputtered up my father and a woman were facing one another waist-high in the water and deep in conversation.

After we left the beach we took a shower at the public bath—me and my father, man-to-man, naked. "You like the sea, eh?" he asked me.

I nodded.

We stopped at a shop. And the salt fish and biscuits we ate that morning sitting side by side on a bench at a plain wooden table in the rumshop is the sweetest food I've ever had, savored that morning long ago and stored in my memory to be retrieved from time to time over the years.

That year during hot-sun vacation in August I taught myself to swim and one evening as soon as Pa came pedaling up the gap and before he had a chance to lean up his bicycle against the house I burst out, "I learn to swim today, Pa. I can swim."

"Yeah?" was all he said. My father was not a talkative man when he was hungry.

We never went to the beach together again. . . .

RADIO ANNOUNCEMENT

[Read by announcer over funereal organ music.]

"We regret to announce the death of Gladstone Augustus Belle, former minister of education, son of Harcourt and Esther Belle of the village, husband of Isamina Springer Belle, son-in-law of Philip and Daphne Springer, and brother-in-law of Samuel Springer. The funeral leaves Simpson's Funeral Home tomorrow afternoon at four o'clock and thence to the Cathedral for service and burial."

II

It was on the morning of Gladstone Augustus Belle's funeral when, from all accounts, the world began to go crazy.

The sun was a golden ball peeping above the treetops when out of a clear blue sky a bolt of lightning lashed like a serpent's tongue and struck old Miss Lord just as she stepped out of her back door in her ankle-length chemise to empty out her chamber pot.

Her next-door neighbor Gilbert, who belly dances in tasseled women's bikinis at a nightclub in town and is better known by his professional name, Miss Betty, saw the silver snake tongue of lightning flick down into old Miss Lord's yard and heard her pot clatter to the ground.

As he told it later, he clapped one hand to his chest and bawled out, "Oh my God! MISS LORD! MISS LORD!"

But Miss Lord was already beyond the sound of human voices; because according to Miss Betty, when he rushed out of his gate door and into Miss Lord's yard and saw his neighbor lying flat on her face with the enamel chamber pot near her hand and the piss that was in it making a damp spot on the ground, his heart start to palpitate and he almost faint with the shock, sohelpmegod. Lightning striking somebody dead is something you does hear about, not see.

So began the day of Gladstone Belle's funeral.

When the news hit the Village my mother said, "That is a bad sign."

But to my mother everything is some kind of sign so it stands to reason that a solitary bolt of lightning snaking through the sky and striking an old woman stone cold dead would be a bad omen. No big surprise. But things got worse.

Not far away and at the same moment the lightning lashed old Miss Lord to the ground and singed every inch of hair off her head, Miss Marshall was struggling to get up off her rheumatic knees after having to hurry through her morning prayers because that fowl-cock of hers was keeping so much blooming racket, as she said later, that she rushed to her back window as fast as the rheumatism would let her to bawl for that blasted cock to hush up and stop waking up the whole blinking place. She pushed her head out the window just in time to see her cock become a feathered tornado spinning then falling with his legs straight up in the air, dead and still rotating.

Seeing this, Miss Marshall bawled out, "Lord have mercy!" and hobbled out into the yard just as the fowl-cock stopped spinning, opened one eye at her and said, "What you looking at?"

Miss Marshall collapsed on the spot. Flat on the ground. She and the fowl-cock side by side.

That is her story. I didn't make it up.

At that very moment, in the house next door, Miss Crichlow's three cats *meeeaaaowed* in perfect three-part harmony and streaked through the back door—*vhoom! vhoom! vhoom!*—one after the other, causing Miss Crichlow to chase after them hollering, "Mary! Martha! Millicent!" following them into Miss Marshall's yard, her heart thumping in her chest, almost knocking her neighbor's gate door off its hinges, in time to see the cats surround the dead fowl-cock and begin licking its feathers the same way they licked their fur. What a strange sight. So strange that even though Miss Crichlow saw her neighbor lying on her back with her legs folded back under her, right next to the fowl-cock and cats, her brain didn't register it right away.

But the moment it clicked in her head that Miss Marshall was lying there dead for all she knew, she turned and ran pelting back into her house for her vial of smelling salts.

When Miss Crichlow fanned the smelling salts under her neighbor's nose, Miss Marshall shook her head, opened her eyes, turned her head, saw her dead fowl-cock lying right next to her and let loose a long *Waaaaauuuh!* and flipped to her feet like an acrobat, rheumatism gone, which caused Miss Crichlow to fall back on her ass and sit with her mouth agape, staring up at Miss Marshall, dumbfounded by Miss Marshall's gymnastic leap.

And hear Miss Marshall: "Gimme some water. Quick!"

"You thirsty?" is all Miss Crichlow could manage to say.

"What you think? Think I want it to bathe with?"

And in the back of her mind Miss Crichlow is saying what an ungrateful so-and-so Miss Marshall is. Why she had to answer her so rude? Some people don't have no appreciation.

But not wanting to make the situation worse by making Miss Marshall more irritable, Miss Crichlow springs right up and rushes into her neighbor's house to fetch a cup of water, all this time forgetting about her cats which had disappeared leaving the dead fowl-cock lying by itself in the yard with its feet still up in the air.

She never saw her cats again, which has become a big source of friction between the two neighbors, with Miss Crichlow saying whenever they have a quarrel, "Is because of you that my Mary, Martha, and Millicent left and en come back!" and Miss Marshall snapping back, "Good! What you need in your house is a man. A big, stiff, strapping man instead of three mangy, starve-out cats." Which, needless to say, never goes down well with Miss Crichlow and starts a whole back-and-forth of cussing and the two of them not speaking to one another for days.

Anyway, at the same instant that the bolt of lightning snaked from the sky into Miss Lord's yard and Miss Marshall's fowl-cock spoke, the clock on the bell tower in the town square struck six o'clock and Henri the undertaker's assistant was just about to step into the room where two coffins sat on their carriages when he stopped in the doorway thinking he coulda swear them coffins was lined up parallel next to one another when he left last night, oui? Now they head-to-head, forming a V, as if the duppies get together in the night to make jumbie conversation. Sacré Dieu.

Bumps raise up on his skin and he makes the sign of the cross.

But then the thought occurs to him, Perhaps Mr. Simpson move them, eh. And right away he chides himself saying, "Boy, is why you so damned stupidy? You stupidy for true, eh." And he begins to chuckle, heh heh heh, nervous.

And he shakes his head like a boxer shaking off a blow and starts to enter the room with the echo of the striking town clock still quavering in his ears when all of a sudden Mr. Belle in the coffin closest to the door sits bolt upright as if a spring that had been holding him down broke, releasing the tension and whipping his torso upright, *boing!*

Which causes Henri to jump and bawl out, "Wah!" while staring at the back of Mr. Belle's jacket and shirt and the safety pins that are holding the clothes together after they had been scissored down the back so they could be fitted onto the corpse that was stiff when the undertaker was dressing it but which is now sitting upright talking like a normal human being, saying in a cavernous voice, "No one knows the truth!"

"Mon Dieu!" Henri yells and makes the sign of the cross again.

By now his knees have turned into jelly, causing his legs to wobble while the rest of him is paralyzed by fright and his hair is tingling on his scalp and his bladder is threatening to release itself.

He opens his mouth and tries to bawl again but he no longer has control of his vocal chords.

His legs are wobbly as they back him toward the door.

As he told me later, that's when his senses came rushing back and he turned and fled down the corridor screaming, "Waaaah! M'sieu Simpson! M'sieu Simpson!"

Mr. Simpson stepped from his office asking, "What's wrong, Henri?"—even in his agitation Henri notices that Mr. Simpson is pronouncing his name "Henry" not "Uhhhnree" as Henri made sure to tell everyone when he first moved into the area although, as he came to find out, he was wasting his time because Mr. Simpson, like everybody else, believed that Henri, first, didn't know how to spell his name right and second, couldn't pronounce it right—You know these French-island people, was what everybody said.

Anyway, Henri rushed past Mr. Simpson standing by the door and into the office. Mr. Simpson turned to face him. "What's the matter, Henri?" he said.

"M'sieu Belle . . . M'sieu Belle . . ."

"Take it easy," Mr. Simpson says. "Cool your passion. What happened?"

After taking a few gulps of air Henri managed to gasp out all in a rush, "M'sieu Belle get up."

"Now Henri . . ." Mr. Simpson begins to say.

But Henri interrupts him with, "And he say, 'No one knows the truth,' " imitating the hollow voice of the dead man. And he continues, "Why me, eh? Why me? I don't know him. I never do him nothing. So why he go frighten me like this, eh?"

According to Mr. Simpson, Henri's frightened face and rhetorical question are making it hard for him to restrain his laughter.

Of course Henri's response to this later was to suck his teeth in one long steups and say, "He was more frighen than me, oui. Is easy to talk now."

ISAMINA

[5 A.M.]
Cock-crow. And Isamina Belle's wakening ears hear the sounds of raindrops pattering on the roof and wind whistling through the seams in the window casing, and she snuggles up with her hands between her knees, comfortable, secure, unmindful of the raw wound of widowhood.

Through the windowpanes she watches the furious gyrations of the tree limbs and dark, gray clouds scudding across the sky chased by wind that whistles and rattles her bedroom window and brings a slight rain chill into the room.

And from years of habit she reaches behind her to pull her husband's arm around her to create with his embrace a cocoon of comfort to add to the raindrops-on-the-roof snugness in their bedroom, but the touch of the bare sheet against her hand reawakens in her memory the estrangement that led to her sleeping alone over the past few months. Bereavement begins to seep in ("Kitten don't bawl till it don't hear it mother call," my mother said when I told her this—her version of You don't miss the water, etc.) as her gaze rests on Gladstone's desk over in the far corner of the room, a neat desk with everything still in place: pens and pencils in a white teacup with a brown capital G on its side, a stapler and staple remover, a rectangular wooden tray filled with paper clips, a medium-sized brown spiral notebook still in the center of the desktop where he had left it (the last of his diaries).

And in her mind she can see Gladstone sitting at the desk like he always did last thing at night and first thing in the morning with his spectacles scotched on the tip of his nose, his pajama shirt unbuttoned and a slight paunch hanging over the waistline of his pajama pants, reading papers he brought home in his attaché case; scribbling, shuffling, tapping papers on the desk, and the rustle of paper or the scratching of a pen, soothing sounds that once would lull her into sleep at night and greet her first thing in the morning even in recent years when quarrels and squabbles were termites devouring the substance of their marriage.

But even that familiar routine ceased the night she told him, "Look, tell me, Gladstone. Do you really want to adopt or not? If you don't want to, say so. Don't keep making excuses."

And after a long silence his answer, something about he doesn't like the idea of adopting somebody else's child and What if it come from a stupid family? What if it has some hereditary disease? What if it is a half-idiot and you don't find out till later? And he's pausing then saying, "But if you really want to do it, go ahead. Don't let me stop you."

That's when she blew up, asking him why he didn't come straight out and tell her from the beginning. Why was he always hemming and hawing with one excuse or another saying, this isn't the right time, or no, he don't want no grown child he prefer a baby they can raise? Why'd he put her through all that knowing he really didn't want to adopt at all? Now here she was, eh? Past forty, and he's saying if she really want it? So what if she goes ahead, eh? Then what? She going do it on her own? Isn't he going to give her any support?

It is after this quarrel that she moved into the spare bedroom and their marriage sputtered along even slower.

So the night he came home from work a couple months ago with the knot of his tie loosened, his shirt collar unbuttoned, his long sleeves rolled up almost to his elbows, his jacket slung over one arm and rum on his breath, she didn't stop to think how unusual this was but instead let loose the anger that had been building up while she was waiting for him, asking him where he went drinking instead of coming home and didn't he remember they were supposed to have dinner with her parents tonight and she had to call them and tell them he had a sudden meeting engagement and couldn't he at least call and say he would be late?

Then something in his expression stilled her tongue. She stared at him as he tossed his attaché case on the couch and plopped down next to it. Nothing unusual about this, because when the two of them were courting she used to brag to her friends about how "quiet and introspective" he was, an intellectual type not given to talking much, attributes that gradually became impediments as time went by when sometimes a whole day would pass with the two of them in the house not saying a word to one another (at least it seemed that way). If she tried to start a conversation he would give her a one-word answer, sometimes no answer at all depending on his mood. Like now.

So she shrugged and started toward her bedroom.

"Your food is in the oven," she said.

"I'm not hungry," he said.

She stopped. Now *this* was unusual.Gladstone was a glutton, plain and simple. There was no nice way to put it. The man ate like he wasn't sure where his next meal was coming from; furthermore, in the last few years he'd developed a habit of eating his food at night, the same habit he said his father had, treating this practice like some kind of family tradition he had to carry on.

When she turned around to face him to make certain she'd heard right she saw him still slumped in the couch with his legs stretched straight out.

Normally she would have continued on into her room and left him alone to brood but something told her that this mood was different. Something was wrong. "What's wrong, Gladstone?" she asked him.

But true to form he continued staring into space.

"Nothing," he said at last.

She shrugged and continued into her room and closed the door behind her.

She fell asleep hearing him at his desk working on the papers he had brought home, as usual.

The next few days went as usual: both of them dressing on mornings and getting into their separate cars and going on their separate ways to work; in the evenings she usually was the one to come home first and by the time he came in she'd be in her room reading or watching TV without really seeing it, using it as a soporific to send her off to sleep.

But that Wednesday evening when he walked in the door she was on her way out and he said as he passed by her, "I resigned." Just like that. I resigned. No discussion, no explanation. Nothing.

She stopped and turned. "What d'you mean, you resigned?"

He shrugged. "Just what I said."

"You resigned," she said. "You resigned. Just like that? Uh? Just like that." And, why didn't he have the courtesy to discuss it with her first, uh? Tell her that. And why was he destroying his career? What were they going to do now? Tell her. She was listening. What were they going to do?

And all he did again was shrug, telling her they'd manage, and "There's more to life than money, Mina."

Which caused her to snap back with, "Yeah? Like what?" and snatch up her pocketbook, jump into her car and drive away with her head buzzing with rage.

When she got back home, he wasn't there. At first she was glad, relieved. She had been careless, carried away by the passion of the moment and hadn't realized so much time had gone by.

But she lay in bed unable to fall asleep. Gladstone wasn't the kind of man to stay out late, not even during the roughest patches of their marriage. That was one dependable thing about him. Every night she would go to sleep with him in the house, feeling secure even in the midst of a stormy marriage.

When she heard the front door lock turning and she looked at the alarm clock it was one o'clock. She heard his footsteps treading heavy and uneven toward his bedroom and heard his labored breathing as he took off his clothes then fell heavily onto the bed. He was drunk. This wasn't Gladstone.

Next morning when she left for work he was still in bed and when she got home that evening he was pulling weeds in the flower garden in the backyard.

Every morning she would leave him still lying in bed and come back in the evening to find him reading a newspaper, doing crossword puzzles, reading a book. This went on for about a week.

After that he began spending time down by the rumshop, playing dominoes, drinking, so that most evenings coming home she would see him sitting on a bench under the tree in front of the shop as she drove by. And she would stay at home and hear his voice among the voices of the men, talking, arguing politics, sports, whatever topic the rum in their heads steered them to.

She had her boutique and it was doing well. But a man is a man. He should be working. Besides, he wasn't an ordinary man. He was the former deputy prime minister, for god's sake, and there he was lowering himself by associating with those men down at the rumshop, letting them drag him back down to their level.

At first she began mentioning, offhand, positions she learned of from friends, family, and connections. No response. Her next strategy was to ask him if he'd found anything yet, slipping the question in cautiously (timidly almost) to avoid igniting his temper, knowing how sensitive he was about the man's position as breadwinner from the beginning of their marriage when he made the firm, unequivocal statement that she was, under no circumstances, to work. He was prime minister's assistant and no wife of his was going to be seen working, he'd said then. Look how things change, eh?

But as the weeks went by she began to lose patience and started to tackle him outright, telling him it was time for him to find a job because "I can't do it all by myself, you know."

Over the years their fights had been sporadic flarings of temper after periods of building resentment. But now? Now they quarreled almost every blessed day.

Finally she said, "I can't take this anymore, Gladstone. I want a divorce."

Then one week later on a pleasant sunny morning she walks out of her house to buy some things to cook and when she comes back her husband is dangling from the rafters.

Funny how things happen, eh? Two nights before he killed himself, as she lay awake in her bed, he came into the room and she pretended to be asleep. But he must have known by the shallowness of her breathing that she was awake, because he said, "I know you're not sleeping."

He lay beside her. When she opened her eyes and looked sideways at his face on the pillow, she saw something she never expected ever to see. In the moonlight coming through the window and falling on his face a tear coursed from the corner of his eye down into his ear. Tears shed too late.

To this day, she won't say what she and Gladstone talked about that night. Won't pick her teeth to say a word.

But one thing she does admit is that on the morning of the day of her husband's funeral, finally the thought really occurred to her that two days ago she had a husband, albeit one she was about to divorce, and now she was faced with the absolute finality of widowhood.

And for the first time since she discovered him hanging from the rafters above her head, tears blurred her vision, overflowed and tickled her cheeks as they flowed down her face and made a damp spot on the bodice of her nightgown.

She grabbed her belly and rocked back and forth, moaning "Gladstone . . . Gladstone . . . Gladstone" to the image of him in her mind, her recollection of him as she'd last seen him alive two days ago (slouched at the dining table with his elbows on the tabletop and holding his head in his hands).

That was going to be her last day in their house. Her suitcases were packed and her father and brother were coming that evening to help her move, mostly her clothes, back into her parents' house—for the time being, until she found a place of her own.

Some soft spot inside her had given her the idea to cook one last meal before she left, a peace offering of sorts, because all of a sudden she didn't feel like quarreling anymore.

So she went down the road to buy provisions and when she returned Gladstone was dead.

It was a day like any other: the hawkers sitting at the roadside with their trays of ground provisions, fruit, vegetables; Miss Vanterpool, who she usually bought from, giving her an extra slice of pumpkin and waving her hand when Isamina said thanks.

The road was damp with the rain that hadn't long stopped falling; the air had that fresh, fecund, postshower aroma of warm, moist soil. A cool breeze ruffled her dress and caressed her; the sun warmed her skin.

It was a good day to be alive, but apparently not for Gladstone.

So here she was a couple days later on the day of his funeral wishing she'd decided to make one more effort to keep her marriage together instead of packing her belongings to leave, wishing she could reel back every harsh word she'd ever shouted at him in haste, wishing she could undo every single wrong she'd done in their years of marriage. But it was too late.

Worse, she felt as though life was a vehicle in which she was passenger, not driver, occasionally happy with the ride but more often smashing headlong into quarrels and arguments she saw ahead but could not avoid.

She wished they'd remained the happy couple they'd been in the early years when they were like two children skipping along a sunlit road toward a distant, hazy horizon.

Instead here she was, a widow gazing at her dead husband's hairbrush on the dressing table, in a house pregnant with the silence of death and really appreciating for the first time how fragile like a spider's web life is and that all we mortals have is the present; because yesterday is a memory and tomorrow is perpetually beyond our grasp.

Dear diary,

I am enmeshed in circumstances where murder and disappearances are normal, politics is a violent game played by ruthless men, truth is hidden by a fog of gossip and rumor, and I am in the midst of a cabal of crooks. Most unbearable of all is my chagrin at the growing realization that this is the way it has always been. Too late have I begun to discover the twofold nature of ambition: at once the fuel that can propel one toward higher achievements but at the same time the deadliest of narcotics; at best a nurturer of naïveté, at its worst a destroyer of conscience, deadening the soul to inconvenient truths.

It appears that for weeks the residents of Spring Garden have been complaining to the police about noises they've been hearing at night in a house in the neighborhood and the stink of death and decay that has been forcing them to pinch their nostrils every time they pass by the house in question. And this afternoon was the first time I heard about it.

I wish that time really was regulated by clocks and could be set back to the moment this afternoon when I heard the ruckus outside my office—a man yelling, "I pay my taxes! I want to see the minister!"

Because if I knew then what I know now I would have remained insulated behind the door of my office. Instead, I opened it and came face-to-face with a tall, gray-haired man in a khaki shirt and dungaree pants looking full into my eyes with his hat in his hand and saying, "Mr. Minister?" a man who could've been my father, a man who led me to a discovery that has caused me to question my entire two decades of public service.

But not knowing then what I know now, I signaled Miss Slocombe that it was okay and led the man into my office to an encounter that has left me laden with the burden of knowledge.

But perhaps that was my destiny. Because even though I have no jurisdiction over police matters, something about the earnestness and desperation in the man's face made me reach for the phone and call the guardhouse in Spring Gardens when he said, "The police en paying we no mind. We is only small people."

He declined to sit beside me in the back of the car; preferred to sit in the front with Sam the chauffeur. And when we reached Spring Gardens he pointed the house out. "There," he said.

A police jeep was already parked in front of a pink bungalow with wrought iron bars at the windows and door. Four constables and a sergeant, all standing around the jeep, straightened up as soon as my car pulled up. The sergeant came over toward us.

"Mr. Minister . . ." he began to say.

But I interrupted him with a terse "Let's go" and strode toward the house.

Never will I forget the stench, so strong that I dragged my handkerchief from my pocket and covered my nose.

And when the police broke open the door I stood transfixed in the doorway. Death has a magnetic attraction. A hundred horses couldn't have hauled my eyes from the scene before me: blood stains splattered on the walls; teeth scattered on the floor like pebbles; the room empty and unfurnished except for a bed with a mattress stained with blood and urine. And a single chair.

In my memory I still smell the pervasive odor of blood, piss, and shit, the stench of death.

When I stepped back out into the sunshine, I stopped on the steps, looked from the crowd that had gathered in the street back into the house at the five policemen grouped together murmuring and glancing at me and seeming not to know what to do. I stared again at the blood-stained evidence of the butchery and brutality wreaked in that house that from its exterior seemed like any respectable middle-class residence but whose threshold marked entry to a sinister universe separate from this world outside of sunshine and people with curious faces.

Sam the chauffeur is a garrulous man but this afternoon we drove back to the office encased in a cocoon of silence and thought.

I told Miss Slocombe not to have me disturbed, and for the remainder of the afternoon I could do nothing but stare through my ninth-story window at the esplanade and the people strolling along it; the bandstand; cars, trucks, bicycles, a donkey cart, men, women, children, passing on the street; normal people living normal lives; the sun sliding toward the horizon and glistening on the sea on what to others seemed a normal day.

Rumors of political violence and intrigue are commonplace here but I've never been a believer. Always I've said, show me the evidence. People gossip, embellish, and create excitement out of the most trivial circumstances. That is the way of this world.

But rumors have been increasing recently. That I can't deny. Each day new ones circulate. Some of them I've heard. But rumor mongering is endemic in this small country of ours and idle talk is the gravy that adds flavor to otherwise uninteresting lives.

However, what I've seen today no longer can be dismissed as idle talk. Perhaps it's the evidence I've been requesting. But evidence of what? That's the question. And whom can I approach for answers?

As we were on the way to Spring Gardens, I remember Mr. Jenkins sitting next to Sam in the front seat and saying, "Somebody see them taking the photographer in there, you know. Nobody en see him since."

And even as I asked him what photographer, I knew, and saw Sam glance at me in his rearview mirror.

And I thought of Cynthia, remembering years ago, young, in my new job as assistant to the prime minister, running up the front steps of government headquarters and meeting her on the way out leaving for the day.

I remember her asking me if I was working late again.

And I, so full of enthusiasm, in such a hurry, all I said was "Umhum" and kept moving.

I still can hear her saying, "See you tomorrow," her high heels clicking down the steps, a car door slam. I never looked around. I should have. Should have said something.

I was about to leave the office when I heard the seven o'clock news on the portable radio on the bookshelf: Cynthia had been found dead in a cart road.

I remember the shock. I remember whispered rumors about political involvement. First the photographer who had taken a picture of the prime minister that showed two ragged children and the devastation of the hurricane in the background had disappeared and was never seen again. Now Cynthia the prime minister's secretary found dead in a cart road.

There even was a court case—a man on the Hill, where Roachford grew up, arrested and jailed for confronting the P.M. in a rumshop and insinuating that he was involved.

But back then Anthony Roachford was a god, a mentor, a colossus who strode the halls of the government building and won elections by landslides, until I discovered that what seems unblemished when viewed from a distance reveals its flaws upon closer admiration.

Anthony Roachford is venal, authoritarian, and power hungry. That I've long since found out. But is he murderous? Even now I find that hard to believe. Perhaps I'm still naive. And naïveté is not to be cherished. But whom can I turn to even as storms of controversy rage and I feel as helpless as I did as a young boy fleeing from a house battered and decapitated by hurricane winds?

"Storms"
by Gladstone Belle

Skies dark, brooding, gray as slate
air still, heavy and morning warm
says Pa, "the stillness right before the storm"
But
afternoon nature later rumbles,
rains and rails, lightning lashing
nighttime blackness finds us
huddling
from winds that whip and roar;
trembling
from chill and fear of
screeching nails ripped
from rafters as
trees crash
branches crack, anguished, fractured and amputated; now
running
in lashing rain, lacerating lightning
midst sailing sheets of galvanized guillotines
unseen and all the more frightening, then
resting
in a church's shelter
feuding
poststorm days later
as tempers flare and
neighbors share
cramped quarters and
scarce water and
politician's promises of
relocation and
compensation and
a new house with
a piece of land
to grow
a little kitchen garden.

DEBRA

[9 A.M.]

In a small house not far from the bungalow where Isamina is mourning and reminiscing, Debra is sitting in her back door wearing a sleeveless flowered frock and plastic beach sandals with her hair plaited in schoolgirl braids, catching a little morning breeze, watching her ducks flap their wings in the little cement pool her man Carl built not long ago and thinking, Who woulda thought that she, Debra, would be sitting here today hours before Gabby funeral? That Gabby would tie a rope around his neck and hang himself?

But that is the kind of thing that does happen when you climb out on flimsy limbs to pick fruits your hands can't reach from standing on the ground. Your feet lose touch with the earth and sooner or later you fall flat on your ass without even reaching the fruit you try so hard to pick, or if you reach the fruits they so damn rotten you can't even enjoy them.

And that is what happen to Gabby. Because people like Isamina Springer en nothing but flimsy limbs that poor people can hurt themselves trying to reach. If Gabby wasn't so grasping and greedy he mighta been alive today. He shoulda never married that girl.

First time Debra clap eyes on Gabby was the day he and his family come riding up the gap in a jackass cart and stopped in front Miss Mimi house and moved in with the few things that survived after the hurricane blow off the roof of their house and then flatten it.

Sonny-Boy (who she had to call Mr. Belle then out of respect) walking next to the donkey and holding the halter; Miss Esther riding on a front corner of the cart with the reins in her hands and a little bat-ears boy sitting with his legs dangling at the back of the donkey cart.

"What you name?" Debra ask him later.

"Gladstone," he say.

"Gladstone who?" she asked.

"Gladstone Augustus Belle." And he saying this with his chest puff out like his name was something to be proud of.

That is how she gave him the nickname Gabby, after his initials GAB, to puncture some of the air out of his little pigeon chest and cut him down to size, the nickname that he carry to his grave.

The first few days after he and his family moved to the village he would come across the road and the two of them would play jacks and hopscotch. Until the afternoon the boys come down the gap. Gabby was fickle and unreliable from small.

After the boys find out what his name was and where he come from and, How come all-you living at Miss Mimi? and, What Miss Mimi is to you? (Me grandmother, Gabby tell them), they finally say they going in the woods, You coming?

Next evening when she go over to his house to call him out he telling her from the window that he en playing no more girls' games.

Couple days later he getting with the other boys and calling her Picky Head because of her short hair. So when he come back to her not long afterward trying to make friends again she tell him go back with the boys with his little knock-knee self.

So to her he become just another one of the boys running about the village. Nothing special.

She remember when he pass the exam for secondary school and stop keeping company with the same boys he abandon her for and instead, all of a sudden, he and fat, sissy Gilbert who start going to St. Christopher Secondary the year before is the best of friends (the same Gilbert who does belly dance at a night club in town now and who everybody know as Miss Betty).

She remember on evenings Miss Esther hollering, "Glaadstuuu-uuhhhn!" and him bawling, "Yes, Mummy!" and running pelting home with his knock knees and you wouldn't see him outside the house again till next evening when the same thing would happen, till after a while he stopped coming out altogether, so that the only time you would see him he would be looking out his front window like a monkey in a cage, or walking to school on mornings and coming back in the afternoon.

She remember too that the joke in the village was that the biggest thing about him was his lunch box. Even bigger than his big head.

But then one day she notice how he change: his body thick; his behind big; his voice deep but cracking with sudden screeching notes, like a snake busting out of its old skin. And all of a sudden her heart pounding in her chest every time she set eyes on him. Funny thing about his voice, though, is that instead of staying deep, it went right back to his high-pitched, boy voice. But that was later.

She hear her mother say to a next-door neighbor one day, "Miss Esther like she feeding that boy growina."

She daydreaming in class about the way he does walk and talk and the way he does part his hair in the middle and the teacher bawling, "Welch!" and she snapping awake from her daydream and having to walk up to the front of the class to hold out her hand for lashes with the teacher ruler while the rest of girls in the class giggling.

She watching him play cricket on the pasture with the rest of boys (by this time is about three years he in secondary school and his mother ease up on him) and her eyes taking in the way his old khaki school pants gripping his buttocks and she feeling guilty because girls shouldn't think about things like that.

One moonlit night she in the crowd on Miss Vivian front steps listening to some story somebody telling (she can't remember who) when all of a sudden Gabby sitting next to her. Her heart thumping. Next night the same thing. First time since he passed for secondary school that he come back to where everybody does gather in front Miss Vivian house to tell stories. And he sitting near her and her heart pounding and her breath coming short.

About the third or fourth night his hand slipped around her waist. Just so. Not a word. Just his arm around her waist. And right away without thinking she doing the same while the moistness between her legs dampening her underwear, her heart thumping and excitement is a band tightening around her chest and making her breathing difficult, giving her shortness of breath.

That was the first night she, her best friend Yvonne, and Gabby walk home together in the dark. Yvonne gone in her house and she and Gabby walking the rest of the way, silent. The only sounds is their footsteps in the dark.

She reach her house and turn to go home and figuring Gabby doing the same, but as she walking by the side of her house toward the back gate she hearing footsteps hurrying behind her. She look over her shoulder and it is Gabby trotting toward her.

That was the first night she kiss a boy. Her back against the side of her house, Gabby pressing against her and his tongue like a tasteless piece of meat in her mouth, his hands groping under her old school uniform and tugging at her panties and she grabbing his hands and stopping him.

One night he kiss her neck and her knees wobble; she feel like she going faint; fingers slipping under the leg of her panties; she panic and tighten her grip on his hand and it is a struggle to stop him.

One evening she's sitting on her front steps when she see him coming toward her down the gap. When he reached in front her steps he stop. "Hello," he said.

And she answered back Hello while her heart thumping in her chest.

"I want to see you tonight," he say.

"All right." She manage to squeeze the words past her heart that seem to be up in her throat.

"Down by the pasture," he tell her.

And that night when everybody sitting on Miss Vivian steps she and Gabby meet by the big tamarind tree at the edge of the pasture.

And they holding hands as they walking to the middle of the pasture. The full moon turning the grass almost silver-gray and the few trees around them is black shapes casting black shadows—the short, prickly dunks tree where Miss Esther few sheep does lay down and shelter from the sun every day; the spreading evergreen where the boys not too long built a tree house.

Soon after they sit on the ground the sound of two voices and the *ticktickticks* of a bicycle reaching them in the dark. A man and woman approaching.

The couple stopping under a tree a few yards away. Voices whispering. A woman giggling. The man voice is a low drone.

Then silence.

Silence where Debra can hear the beating of her heart, the chirping of crickets, a woman's voice back in the village shouting to go and wash your nasty feet cause you en getting in my bed so.

And in this stillness, new sounds from the woman over under the tree: moaning, groaning, sighing, sobbing, voice trembling; a drawn-out "yes" and "oh God." Pain but something more than pain—pain and pleasure, a puzzling contradiction. Sounds new to Debra's ears and stirring strange, strong feelings inside her, a tumult causing her heart to pound as if it going explode; her breath coming short; a sensation she can't describe spreading all over her and moistening between her legs more than on the nights when she and Gabby was alone in the dark at the side of her mother house.

And as hard as she's peering into the shadows under the tree her eyes only seeing indistinct darker-than-the-surrounding darkness shapes while Gabby hand reaching under her frock, grabbing the waist of her panties and pulling and tugging. Other nights she would've grabbed his wrist and whispered no; other nights they would've been standing at the side of her mother house. But tonight she sitting on the pasture still warm from the heat of the sun and no isn't a word that's even at the back of her head so she raising her behind off the ground and her panties sliding down her thighs past her knees down along her legs and settling around her ankles and as the woman moaning groaning sighing growing louder nearby under the tree and Oh Jesus God . . . Oh Jesus God repeated over and over while Debra kicking her panties from around her ankles and her legs open and Gabby pushing them farther apart and the grass warm under her bare buttocks and she find herself resting on her elbows and then lying back as Gabby pushing against her arms and just as her back touch the warm pasture OOOHHGAWD PHILBERT . . . OOOOOHJEESUS the woman under the tree bawling and Debra heart leap and an electric tingle course through her body and now she know the man in the darkness is Philbert who not too long ago come back from picking fruit in America and this recognition giving her imagination something more to work with as the fast creaking of the springs of the bicycle seat and the woman moaning and sighing Oh God, Philbert creating in Debra's head a mental picture of the woman with one leg over the bicycle seat widening her up to Philbert who grunting now and causing the woman to let out one long last, shuddering . . . s-s-sigh.

The couple walking away. Their voices fading. And Debra gradually becoming aware of her surroundings again: the moon, which is a silver ball dimming the stars, the cool massage of the wind against her flesh, Gabby head almost blocking out the sky, the rustling sound and the hasty movements of Gabby's hands fumbling with his pants.

Young and foolish, she didn't know what to expect.

She didn't expect pain or the wetness of blood.

She didn't expect the silence that rise up like a wall between them when they walking back toward the houses in the village.

She didn't expect that when they reach the road all Gabby would say is See ya and walk off leaving her alone in the dark.

She didn't expect that what she thought would've been a happy night would leave tears welling up hot behind her eyes as she walked toward the group sitting on Miss Vivian steps.

She sat down with her arms wrapped around her knees and with pain between her legs, hearing voices only as background noises until it was time for everybody to go home.

Next morning she looked out her front window just as Gabby was passing by on the way to school.

She hissed "Ssssst" to get his attention, expecting a smile, expecting him to stop and chat her up because her mother was in the backyard and wouldn't be able to quarrel with her saying, How many times I warn you about talking to boys? If you bring any bundle in this house I going send you packing off to your worthless father.

But instead Gabby keeping his head straight like he en hear her, like he en notice her looking through her window. And in the days and weeks that followed never picking his teeth to say another word to her as if after she got up off the pasture and brushed off her dress she caught some kind of disease he didn't want to catch.

It is only years later—after he went away and come back, after what happened between them as children was something she stopped thinking about long ago—it was only then that she find out why he stopped speaking to her after that night on the pasture: he was frightened she was pregnant. "I was young and foolish," he tell her one day when they were lying back in the backseat of his car half-naked and still sweating. But that was Gabby. Always had a excuse for everything, always had a plaster for every sore.

Like when he tear down his grandmother old house after he get the job with the prime minister.

Debra watch a government lorry with men in the back come up the gap one morning and stop in front Miss Mimi old house. Quick so the workmen knocking down the little one-room wooden house that Gladstone used to live in when he and his parents first moved to the village after the hurricane.

Next day two lorries delivering building materials and over the weeks a bungalow going up, causing Debra to remember Miss Mimi one-room house: sideboards gray with age and weather; tin patches on the shingle roof; the wood door where you would see Miss Mimi from her shoulders up looking at the world outside through the top half propped open with a stick and the rest of her out of sight behind the closed bottom part, right up to the day she died. Miss Carter say she pass around forenoon and see Miss Mimi looking out as usual and when she ask her "How you keeping, Miss Mimi?" Miss Mimi say, "Not too good, girl." A hour later when Miss Esther come over with her mother-in-law food and unlatched the door and step in the house she find Miss Mimi lying on the floor, dead.

Now the house gone and with it the last remnants of Miss Mimi, so that when you pass by there's nothing to remind the living that there ever was a Miss Mimi or a Mr. Belle, Gladstone grandfather who worked at the sugar factory till the rollers crushed his hand like it was just another cane stalk and his screams mixed with the thunder of the machinery and his blood added color and flavor to that year's cane juice.

Not even the bare house spot remain. Nothing.

All the memories of the years Miss Mimi lived in that house with her family and then by herself in her old age, then with her son and his family till they catch themselves and get their own piece of land and moved out, memories seasoned into the very wood of the house and ground into the floorboards Miss Mimi scrubbed on her hands and knees, memories sprinkled in the dust under the house and bleached into the groundsill stones that the house sat on, memories of a lifetime, all torn apart by hammers, ripping irons, and workmen's hands tough with corns, memories hauled away in the pieces of broken lumber and scraps on the back of a lorry.

And one day standing in their place is a brand new almost shining cement bungalow with wrought iron bars on the windows and doors, and wrought iron gates in a stone wall topped with glass bottle, and a lawn that men bring on a lorry and lay down like a carpet. A new house with no history.

Meanwhile all that is left to remind generations of Miss Mimi is in a dump heap somewhere. Gone. Like Miss Mimi who used to call Debra Little Deedee and give her sugar cakes, who would call her and ask her what she learn in school today. Miss Mimi.

And years later when she finally got the chance to ask Gabby why he do that, why he tear down his grandmother old house and throw it away, why he couldn't at least give it to somebody who would've been glad even for a old house like that, at first he look at her with a half-smile like she was half-cracked, then when he see she serious he say, "I couldn't bear looking at it. It reminded me too much of Grandma." Just the kind of thing you would expect a politician would say.

Seeing that old house being torn down started her thinking, wondering if anybody would be around to prevent the same thing from happening to her: all the evidence of her pains, joys, hardships, laughter, tears, her life, everything ripped to pieces by ripping irons and hammers and tossed on top a lorry headed for the dump heap and replaced by something new. Would she have anybody to stop that from happening to her or would her children be like Gabby, wiping out her past like it was writing on a slate? That is a sad thing to think about, eh?

When she got laid off from the garment factory and Carl say, "Why you don't go over by Gabby and see if they want anybody to do servant work?" she had strong reservations about being a servant to somebody she grew up with. She didn't feel comfortable with the idea. But reservations is a luxury poor people can't always afford.

The little money Carl was working for at the garage could barely keep hunger from tying up their bellies. If it was only she and Carl they probably coulda managed, because adults can band their bellies and get by. But she had little Carl Junior to think about, only four, too small and innocent to suffer because of what grown-ups think about one another.

As the old people say, trouble don't set up like rain, and when it come it does fall bucket a drop. And that en only old people talk; it is a true fact. But it is also true that sometimes you can see rain coming but en got the sense to shelter from it. That is the way she was with Gabby.

The very said day that Miss Belle hire her, she in the kitchen turning off the stove under the food when she hear a car pull up in the carport. Gabby come home for lunch.

She reaching up to get the plates out the kitchen cabinet to get ready to serve the food when she hear footsteps coming in the kitchen and Gabby breathing close behind her.

"Debra?" he said.

She turned around. "Yes. Is me."

If she knew good for herself she would've walked out of the house right then and not come back, because she and Gabby staring into one another's eyes and it is as if the world stopped and she saying to herself, Debra girl, what wrong with you? When God was sharing out sense he decide not to give you none? and she hearing Miss Belle voice coming from the bedroom saying, "Gladstone? Is that you?" and Gladstone eyes locked on hers and he saying, "Yes, Mina. It is me."

It is like she catch a fever. That very same Saturday, she and Gabby driving on the coast road and they pulling off onto a dirt road that winding uphill between the casaurina trees, till the main road is a winding ribbon far below and the only sounds around them are the soughing of the casaurinas and the twittering of birds.

She think that is the day little Shirley came to life inside her, produced out of the two of them fumbling, grappling, panting, moaning, and "Oh God, Gabby. Oh God" and "Yesss, Debbie" and sweat running into her eyes and dampening her hair and her legs wrapped around his waist.

It was hard working as a servant in a house where she sneaking away with the married man every chance she get, even though she telling herself she had him first—from when he was a boy turning into a man and she a girl just getting breasts and feeling urges in her body she never felt before. Like that was a good excuse for what she was doing.

It was hard trying to keep things looking innocent in front Miss Belle, not because she didn't want her to know but because of the exact opposite. Isamina Springer. High-class Isamina Springer. Every day Debra had a strong urge to let her missis know that she, Debra

Welch, had Gladstone first and have him still, just to see the expression on her face.

The hardest thing was horning Carl, who is a good man, the father of her boychild, the man she'd been living with ever since she was old enough to leave her mother house, a man she suffer through all sorts of hard times with. And there she was, going through all this deceit, this two-timing, scheming, peeping, and dodging for what? Knowing that when all was said and done she still going to be Debra Welch with a child that Carl think is his, and Isamina Springer still going be Mistress Belle. And Gabby still going be the worthless unreliable bitch he always was who, if she know him, and she think she do, probably wouldn't own up to his child when he find out she pregnant for him.

So when he catch her oneside and telling her to meet him by the race pasture as usual, she finding all kinds of excuses. And when he come up behind her in the kitchen and caressing her hand or trying to kiss her she brushing him off. After he finally realize that she really en want nothing more to do with him he making a point of ignoring her, talking master-to-servant sharp with her, causing Miss Isamina to rebuke him one day with, "Gladstone, why you being so rude to Debra?" Acting as if he was the one that end it.

When her belly begin to show she never tell him what she know for certain—that the child is his.

She keep working almost up until it was time for the baby to born and when Mistress Belle ask her the day she was leaving when she coming back she look her full in her eyes and say, "I en coming back."

Sometimes she does see Carl looking at Shirley hard, like if he trying to see his features in her (at least that is the way it look to her). But up to now she don't know if Carl suspect anything about what happen between her and Gabby. It is hard to know what Carl does be thinking.

Now Gabby dead, lying in a coffin down at Mr. Simpson funeral home.

Perhaps she shouldn't have told him that Shirley was his daughter. But what else can you do when your daughter come home and tell you that the man who was your first boyfriend, the man who is old enough to be your daughter's father, the man who really is her father, offer her a lift in his car and when she asked him where he going he say, just for a drive, and they end up in a lonely spot and, He pull me over the seat, Ma. He pull me in the backseat. And she's looking at her daughter and wondering how somebody could pull a big, strapping, voluptuous girl like Shirley over into the backseat of a car. But she is her mother, so she marching the girl to Gladstone house but he denying it.

What can you do when you look in his eyes and en sure if to believe your own daughter? She en had no choice but to face him away from the eyes of everybody, not to accuse him of rape but to tell him what a slimy bitch he is for screwing his own daughter, because he had to know. He had to see the resemblance over the years.

And when she see him rest his forehead in his palms and shake his head she feeling all kinds of emotions mixed up inside her: blind fury at a man that would screw his own daughter, their daughter; anger with Shirley and her flirtatious ways that Debra always warn her about; anger with herself for being confused when she should be single-minded and focused in her anger.

Now Gabby is dead. Hanged himself. And her mind is just as confused as ever.

CARL

[11 A.M.]

And in town a fifteen-minute bus ride away, Debra's man Carl is sitting on a greasy bench in the garage where he works as a mechanic.

As he told me later, he's unwrapping the fish sandwich Debra fixed for him that morning when a mind tell him to look up and so help him, he nearly wet himself. Gabby standing right there in the doorway, a dark shape with the glare of the midday sun behind him, and his lips moving but with no sound coming from them.

Chilly bumps on Carl arms, his balls tighten up and his scalp suddenly prickling as though a swarm of wriggling insects crawling through his hair.

He trying to bawl but the only sound coming from his throat is a weeping groan like the noise his father used to make at night before Mum would shake him awake saying, Wake up! Wake up! Duppy riding you!

But this en no dream. It is broad daylight and he staring eyeball-to-eyeball with a duppy that should be resting itself in its coffin down at Simpson funeral parlor but instead standing up in the garage door in broad daylight frightening the piss out of a man.

And a voice right by Carl shoulder shouting, "HEY! WHAT WRONG WITH YOU, BOY? YOU SEEING DUPPY?" causing Carl to spring up off the bench, almost shitting his pants with fright and dropping his fish sandwich on the floor, his good fish sandwich his mouth was watering for couple minutes ago. He whipping his head around to see who it is frightening him like that but it is only Grantley, one of the other mechanics in the shop grinning and saying, "Boy, you look like you seeing duppy."

Carl is a peaceful man but the blood flying to his head and, so help him, only God knows what hold him back from knocking Grantley flat with a cuff.

So he picking up his fish sandwich and dusting it off with one eye on the doorway and seeing Gabby floating backward then vanishing altogether.

And fright and vexation making him holler at Grantley, "Boy, what the rass you doing creeping up on a man like that, eh? You stupid? Eh? You blinking stupid?"

And Grantley looking puzzled and hurt, then steupsing his teeth and walking off muttering something about you can't make a joke with some people. Some people don't know how to take a joke.

And as the fright wearing off Carl feeling bad about snapping at Grantley like that.

He sit back down on the bench and bite into his sandwich but it taste like sawdust. His hands shaking and he saying to himself with his mouth full, "Jesus Christ, boy. You better get your eyes check." But he know nothing en wrong with his eyes. He know what he just see. A duppy in broad daylight—Gabby that hang himself, who burying this afternoon.

As soon as he got in the house from work two days ago, the first thing Debra say was, "Gabby hang himself."

It take a couple seconds for the words to sink in, then he grunt, "Hm."

What else he could say? Plus whoever hear about a man having conversation on a hungry belly?

But Debra jump on him like a sitting hen snapping, "A man dead and that is all you got to say?"

Well. The words shoot right out of his mouth before he could stop them: "Gabby was *you* friend," he hear himself say. "Not mine." Years of pent up suspicion rising up in his mouth and gushing out like vomit. Because Debra's words and her attitude is like rough hands ripping the scab off a sore.

His father always used to tell him, "Boy, you got a memory longer than a donkey prick. You don't forget nothing." Which is true. And it is a curse. Because as much as he would like to forget it, as much as he tell himself it en important, the thought of Gabby and Debra down on the pasture years ago still does pop up in his memory every once in a while, even though he know that what Debra used to say, before she got tired of saying it, is true. "Me and Gabby was children, Carl. What happen between we long ago en got nothing to do with you and me. That was before you."

But even that is small potatoes longside the suspicion that gnawing inside him like a cancer all these years. He can't ignore the resemblance he see every day between his daughter Shirley and Gabby.

When Debra was doing servant work over at Gabby and his wife, Debra all of a sudden take up needlework—needlework! Blasted woman wouldn't pick up a needle to darn his pants but all of a sudden she saying she going over by her cousin to learn how to make dresses.

At first he en think nothing 'bout it, figuring is good she finding something new and useful to interest her. See how stupid we men is? But one night after Junior sleeping strong he decide to get on his bicycle and ride over by the cousin house to bring home Debra, to save her from walking home by herself. The cousin come to the window and when she see it is Carl, surprise stamp all over her face.

"Tell Deb I come for she," he say.

The cousin, Sheila, hesitate little bit then say, "She not too long left. Not too long. You en see she? I surprise you en meet she on the road."

When Carl get home, no Debra. About a hour later she come traipsing in and when he ask her, "Where you been?" she say, "At Sheila, nuh? Where you think?"

"You en been at no Sheila," he say. "I went there to pick you up and you wasn't there."

And she explode. "You spying on me? Eh? You spying on me? You don't trust me?"

And by the way she attacking him, which is unusual for her, by some little thing in her voice, her expression, a small voice in the back of his brain telling him: She guilty about something.

But it is funny how love for a woman can blur your reasoning and make you doubt what you see right before your eyes. When people say the man is the last to know, that en true. The man is the last to believe.

So it was with him. When Debra tell him, "You want to know where I was? Eh? You want to know? I was at Sheila but I left before you get there. And since the night was so nice I decide to take the long road home to walk and think little bit and straighten out some things in my head."

The straightening-out-things-in-her-head statement put such a worry inside him that he decide not to ask her what long road it was that she take. When women begin talking about straightening out things in their head you better watch out. They thinking about leffing you.

When Shirley born months later, he find himself searching hard to find his features in her.

And he hearing the gossip, the snickering behind his back. One night down at the rumshop in the heat of an argument Carl tell Delroy he always arguing about things he en know nothing about and Delroy steups his teeth and say, "But I en wearing Gabby jacket, though" and turn to the other fellows, laughing, and the fellows looking embarrassed.

Blood fly to Carl head but his emotions were so jumbled up that they immobilize him and clamp his mouth shut. He vex with Delroy for embarrassing him; he vex with himself for putting himself in a position for people to ridicule him; he vex with Debra for what he strongly suspect she do and which everybody seem to know she do. But that is the thing with people: they know too much.

He trying to tell himself that what Delroy say en bother him. Delroy en too bright, he telling himself, that is why he got to stoop to gossip and ridicule to win arguments.

He try real hard to ignore the gossip, telling himself that when people don't like to see you living good they does try to stir up all kind of trouble for you. People don't like to see you happy.

After a while the talk die down as the Village find other things to occupy itself with. Funny how the Village is like one whole living thing sometimes, eh?

But Gabby was always there between him and Debra, present in memories that keep pestering him like sandflies: the time he went over by Debra cousin house and she wasn't there; Saturdays when she would leave Junior with her cousin and go in town and come back later looking happy and humming; the night she keep asking him why he en going down by the shop tonight, getting more and more irritable, pacing around in the house, jumping like a dog bite her ass when a car horn blow outside. And he wasn't man enough to look out to see who it was, though he suspect.

And as time began to go by and the older Shirley get, the harder it was for him to see any features in her that look like him.

His own family calling him all kind of bewitched, stupidy this-and-that. His brother Stanley telling him, "That girl en got none of we family features. You can't see that? That girl en a Bostick." His father stop speaking to him altogether, saying he is a disgrace to the Bostick name.

And he blaming himself—imagine that?—saying if he didn't put the idea into Debra head to see if Gabby wife would hire her to do servant work, perhaps none of this would happen. What devil got into him? What foolishness take over his brain to put Debra and Gabby together like that? They were catching hell, true, but they coulda managed.

But sometimes he think that what his uncle Harold say is true: "Boy, all you want now is a saddle. That woman riding you like you is a born jackass." And Uncle Harold going on to say how he shame to see his nephew turn out to be so dotish and bewitched. Carl en a Bostick man. He, Harold, shame to show his face with people talking about his nephew so.

But Carl figuring Uncle Harold should be the last one to give anybody advice, seeing that no woman ever live with Uncle Harold for more than a year. The last one—a healthy-looking, hardworking, country woman name Rita—pack her things and leave, calling Uncle Harold a cheap, spiteful, old this-and-that who want to treat woman like a slave in this day and age and who think that all woman good for is lying down on their back, and cooking and cleaning for him. He en know this is a new day? she saying.

But the more Carl look at Shirley the harder it is to ignore what everybody saying.

Nobody in his family en got the kind of round features and wide mouth that Shirley got; nobody en short and stumpy like she turn out to be. Still, he try to treat her the same way he treat Junior—like she was his own flesh and blood, without any doubts. But sometimes he would be laughing and skylarking with her and he would notice her features or something in the way she laugh that remind him of Gabby, and the laughter would freeze on his face. His skylarking would fizzle out. Because he en Jesus or Mohammed or any of them fellas; he en no prophet or holy man. He is only a man that love his woman ever since they was children together, love her so bad she feel like a part of him. But Shirley ent.

So as Shirley get older she become more quiet around him, no longer laughing with the open face of a child but acting toward him like a puppy with its tail between its legs, a puppy that get kick too often. And that hurt him. It really hurt him, because he en a brute-beast. He is a human being that want to hug her especially when she sad or disappointed but he can't bring himself to do it; sometimes he want to laugh and frolic with her but feeling tense in his face whenever he try.

At times like these, and other times too, he would see Debra looking at him and Shirley but never saying nothing to him until one day (Shirley musta been about seven or eight) Debra catch him after he walk out of the house and sitting down under the tamarind tree in the yard whittling a stick and say to him, "She is you child too, you know."

He look up in her face and want to say, "Me child? You telling me that girl in there that look the image of Gabby is me child?" But he looking at the little frowning, worry wrinkles between Debra eyebrows, the slight sideways tilt of her head and the droop of her shoulders (as if her body saying sorry and asking for the forgiveness her mouth can't ask for); his eyes taking in the way her arms hanging straight down by her sides, her fingers playing with one another, her toes scuffing in the dirt. And the harsh words choking up in his throat. And he look off, silent, feeling her presence but not looking at her, feeling her turn and walk away and wanting to stop her with, Come back. Leh we talk about this. But he can't. His hands whittling the stick by themselves.

All of a sudden he wake up one morning and Shirley is fifteen, changing from girl to woman with voluptuous, tumbling buttocks and curves that making the young boys in the village goggle-eyed.

But it seem like it en only the young boys blood that the sight of Shirley ripening body set to pumping.

Although now he don't know what to believe. It wouldn't be the first time a young girl put the blame on the wrong man to protect herself or some young boy her heart beating for. It wouldn't be the first time. But how can you know? Gabby never say a word to defend himself when Debra walk up to his house and face him. All he say to her in a real soft voice and with a hurt expression on his face is, "You really believe that, Debra?"

And something (perhaps something in his voice, his expression) cause Debra to pause little bit. But only a instant before she say, "Yes I believe it! My daughter en a liar!" And the rage in her causing her fists to clench and veins to show on her neck as she saying, "You should be shame of yourself! Big man like you with a young girl like that! You en shame?" And she ignoring Mistress Belle standing in the gallery and she continuing, "I want satisfaction! I want satisfaction for what you do to my child!"

And the whole village looking on in silence as Gabby shake his head and say, "You really believe this. You really believe I would do something like that to your daughter?" and turning with his head bent and walking back into his house. And the silent crowd exploding with indignant talk, everyone at the same time saying:

"You hear that? You ever see such a bold-face . . ."

"Girl, there en no justice in this world . . ."

"If she was my daughter the police van would be coming for me . . ." A man's voice.

"I woulda slice him up like he is a tomato . . ." Another man's voice.

And Carl hugging Debra shoulder and telling her, "Come. Come leh we go home."

And another man, Booboo, saying, "Girl, you need a man. A real man that would represent you . . ."

And for the first time since he was a boy blood flying to Carl head and he turning to face Booboo and his fist connecting to Booboo head and Booboo staggering with a shocked look on his face and Carl stepping forward and his arms operating by theyself, wild, swinging, not with control, not like a boxer, but swinging from his shoulder sockets with force, with rage, causing him to connect with Booboo head with the inside of his arms, his fists, not feeling a thing as Booboo backing back, too stunned to defend himself. And just as sudden as his rage explode it subside. He stop, his arms hanging at his sides, staring at Booboo puffy eyes and slump-down shoulders and he turn away saying, "Debra, come."

Later Debra tell him the crowd open a way for them to pass. He en remember that.

Couple days later he in the rumshop leaning against the counter with his elbows on the countertop, his hands playing with the glass he just empty with one toss-back of his head when he hear Booboo say, "You want one of these?"

He turn his head. Booboo, with his face still puffy, saying to him, not meeting him eye-to-eye, "You want one of these rums?" and giving the bottle a slight push in Carl direction.

Carl look at the other fellas around Booboo—skinny-ass, red-eyed, puffy-faced Seymour that live down in the bottom and does work on a lorry—always drunk; Man Rat, husky, with his shirtsleeves rolled up as far as they can go to show off his biceps—he does work down at the docks; and Philbert who does do seaman work—is almost a year now since he come home from his last boat. They looking at Carl to see what he going do.

"That's all right," Carl say. "I just had one." And he walk out the shop, hop on his bicycle and head for the beach where he sit down till the sun almost finish sliding behind the horizon, thinking seriously about leaving the village, leaving the whole blooming country, perhaps boarding a schooner and getting off down the coast, or paying one of the fishermen a few dollars to take him out when he going fishing, across the water to the land that on a clear day look like a dark, slumbering, giant reptile lying on the ocean.

But over the last few weeks that feeling to flee gradually subside as he come to acknowledge that he was born and raised right here in this village and this is where he belong. How he can leave Debra and Junior, his own flesh and blood? How he can leave Shirley even, now that she in the middle of a storm of gossip?

Plus, something else happening that giving him a little satisfaction every time he see Gabby driving by or in his veranda.

Mistress Belle peeping and dodging every chance she get, horning Gabby, getting less discrete as time going on so that one night not long ago he coming home from a political meeting and see a man easing out of Gabby front door on tiptoes. That night the satisfaction in Carl belly open up a twisted grin on his face.

Now Gabby hang himself. And Carl wondering if Gabby find out his wife was horning him and couldn't take it; or if what Shirley accuse him of is true—that he ask her if she want a drive, carry her to a lonely spot and force himself on her—and now he can't face it; or perhaps it is the political rumors that seem to be growing every day, rumors about politicians involved in murder: like the murder of the Gittens girl (who used to be the prime minister secretary); the disappearance of the photographer after he took a picture of the prime minister with two half-naked, hungry children in the background; the body two tourists find on the beach not long ago; all kinds of dealings people saying the People's Lawyers Party involved in.

As for what Shirley accuse Gladstone Belle of, Carl looking in her face for answers but can only see the slyness of Debra in her, the Debra that Carl would see holding Gabby hand and going behind her mother paling at night, who let Gabby take her on the pasture just because Gabby was a high school boy all those years ago when they were all youths together, the Debra that Carl like from ever since he can remember, and who he still love so much that even the stamp of Gabby features in the face of the girlchild Debra say is his en strong enough to rip the bond that tying him to her.

When he was alive, Gabby and Carl never talk man-to-man, hardly ever say two words to one another. Yet now he dead Gabby appearing in broad daylight before Carl with apology on his face and his mouth moving as if he trying to say sorry. But sorry for what? For Debra? For Shirley?

If it is for Debra, he en got nothing to apologize for. Carl en got no grievance against Gabby. Gabby didn't force her to spread her legs. That was her choice.

And if it is Shirley he apologizing for, well what he expect from Carl? Shirley en Carl pickney; she is Gabby daughter. And it is hard for Carl to believe Gabby didn't know that, didn't see his features in the girl the same way everybody else did. Perhaps he didn't do it.

Something about Shirley story en sound right.

As Carl is telling me his story, a lorry stops in front of the shop. The driver gets out, but before he can begin talking Carl motions him to talk to Fitz who owns the shop.

Fitz and the lorry driver come back out with Fitz telling him the boys at lunch and he can either wait or come back later and he'll get one of the boys to look at his radiator.

"I'll wait," the driver says, and tells the two men standing on the lorry platform he going down the road to get something to eat. "All you want anything?" he says.

One man says a cheesecutter and a Ju-C, his partner requests a hamcutter and a mauby. The driver takes their money and begins walking knock-kneed down the road to the shop at the corner.

The two men are sitting at the back of the lorry with their feet dangling.

One of the men says, "Is a shame Gladstone Belle kill himself, eh? He was a good man. Too good for politics."

The partner, a tall, thin, light-skinned man with his shirt buttoned up to his neck hawks and spits over the side of the lorry and says, "Them is two words that don't go together: good and politics. If he was so good he wouldn't a been in politics."

The first man, a short, jet-black muscular bare-backed man picks his teeth and drawls, "Gladstone Belle was different. He had some good ideas."

"Good ideas in a politician is as useless as black-eyes-and-rice in a bucket of shit." The tall man says.

"And what that mean?" his partner asks him.

"What you think it mean?" the tall man replies.

The short man steupses his teeth. "That is the problem with unna. All-you listen to too much he-say she-say stupidness instead of judging people for yourself," he says.

"And you different," the tall man answers back.

For a few minutes they say nothing to one another. Then the tall man starts talking about cricket and the subject of Gladstone Belle becomes words dispersed like clouds by the wind.

I walked away from the garage where Carl worked, thinking of conversations I'd also had with Isamina, Debra, Miss Esther, Sonny-Boy, and others, assembling in my head the fragments of perceptions that together comprised the man we all knew as Gladstone Augustus Belle.

And I began to appreciate, perhaps for the first time (I had never considered such matters before), that one's identity is less a fabric of one's own weaving and more a patchwork of perceptions, quilted fragments of rumor, gossip and opinions that could very well be erroneous. And if they are, what then?

I also found myself wondering why when Sonny-Boy came to me with his son's journals suggesting that maybe I could do something with them, why didn't I tell him what was on my mind, what was on the tip of my tongue to say: that he was no longer in America where biographies seem as common as comic books, where every person of fame or notoriety, no matter how transitory and inconsequential, no matter how feeble-brained they may be, consider their lives worthy to be transcribed onto the pages of a book?

His son had enjoyed a distinguished public career, true. Deputy prime minister among other achievements. But in a land of rumor, gossip, and hearsay, everyone is a biographer. That is what I wanted to say but could not, realizing that the gray-haired man with bags under his eyes standing before me was merely seeking immortality as we all do. Sonny-Boy, a man of humble birth with his nose pressed against the windowpane of history, a man with no memorable achievement to gain him admittance, a man who had seen his chances of living forever in the genes of his son and his son's sons and *their* sons slip away with the death of his only boychild.

So is that why I undertook this endeavor: to satisfy the desires of a sad old man? No. Life is a little more complicated than that.

Initially I'd begun talking to friends, acquaintances and family of Gladstone hoping to garner an unwritten suicide note from among their collective remembrances, hoping to discover reasons other than the relationship Isamina and I had shared. So when Sonny-Boy offered me access to his son's personal thoughts via his diaries and journals it was as though an open door of discovery had been presented to me.

But discovery can be an illusion. Just ask old Christopher Columbus.

Because recollecting my own memories of Gladstone, never mind others', was like tugging at several protruding ends of a mass of knotted twine.

I remember, for example, one August vacation day not long after what turned out to be our final day spent together as childhood friends and just days before the beginning of the school term, my mother watching through her front window as Gladstone walked by and she said, "Soon that boy en going fart pon we." I didn't believe it.

But one evening less than a month later as I'm passing by his house I see Gabby at his front window looking out and I wave and hail Hello as usual. Gabby waves back. Normal routine.

This time, though, Miss Esther comes flying out of her house like a sitting hen, bawling and carrying on about the low-class people around here that want to drag her son down to their level because they en got nothing and en want her son to get nothing and, The next time I catch any of all-you runagates, hooligans, and harlots in front my house talking to my son I going bring out a pan of hot water and scald unna like a dead fowl, so help me God!

Which caused me to glance around to see who she's talking to.

But there's no one but me in the road.

My brain becomes a maelstrom and I'm speechless, staring aghast. Gabby and I have grown up together, sometimes late at night my mother having to tell him, "Boy, it getting late; your mother going soon start hollering for you" and it is like she and Miss Esther have a system of telepathic communication because right then Miss Esther's voice would ring out from two houses away, "GladSTUUUUUUHHHN!" And the same thing would happen when late night found me over at his house with Miss Esther saying how it's time for all-you to be sleeping and tomorrow is another day, and she would be smiling when she's saying this.

But now less than a month after he has begun secondary school I'm rooted to the ground on my eleven-year-old bare feet hearing this woman, this screaming stranger, carry on about hooligans and harlots dragging her son into the gutter. And she's talking about me.

Perhaps it was at that moment that I first began to understand how truly illusory is that state we call friendship; then again, perhaps not. Because at that age one doesn't ponder deeply on such things.

Over the years, however, I definitely have learned to avoid the disappointment of reaching for human friendship only to taste rejection like sand in my mouth because what was mistaken for congeniality was merely a mirage and not the oasis envisioned.

Was it Gabby, my former childhood buddy whose actions led me to this realization or was it his mother, Miss Esther, who simply wanted the best for her son as she saw it? And what the hell does it matter?

One day a few months after that episode with Miss Esther, I was home from school, sick with the flu, and I heard Gabby's voice at the front window telling my mother he heard I was sick and asking her how I was feeling and if he could come in to see me.

I still can hear the surprise in Mumah's voice as she said, "Yes . . . Yes . . . Come in."

That day Gabby sat on my bed talking and laughing and when it was time for him to leave he all of a sudden got serious and said, "You know, you's the best friend I ever had."

And for a moment we are back to the days of elementary school together, going to private lessons, planning for the future.

But when he left the moment left with him. For that's all it was—a moment.

Years later, days after he won his first election, the news spread all over the village that Gabby had been given the portfolio of minister of recreation and sports, the youngest minister in the cabinet.

Big jubilation broke out. Because in spite of what some people had come to think of him over the years he was the first—the first among us to hoist head and shoulders above the clouds and savor the air breathed by those in high professional and political positions.

That night Mr. Thorne's shop was packed with celebration. And in the midst of all the talk and laughter Gabby turned to me and said, "How you would like to work with me in the ministry?"

I looked at him standing in front of me with a rum glass in his hand and his face shining with sweat and I said, "You making joke, right?"

He gave me a steady stare then turned back to joking and laughing with the men.

To this day I remember that incident and it's like picking at a sore, because I still wonder whether he was serious that night or if it was the rum talking.

I never told my mother this because I knew what she would say: You so useless you can't even grasp an opportunity.

Now I'll never know.

Then there is the day of my uncle's wedding. Uncle Sharkey. Actually, his name was Douglas but nobody called him that.

It looked like the whole village was there: men drinking rum and talking loud; women off by themselves talking and laughing; little children scooting and scampering, playing and hollering.

Time for the toast and people begin looking around for Boy Blue the speechmaker. Finally a voice yells out, "There he is! Hey, Boy Blue! . . . They waiting for you!"

The noise quiets down.

And Boy Blue begins his speech bawling like an officer in the regiment. "Here we are!" he starts out, "on this auspicious occasion . . . !" (In the world of speechmakers in this country, every occasion is auspicious and every wife lovely.)

Now, normally the crowd would be going wild at this beginning, clapping, urging on Boy Blue with, "Words, man. Give we the big words!" And Boy Blue would be making up all kinds of multisyllabic words that never saw a dictionary and don't make any kind of sense. But they sound good. And the crowd would be in a frenzy, especially if the liquor was flowing, as it was that day.

But all of a sudden a slurring voice is drawling out, "Whyn't you shut up! Shut your damn beak! Always talking stupih . . . stupidness! En making no blaaasted sense!"

And right behind this voice comes total, stunned quiet, leaving Boy Blue standing in front of the crowd frozen and blank-faced.

Because for years now, as long as most people can remember, Boy Blue is the official toaster for miles around. No dispute, no contest, even though nobody ever had a clue what he was saying, with some people thinking his words were too high for them and others being plain skeptical. Like my father who one time I heard say, "I got a feeling Boy Blue does make up them big words he does use, but they sound good, though. And they does really suit the occasion."

So Boy Blue was king of the village when it came to speechifying till the day Uncle Sharkey got married and the sound of a drunken voice hit the crowd like a deluge of ice-cold water and broke the spell.

One solitary voice in the gathering came to Boy Blue's defense saying to the drunken voice, "Aw, shaddup, let the man talk."

Meanwhile Uncle Sharkey is frowning, at first angry, then thoughtful. Then he snaps his fingers and says, "He right, you know? He damn right." And his eyes search the crowd and light on Gabby and he says, "Gabby. Come up here."

So now Gabby is weaving through the crowd and everybody is silent as Uncle Sharkey lays his hand on Gabby's shoulder and says to the gathering, "This is a Wilberforce boy." Then he turns to Gabby. "Go ahead, boy," he says. "Show them how to make a speech. Talk your high school talk."

Now everybody's eyes are on Gabby up there in front of the whole village in his short-pants suit looking nervous with his hands behind his back, one shoulder up and the other one down, shuffling from one foot to the other. And everyone is probably figuring, what the hell this little boy can say on a big occasion like this? At least with Boy Blue they know what to expect.

Gabby starts out in his little, high-pitched voice with, "Ladies and gentlemen, we are here on this auspicious occasion to celebrate the marital bliss of our good friend and neighbor . . ."

Well the whole place break loose. People bawling for murder, whooping, throwing their hats in the air to hear this eleven-year-old boy talking so sweet.

And Uncle Sharkey going, "Shhhhhhh! Shhhhhhh! Let the boy talk, nuh!" till finally everybody cools down, listening to Gabby make this mellifluous speech with real words that they can understand (some of them anyway) but which put together so sweet they sound like music.

And for days all people talking about is how Gabby mash-up the place with the sweetest speech they ever hear. The boy going be a lawyer and a politician, some saying. And somebody say, No, a radio announcer. But that remark bringing ridicule on the person that made it. "Anybody can be a radio announcer," somebody says. "That is something to wish for the boy?"

And for the whole week Boy Blue is passing Gabby and keeping his head straight, not answering when Gabby says "Good morning" or "Good day, Mr. Goldbourne."

And for people this is a big joke to see a grown man acting like that: refusing to speak to a little boy young enough to be his son.

Boy Blue couldn't take the ridicule. One night not long after the wedding a lorry shows up in the village and Boy Blue and the two men on the lorry begin to load Boy Blue's few pieces of furniture, clothes, and odds and ends onto the lorry.

Next day the news get around that Boy Blue moved to town.

Years later, after Gabby came back from overseas he came up to me one day and said, out of a clear, blue sky, "Remember the speech I made at your uncle's wedding?"

By then the consensus was that he came back from Away half-mad, so I'm searching his face for the lunacy behind his question; but he appears to be serious, so finally I say, "Yes." Though I'm still wary.

"I always thought you would've made a better speech if he'd asked you," he says.

Well needless to say I was stunned.

But that was Gabby—always unpredictable.

After Boy Blue moved to town, it wasn't long before he became nationally popular as the M.C. for the People's Lawyers Party, warming up crowds at political meetings with his nonsensical speeches.

To this day, as old as he is, he still is so popular that he's getting all the women he wants, young and old, while Gabby is lying in the cemetery for reasons nobody knows and his former colleagues have concocted an official tale nobody believes.

SERGEANT STRAKER

[11 A.M.]

Down at the police station in Spring Gardens on the day of Gladstone's funeral, Sergeant Straker and two constables are sitting at a table by the side window playing dominoes. One of the constables glances up at the clock on the wall and says, "Almost time for them to put down your boy Gladstone Belle, Sarge."

Sergeant Straker's only answer is to grunt and stare at the dominoes cupped in his palm.

These young fellas. Think they know it all. They listen to rumors and wild talk and they believe they know. But he can't really blame them because it is easier to run with the herd than it is to find your own way. Even he sometimes finds himself jumping to conclusions along with everybody else.

Like the last time he talked to Gladstone Belle the day he rushed out from the house in Spring Gardens with his hands to his mouth, bending over in front the house like he wanted to vomit.

With everybody looking on the sergeant couldn't hold back his scorn as he looked at the deputy prime minister acting as if he didn't know about the goings-on at the house.

These fellas. Keeping company with jailbirds like Peewee, inviting them to their private big-shot parties, looking the other way when election time come around and these jailbirds and vagabonds going around intimidating people, telling them vote for the PLP or you know what go happen, vote PDP or you going be sorry. And people so frigging frightened elections is a farce, even though Roachford always quoting some foreign organization that years ago list this country as one of the freest and most democratic nations in the world.

And even when it en election time these stupid little gangsters and criminals waging vendettas in the name of whichever party they attach themselves to, killing one another and innocent people in the name of people who don't care if they live or die. Anything more stupid than that?

Then when politicians like Gladstone Belle come face-to-face with the brutish handiwork of thugs like Peewee and his friends they acting like it turn their stomach, like it is some kind of revolting shock.

For years people in the neighborhood shunning this house in Spring Gardens. The sergeant and his men suspect what's going on. But what they go do? Stick their necks out and get them chopped off? They is policemen, yes. But policemen is small fry that can get eat by the big sharks just like anybody else if they not careful.

But perhaps people finally getting bolder. What Mr. Jenkins did—going to Gladstone Belle's office to complain about the house—would never have happened years ago. Although, seeing what happened to Mr. Jenkins afterward, it may not happen again for a long time either.

From the moment word came to him years ago that Peewee was renting a fancy bungalow in Spring Gardens but nobody en see no furniture moving in, the sergeant suspect something illegal was going on in that premises but he en had no proof. But he knew Peewee.

He and Peewee grew up together. From when he was small, Peewee make up in spite for what he lack in strength. A bony little runt that couldn't beat none of the other boys his own age, who would run for rocks and start pelting if he and anybody get in a fight. Couldn't fight hand-to-hand. A real little weakling.

Later he begins walking with a knife in his pocket, swaggering and threatening to "slice you open and cut out your guts like a fish"—his favorite words—every time he and somebody had a quarrel. So without anybody actually saying anything, the fellas began to shun Peewee. They ban him; because nobody doubt he would really use that knife, which means either you would have to find something to defend yourself with (and get yourself in trouble over a little shit like Peewee) or risk getting cut with Peewee knife.

So Peewee name would be the last one anybody would call whenever they picking sides to play a game of cricket or football; he would always be at the fringes of conversations with his rotten-teeth self; none of the girls liked him—the only girl he ever got pussy from as far as anybody know, was half-foolish, butter-teeth Marlene who her mother wouldn't let out of the house out of fear she would bring home a big belly. But one day one of the little boys catch Peewee climbing over the paling when Marlene's mother wasn't home. And when the fellas laughing at him he throwing out his little chicken chest and boasting about how big Marlene legs is and how they roll around in Marlene mother bed and Marlene bawling and grabbing the sheet in her fists when he giving it to her from behind. Which caused some of the fellas to swallow their pride and investigate to see if what Peewee say was true.

When Peewee finished elementary school he began hanging out in town every day, a wharf boy during the day, bare-backed with only a old khaki short pants on, diving for coins the tourists tossing from their yachts, and at night liming in Drake Street where the whores, sailors, pimps, roughnecks, and petty criminals mixed up altogether in a stew of iniquitous humanity. And the boy en no more than a fourteen-year-old runt with rotten teeth and a cigarette in his mouth.

Next thing the sergeant heard, Peewee in jail for stabbing a man in a fight over some whore. By the time the sergeant joined the force, Peewee was a regular jailbird with a violent reputation.

So you can imagine the surprise it caused when Peewee began to show up at political meetings helping to set up the lights and microphone and odds-and-ends like that, hanging around the politicians, talking and laughing with them—even the prime minister—like he and them is pals.

And Peewee telling people he is a bodyguard for the PLP politicians. Of course everybody know what that mean: Peewee is a political gangster.

The week after the prime minister picture appeared in the newspaper with two ragged children and devastation from the hurricane in the background, Rudolph Brathwaite, alias Al Capone, got drunk at a rumshop in town and bragged about how he and his friend Peewee cut off the photographer's hands in a house in Spring Gardens and drink a whole bottle of rum while the photographer bleeding to death and rolling around on the floor and hollering behind the gag they stuff in his mouth.

You really can't hide nothing in this country, so the news reach the sergeant ears (he was a corporal then) and he canvasing the neighborhood asking people if they heard or saw anything strange at the premises in question.

Mr. Ward who lived next door whispered, "Don't tell nobody I say this, but one night last week I get up to pee and hear a lot of racket coming from that house, loud voices, like somebody arguing."

Miss Gilkes who lives at the back of the house said she saw Al Capone coming out the back door of the bungalow with the photographer. "He en had no hands," she said.

"What you mean he en had no hands? Who en had no hands?" the sergeant asked her.

"The man with Rudolph," she said. "All he had was stumps. With blood dripping from them and with a rag around his mouth to keep him from hollering, I figure."

But it is hard to go by what Miss Gilkes says because, as everybody knows, she's mentally unstable, always in the habit of running out from her house naked as she was born hollering that some dead man or the other just raped her. The last one, according to her, "sneak up behind me and torpedo me like a submarine."

But the fact is that no one ever saw the photographer again—except if you want to count half-cracked Miss Gilkes.

A couple days after Al Capone bragged about what he and Peewee did, two little boys found him lying facedown on Brighton Beach, dead with all his clothes on, even his shoes—Al Capone who lived off the whores on Drake Street, dressed like a pimp in the movies and wore gold chains and bracelets like they cost a penny apiece; the same Rudolph Brathwaite you would see driving the prime minister private car from time to time. What it is about these government ministers letting these crooks drive their cars, eh? For the crooks it show everybody they have connections. But it always puzzle the sergeant what the ministers get out of it. Even Gladstone Belle, who the sergeant thought knew better.

When the sergeant saw Peewee driving Gladstone Belle Mercedes, he wasn't sure Gladstone knew who Peewee really was, so he figure he ought to warn him.

One day the sergeant is walking along Main Street when he sees Gladstone Belle coming out of DeFreitas Department Store, so he calls him aside and lowers his voice and tells him how he saw Peewee driving his car the other day and, "You know he's a jailbird?"

Gladstone Belle looks him in the eye and says, "I know."

Well, that one knock the stuffing out of the sergeant and he wants to say, You know? Then why you letting him drive your car, then? But it's not his place to ask, so he just mutters, "Just thought you'd like to know" and Gladstone Belle says "Thanks. Thanks for your concern." And that was that.

And as Gladstone Belle walks away the sergeant reminds himself that though Gladstone Belle has a reputation for being an eloquent, flamboyant speaker in public, everybody says that in private he is reticent and shy as a virgin (at least *some* virgins). But the sergeant expected a different reaction—some kind of explanation for why he would associate with a low-life criminal like Peewee. But nothing. Only thanks.

So the sergeant continued on his way shaking his head and thinking, What a shame.

Because the first time Belle ran for a seat in the House, the sergeant would go to political meetings just to hear him talk, not the usual gossip and mudslinging but sensible talk about what the country need, about what he, Gladstone Belle, planned to do not only for his district but for the whole country: new health clinics; free bus tickets for old-age pensioners; community centers to keep the youths off the street; school lunches because children can't learn on a hungry belly. Things like that.

But then he got elected. And perhaps what the sergeant's old grandmother used to say is true: If you sleep in a goat pen you bound to wake up smelling pissy.

Although the sergeant got to admit that every Tuesday evening when the radio broadcast the debates in the House of Assembly he always would make sure to be near a radio.

The sergeant remembers one debate in particular. The honorable member for St. Augustine parish introduced a bill to raise the representatives' salaries.

People listening to their radios and figuring this one will pass easy as usual. That is the one sure thing you can always bet on.

But then another voice coming through the radio speakers, a high-pitched, almost girlish voice. Gladstone Belle asking the honorable member from St. Augustine how many cars he have.

A long pause and then, "T'ree." In a soft voice.

"I didn't get that. How many?" Gladstone Belle asked.

"T'ree! I said t'ree!"

"So you have three cars," Gladstone Belle said. "Three luxury cars. PLUS, and Gladstone Belle paused here, "correct me if I am wrong, but you have, in addition to your rather comfortable residence, a beach house at Sheridan beach, a . . ."

At this point the honorable member from St. Augustine interrupts, bawling that it eh none of Gladstone Belle business what he got; he work hard for everything he got. Everything. And, You calling me a thief? Eh? You saying I thief the public money? Eh? You accusing me? Eh? Come right out and say it! Say it, if you's a man!

And people who were in the gallery at the House of Assembly say the honorable member from St. Augustine took off his jacket and rolled up his shirtsleeves and rushed toward Gladstone Belle, and the policeman standing at the door with his hands behind his back had was to rush and hold back the honorable member from St. Augustine to prevent him from attacking Gladstone Belle right there in the House.

When everything cooled down and they took the vote, the bill didn't pass. *That* year.

And it wasn't only the backbenchers, fellow ministers and opposition members that Gladstone Belle kept on their toes but even the prime minister, challenging him when he announced plans for an industrial park and tax incentives for foreign companies operating in the park ("What guarantees do we have?" Gladstone Belle asked), when Roachford announced that exploration on the Hill hadn't yielded the expected results and that the company had applied for permission to develop the area into a tourist resort ("And what about the people who live there?" Gladstone Belle asked), and when helicopters were flying overhead while the prime minister announced "assistance from our northern friends . . ." Gladstone Belle stood up in the House and said, "I wash my hands of this" and walked out.

He was like a buzzing mosquito, raising questions, criticizing plans. Every time somebody raised an issue in the House, or introduced a bill, their glances would flick to where he was sitting first before they began to speak. He was young, he was fiery, he was popular, winning his seat in a landslide every time.

The sergeant looked in Gladstone Belle's eyes the day he approached him about Peewee driving his car, thinking he would see the same thing he'd been noticing in politicians, university students, and some young middle-class people: it was as if they felt that their life was too soft and by associating with jailbirds and hooligans some of the street toughness would rub off on them.

But the sergeant couldn't read Gladstone Belle, though he felt like telling him, Boy, you playing a dangerous game. You're a good man. The people around you en no good. I been in the police force for twenty years, so I know. But you's a good man. Don't follow them. But he kept his mouth shut. Gladstone Belle was a grown man and he was a policeman, not a baby-sitter.

A few days after Gladstone Belle came to the house in Spring Gardens, two tourists found the body of a man on the beach with his throat sliced open and his tongue stuffed inside his mouth—the old man that show up with Gladstone Belle at the house in Spring Gardens. Mr. Jenkins.

Soon after this is when a rumor sprang up and began spreading like weeds in rainy season: Gladstone Belle had the old man killed to shut him up, people saying.

At first the sergeant just shook his head, thinking that this rumor was so ridiculous it would soon fizzle out.

But then more rumors began to circulate: Gladstone Belle embezzled petty cash from the ministry; he purchased personal items and submitted vouchers for official expenses.

So one minute Gladstone Belle is a champion in the eyes of the people, next minute the same people dragging his name in the dust and arguments raging.

—I know he wasn't no blooming good. Behind all that talk, all that pretty-pretty thing, he is just another vampire like all the rest of them.

—How you know what people saying is true?

—How you mean how I know? It sound true.

That sort of thing.

There is a saying: When everybody thinks the same, nobody thinks. So it becomes easy for rumors to spread faster than a grass fire in dry season. As he always say, rumor-mongering is like playing rugby with a ball of shit and thinking is a genuine ball you catching and passing on. Worst yet, woe to the man who try to say, Hey! You playing with a ball of shit!

One evening the sergeant is strolling down the street and he notices a crowd. People arguing. Voices raised. Hands waving around. And a man in the middle of the crowd is saying that it sound to him like somebody start the rumor linking Gladstone Belle to Mr. Jenkins's death so as to throw attention on Gladstone Belle and off themselves, "Think about it," he saying. "All these years Gladstone Belle is the only one among them pack of thieves that anybody respect. Now all of a sudden he is the ringleader? I know Gladstone Belle as a decent young man. Know him since he was a boy. Use your heads, man. This whole thing don't make no sense."

Well who tell him say that? Is like the crowd of people turn into a pack of wild dogs. Everybody talking at the same time and somebody saying, "Pack of thieves? What you is? A agitator? The prime minister warn we about people like you."

"What?" the man is asking. He's looking puzzled.

Meanwhile another voice in the crowd is saying that people like him want killing, and another one wants to know if he belong to the opposition party, if they send him up here to spread lies and stir up mischief. You's a PDP man? somebody is asking.

Next thing you know, elbows raising and fists connecting and the poor man is fleeing with the crowd chasing him with a rain of rocks right up to the door of the police station and the sergeant is running behind the crowd bawling, "Hey! Hey!" but nobody's taking him on. And when the crowd reach the police station the sergeant has to shove his way through it and he finds the man inside panting like a racehorse and ashen as a duppy and guzzling down water, cup after cup.

And they had to keep him inside the police station till all of the crowd finally dispersed. But the man should've known better. The district is a Roachford stronghold, elections coming up later in the year, and here he comes airing his dissident opinions. He was lucky to be alive.

All the sergeant could do was stare at him and ask him, "You stupid?" Because although he might have been right, you have to know when to keep your mouth shut.

People disappear, bodies turn up, sometimes so mutilated that not even their closest relatives can identify them. And even though rumors and speculation continue to buzz all over the place like shit flies, nobody has served a day in jail because nobody see nothing. And for good reason.

Now Gladstone Belle is dead and all of a sudden speculation is rampant that perhaps he was involved in "political chicanery" as the newspaper editorial put it, and his wrongdoings crept up on him like Miss Gilkes's duppy rapists and pushed him toward suicide.

Some are saying that it's because he raped that girl in his village and couldn't stand the embarrassment after the girl's mother exposed him.

But the funny thing about that particular affair is that neither the girl nor her mother reported anything to the police. So without an investigation, all anyone really has is rumor and allegation, which is no more than entertainment at the expense of somebody else's anguish.

The sergeant slams a domino on the table, thinking, What a pity. What a waste. Gladstone Belle was a good man who got sucked into a mud hole where he finally sank to the bottom and perished.

And as he glances up at the clock on the wall his instinct also reminds him of something it told him the moment he stepped into Gladstone Belle's house and saw the ex-deputy prime minister hanging from a ceiling joist—something didn't look right. He couldn't put a finger on what it was that struck him as being out of place. But something about this whole setup didn't fit.

And he couldn't help thinking that this is an election year, Gladstone Belle was a thorn in the foot of his former party. And thorns must be removed.

ISAMINA

[11:30 A.M.]
If this were a normal day Isamina would have been closing her boutique and hanging the sign on the door that says: Closed for lunch. Will reopen at noon. But today is not an ordinary day.

So, hours before she is due to bury her husband amid speculation about the reasons for his death, she is sitting on the bed with her robe open, examining the rolls of fat encircling her waist that used to be firm and narrow but which Gladstone had come to look at with profound scorn. "You look pregnant," he told her once. "You need to exercise."

She gazed at her thighs—still firm though broader now. Her face staring back at her in the mirror had long lost the soft smoothness of youth—laugh lines framed her mouth ("There are creams you can use to soften your face, you know," Gladstone said); more gray hairs seemed to be appearing every day (she gave up plucking them, because plucking only seemed to annoy them into returning and bringing along more with them out of sheer spite).

Almost fifty years of her life had gone by and there she was bearing the heavy, mind-numbing burden of widowhood alone with no one around to make her load lighter.

"What?" That is what her father barked when I told him what Isamina said about the burden of her solitary widowhood.

His face turned red and he began to explain that as soon as his daughter called him, yes, the minute he picked up the phone and heard that Gladstone was dead he hopped in his car, he and his wife, and drove down to the village in time to see the mortuary van driving off, and right away, *right away* he offered to handle the arrangements. And this is the thanks he gets? Eh?

Ask Miss Belle, he told me. Ask Miss Belle. She was right there too saying that her family had a plot in the cemetery and she wanted Gladstone buried in his grandfather's grave.

So he offered to drive Miss Belle down to the cemetery to take care of that end of it. His wife volunteered to see about the radio announcement and obituary in the newspaper.

Meanwhile Isamina waited cool till everybody finished speaking then said Gladstone was her husband and her responsibility, but she thanked them for offering to help.

No matter how much he talked he couldn't change her mind. The girl is stubborn. Hard-headed.

That's when Miss Esther got upset, saying Gladstone was her son and he would want to be buried with his family.

According to him, at this point Mrs. Springer (that's how he referred to his wife), not wanting to become involved in a public argument, tugged on his sleeve and told him, Come, Philip, let's go.

And knowing how stubborn Isamina could be and that arguing with her would be like trying to budge a balking mule, he decided to leave but not before telling her that if she changed her mind he was there to help.

All three of them left—he, Mrs. Springer, and Miss Belle. They gave Miss Belle a lift to her house.

That is Mr. Springer's account of what happened, told to me while Mrs. Springer sat nearby nodding in agreement.

Miss Esther, on the other hand, told another story. According to her, when she tell that daughter-in-law of hers about the family plot and say how Gladstone come to her in a dream and tell her he want to bury in his grandfather grave, that girl start screeling. Screeling, eh? Talking about how Gladstone is her husband, *her* husband and how he left instructions that the two of them should be buried together so that they could be together in death as they were in life, so she's going to buy a plot for her and her husband according to her husband's wishes.

And she, Miss Esther, mad to ask this daughter-in-law of hers to show her in black and white where Gladstone left instructions because number one, why would he give his wife those instructions and then turn around and come to his mother in a dream and say some thing else, eh? and, two, everybody know he and Isamina wasn't getting along—she hear for a fact that in the day she walking around like butter can't melt in her mouth but at night she sneaking around with somebody else behind Gladstone back. She even hear the person she horning Gladstone with is a woman. What wickedness, eh? What the Bible say is true. These really is the last days.

Plus the way she screeling and carrying on like somebody want to thief her husband remind you of people you see crying and hollering the hardest at funerals, beating their fists on the coffin and talking about, Put me down with him! I want to go with him! Usually they is the head ones who used to neglect the person when they were alive, or treat them bad. It look suspicious and make her wonder what else Isamina feeling guilty about—apart from two-timing Gladstone, that is.

Gladstone tell her clear and plain in her dream, Mum, I want to bury with Granpappy. But she en want to make a scene in her son's house with him not even cold yet, so she zip her mouth shut and keep quiet for the sake of dignity and decency.

But according to Isamina, what she wanted most from the three people standing in her house hours after she found her husband hanging was some kind of reconciliation, some sense of a family sharing grief. But looking back on it, that was too much to expect: Gladstone detested her parents and Miss Esther, her mother-in-law, hated her guts. So what she got instead was her father offering to help only out of a sense of duty, her mother who probably was glad that Gladstone was dead even though she would never admit it even to herself, and Miss Esther who seemed to think that she was the only one who'd lost somebody she loved.

That is Isamina's story.

But regardless of who you choose to believe, what everyone does agree on is that Isamina band her belly, as the saying goes, and went about making funeral arrangements with such apparent dispassionate self-assurance that people began to talk, saying:

—Look she. Like she in a hurry to put him down.

—Ent? Not a tear in her eye. Is like if she had it plan.

—A little bird tell me Gladstone hair was plait in cornrows when they find him. You ever see Gladstone Belle hair in cornrows? Cornrows good for hiding bullet holes, you know.

—How you know so much about hiding bullet holes?

But as Isamina said later, if she was crying and helpless people would've said she was shedding crocodile tears. Folks will talk regardless of what you do, so it is best to go about your business and not pay them any mind.

And so it was that on the morning of the day of the funeral, realizing that nothing was left for her to do but wait for afternoon, she had the feeling of emerging suddenly from a fog and seeing clearly for the first time that in a few hours she would be putting her husband's body in the ground: Gladstone who sat at the dining table with his head in his hands after she'd finished packing her bags to leave and who tied a rope around his neck and departed this life while she was down the front road shopping for provisions to cook their last meal; whom she told days ago, "I'm not happy, Gladstone."

And she wasn't, and she isn't now, and she's wondering which is worse. Because grief and guilt is a potent mixture. And there is grief, even though her packed suitcases still sit on the floor next to her bed, relics of their domestic rift.

Because you don't share a life and a house with somebody for over twenty years and not feel haunted by the empty space left when they're no longer there.

Even though in the last year or so, the intermittent quarrels they had almost from the beginning became increasingly frequent fights fought with words that inflicted festering wounds that never healed.

From her: "You don't care for anybody but yourself. . . ." "I don't feel loved. . . ." "You don't do anything to please me. It's all Gladstone, Gladstone. . . . I can't take your moods. One minute you're cheerful, next minute you're giving me the silent treatment."

Recently: "I came home from the boutique yesterday after a hard day, tired, head aching from dealing with rude, demanding customers, and I tried to talk to you but you, with your head buried in the newspaper. I come home every day and I don't have anybody to talk to."

And he's accusing her of being a spoiled, self-righteous, bourgeois bitch, a daddy's little girl who likes being in the limelight as a government minister's wife but who doesn't appreciate his problems; a vacuous spoiled brat only interested in things and status and her little teas with her little, empty-headed, materialistic bourgeois friends. And that boutique of hers is only a pastime, a hobby, a toy. And, if she ask him, she should sell it to somebody who really needs to make a living.

This last remark caused tears to well in her eyes because she wasn't anything like that "and you know it. You're only saying these spiteful things to hurt me because you know what I'm saying about you is true. You're selfish, callous, and cold. I work hard in that boutique. Anybody can tell you that."

Most often he would be repentant and his attitude would soften and he would become more attentive for a few days. But then he'd go right back to his old cold, indifferent self, and it would be like nothing happened.

She would never know when he was going to be in a good or bad mood. Sometimes they would go for days hardly talking, with him giving her the silent treatment; bossing her around like she was a child, till lately she put her foot down and demanded respect. "I'm not taking this from you anymore," she told him.

Her rage would simmer inside her till like a volcano she'd erupt with searing words of hurt and anger she'd vented so many times before. Every time it would be the same. He would change for a little while and then go right back to his own selfish, insensitive ways.

But it wasn't always like that.

One of the things she liked most about the early days was the way he would take off early from work and they would go driving, sometimes not coming back home till the bats were swooping in the sky and evening breezes blew with the coolness of menthol.

She remembers one day in particular: the *blam* of the car door slamming in the garage; the twisting of the front doorknob; his rubber soles padding on the tiled floor; his arms around her waist and his body pressed against her back as she looked into the vanity mirror to see his chin resting on her shoulder as he's saying, "Let's go."

They packed their lunch into a basket. Debra, who was the servant then, not pleased and wanting to know, "All-you not eating here?"

"No," Gladstone said. "We're going on a picnic."

They drove along winding country roads with the car windows open. She closed her eyes, lay back her head, feeling the breeze against her face and inhaling the aroma of cane sugar boiling in the factories.

The car slowed; she opened her eyes. Cane fields framed both sides of the highway which converged to a point in the distance.

They turned onto a cart road rutted by years of tractors, lorries, and mule carts hauling cane from field to factory. The car bumped and rocked until finally they reached a spot where the highway was no longer visible through the rear window.

Gladstone switched off the engine. All around them cane blades rustled; a tractor chugged in the distance; a blackbird cawed as they hastened into the backseat of the car her father gave them as a present after Gladstone got the job of prime minister's assistant.

All four doors remained ajar.

And that day with Gladstone inside her, Isamina felt stirrings inside her that she'd never felt before, sensation engulfing her and sweeping her into such delirium that she locked her ankles against the crest of his buttocks, clutched his shoulder and closed her eyes as his breath rasped near her ear, feeling him hard inside her, aware of the leather seat slippery beneath her sweating body, the rustling of cane blades, the soughing breeze sweeping through the car, acquiring awareness of what her girlfriends carried on so much about, even as a moan welled within her, "Oh, Gabby. Oh Lord, Gabby" (and mind you, she never called him Gabby). But just as she's about to hurl a cry from the depth of her gut past the back of her throat to vent the passion building in her Gladstone utters one long groan and collapses with his chin resting on her shoulder, leaving her writhing, clutching his shoulders and squeezing her eyes tightly closed, attempting to hold on to the feeling, until finally she relaxes. No use.

Gradually she becomes aware again of her surroundings as the delirium fades and the feeling is that of teetering on the brink of a precipice of passion as she lies with Gladstone still folded in her arms and scissored within her thighs.

Gladstone was the first to get dressed as she lolled in the backseat naked, caressed by the breeze that flowed through the four open doors of the car.

But back then she wasn't bitter, because the fun of those afternoons was more than the hurried undressing and sweaty grappling in the backseat of the car. It was the excitement of taking off in the middle of a working day, carefree, driving with no planned destination, enjoying the breeze, the countryside, and one another's company.

On that first day they sat in the car in the midst of the canefield and ate the lunch Debra had packed.

Then Gladstone drove to a fishing village and they watched the fishermen unload their catches, then sat on the beach and watched the seagulls swoop and glide while the market women and fishermen haggled over prices.

The sun was a big red ball sliding below the horizon when they got up, dusted the sand from their clothes, and drove home.

Sometimes they would drive along the windy east coast road inhaling the salty sea mist caused by white-capped waves that rolled shoreward and bashed against rocks so glistening brown and huge they must have seen the flailing arms and heard the gasps of drowning crews of sailing ships of centuries past.

And on those carefree days she would tease Gladstone, asking him, "Boy, you don't have no work to do? What kind of job is that you have?" And he would throw back his head and laugh and say, "Work can wait. If I die tomorrow they will find somebody else."

One day they parked in the middle of an open pasture with two scrawny cows grazing nearby. The cows raised their heads and stared but then resumed munching the grass that was so scorched by the sun it was no wonder that the poor cows looked so malnourished.

That day sweat burned her eyes and she clutched the edge of the car seat while behind her Gladstone grasped her hips as his groin rammed against her bottom as he pistoned inside her.

Afterward, she and Gladstone stopped by a roadside rumshop and drank rum-and-cokes in the quietness of the afternoon, sitting at a table under a tree in front of the shop—she sipping, Gladstone throwing his head back and tossing the liquor down.

That was the first day she saw his anger. People say trouble don't set up like rain but that's not always true. Sometimes it does; we just don't pay attention.

They were driving along listening to the music on the radio and watching the sun glint on the sea when suddenly Gladstone shouted, "Shit!", wrenched the steering wheel, and the car swerved.

She looked up in time to see a small truck zooming from a side street.

Gladstone stamped on the brakes, her body pitched forward, the little white truck came so close to the front of their car that she swears to this day that she saw red veins in the whites of the driver's eyeballs.

They missed the little truck which turned, straightened up, and kept hopping merrily along blowing light-blue smoke from its tail.

Their car smacked into a tree. The damage was slight—just a small dent on the front fender—but Gladstone's fists balled up and his face grew tight with fury and he clamped his mouth shut. They drove home in silence. The ticking of the clock, the sound of Debra moving around in the kitchen and the clacking of their forks against their plates were the only sounds during dinner.

When Debra said Good evening before leaving, only Isamina answered, Get home safe.

Later as she sat in the veranda listening to the crickets and watching the fireflies flicker in the dark, Gladstone came from the house and leaned against the rail with a rum glass in his hand.

"That damned man got me so vex today," he said. "Didn't even stop to ask if we're all right."

She heard the apology in his tone, but let the silence stretch until finally she said, "So you take it out on me, Gladstone?"

It wasn't long after this that she told Debra not to bother making any tea for her on mornings because she wasn't keeping it down anyway.

But what should have been a blessing in their house almost eight months to the day after their wedding day turned out to be the beginning of the slippery slide that ended two days ago, when she stepped back into her house to find Gladstone hanging from the rafters in her bedroom with a deathstare fixed upon the three suitcases she had finished packing the night before.

"Fallen Fruit"
by Gladstone Belle

Squat, spreading,
Young, expecting
bare bulbous nectar breasts
that ooze when sucked
of ripe, sweet, juices
fecund female
sighing, breezy rustling
cracking, snapping
in stormy wind
dropping
acid premature
pale-green fruit,
not sweet
not ripe
not juicy.

It was about nine o'clock when the pains first hit. "Gladstone," she said. "I think it is time."

He didn't even look up from reading his newspaper. "Time for what?" he asked her.

"The baby," she said. "I think it is time."

"You sure?"

"Yes, I'm sure," she said. "Call a taxi."

"Where we going get a taxi this time of night?" He said this still with his eyes down in the newspaper. "Call your father. He just lives up the road, fa Pete's sake."

She didn't want to call her father—she was determined to be independent. And she wasn't in a mood for arguing with Gladstone either, but she couldn't help reminding him that if he hadn't gotten into the habit of drinking with his coworkers on evenings after work and if he hadn't wrecked the car in an accident two weeks ago he wouldn't have to call a taxi to take his wife to the hospital.

But he started raising his voice and saying how accidents happen and why she had to bring up the same thing over and over again and "What happen, happen. It's not the end of the world, fa Pete's sake!"

But the pains were wrenching her insides, so to pacify him she sighed, "All right. I don't want to fight. Just call a taxi for me."

And right at that moment she felt an urgent need to pee and rushed to the toilet.

They ended up leaving the house to catch a bus to go to the hospital. "Just like I said," he told her when she came from the toilet. "I can't get any taxis this time of night." And he's grumbling about wasting money on a taxi when she could call her father and why didn't she go home to her mother when the time was getting near like he suggested? Her mother was a woman and would know what to do when the time came. But she wouldn't listen to him. She *never* listened to him.

So she wondered if he'd tried at all. He just didn't understand—she was a grown, married woman, not the spoiled little girl he thought she was. Her place was with her husband.

Twenty years later on the day of his funeral she still wonders whether or not he was lying that night, whether he really did try to get a taxi.

But that night with labor pains bending her over she didn't argue.

They walked past the men seated around the table under the streetlight slamming dominoes, past Stella selling fried fish at her stall, down to the bus stop on the main road.

As soon as they reached the bus stop she felt the urge to urinate again, so she slipped into the darkness of a yard nearby. And while she stooped within the shadow of a tree the top half of the back door of the house opened and a woman's silhouetted head peered into the darkness of the yard and the woman shouted out, "Who that out there?"

She tried to stop peeing but couldn't. She glanced toward Gladstone standing at the bus stop. He'd heard the woman shouting and was shifting from foot to foot and staring down the road.

When Isamina stepped from the darkness, the woman yelled out, "What kind of nasty slut you is, pissing in people yard?" And Gladstone shoved his hands in his pants pockets, hunched his shoulders, and faced away from the yelling woman with his back also turned to Isamina while Isamina tried to hide her face with her hands.

The woman recognized her anyway and to this day Isamina still cringes when she recalls the embarrassment of the woman going around telling everybody how Isamina Springer stoop down in her yard and pee so loud she could hear it all the way inside her house because, "Is like some sluice gate open in my yard." So embarrassing.

When the bus reached in town, the half-mile walk to the hospital was like a hundred-mile trek with her stopping every few yards and holding her belly and bending over while Gladstone is standing with his hands in his pants pockets waiting for her to straighten up and continue walking.

She wasn't in the hospital an hour before out of her gushed a lifeless, slimy mass instead of the screaming bundle of balled fists and kicking feet she had spent eight months hoping for.

First thing Gladstone asked when they allowed him into the ward was, "What is it? A boy?"

———

Twenty-odd years later on the day of his funeral, the memory of that night brings back such hot fury that she gets up off the bed and strides to the wardrobe and begins to rip Gladstone's clothes off their hangers and fling them on the floor.

She tries to wring the wedding band off her finger and toss it in the yard as far as her strength can allow but it remains stuck just like the conflicting emotions that have stuck with her all these years.

Dear diary,

Lately I feel like a man clinging to a vehicle as it careens toward eventual and inevitable destruction after twenty-two years of good times, bad times, changes, disagreements, quarrels, and venomous fights:

—I want a baby / —I don't like adoption;
—I want to find myself / —What d'you mean? You lost?
—See? You don't respect me / —You don't give me any moral support;

Two nights ago on my forty-eighth birthday came the final collision that has caused us both to be hurled in different directions with me landing in this abyss of pending aloneness and despair.

I would like nothing more than to say to Isamina, I'm sorry:

> sorry for years of conflict, tension, unnecessary battles, unrepentant eruptions of anger;
>
> sorry for too-frequent bouts of undemonstrativeness like on that long-ago night of our still-born child, a night that remains a ghost haunting my conscience;
>
> sorry for not enough moments of shared joy over the years of our fleeting lives;
>
> sorry for barriers raised and access denied;
>
> sorry for the pain placed in your eyes two days ago when on my birthday you took me to a restaurant in celebration but in my mood I snapped harsh words to a question I cannot even remember and saw your smile melt and pain settle behind your downcast eyes while I restrained my contrition behind a stern mask and clamped my apology behind frowning lips;

sorry for not saying I'm sorry, even though often I wanted to but never did and can't even now.

And why? Growing boys learn from grown men, they say. The cub observes and imitates the lions in its pride but when grown often must adapt to new circumstances—such are the requirements of survival. And this old lion has adjusted over the years. I have tried. But not enough, perhaps.

Then there were those times of retaliation in instinctive defense against the wounding words of domestic battle. But pain inflicted in reflexive retaliation hurts no less than that caused by aggressive anger. So, knowing that my lashing out often was but a reflex brings no solace. And the memory of times when manly pride restrained apology brings only remorse.

Like most I've lived as though time were a reel that can be rewound, a road one can retravel after having learned its bumps and bends. Now, too late, I know that's not so.

Monday morning. Warm. Tranquil. High above a hawk swoops and soars. Birds flit, twitter, whistle and chirp, as colorful as the rainbow arcing across the morning sky and as melodious as the rippling symphony of clear water flowing past my backyard from distant hills moulded by some long-ago cataclysmic upheaval but which now lie on the landscape like mammoth beasts.

The nine o'clock sun is a pleasantly warm orb, not yet scorching, in a sky as blue and vast as infinity, washed clean by a sudden downpour that dampened the earth and left behind a steamy, earthy aroma that now rises to my nostrils like the scent of freshly brewed coffee while a breeze tickles the tree leaves like a lover, flutters the window curtains, caresses my skin and brings with it the essence of cane syrup boiling in the sugar factory a few miles distant upwind, the whiff of cane fires, and drifting flakes of black cane ash that float and alight as gently as butterflies.

To the sparrow that has just lit on my windowsill, twigs grasped in its beak, this is a day of life, nest-building and beginnings. For me it is a day of misery, melancholy, and endings.

Last Friday saw the beginning of my forty-eighth year, a birthday that should have been spiced with the flavor of celebration but instead ended with the bitter taste of pain in the eyes of Isamina inflicted by intemperate words born of my brooding mood.

But such has been my fate of late, to be severed from the lives of those I love.

My daughter, yelling months ago on the sidewalk of a New York street, "So now you want to be a father? Telling me how to live my life? Where were you when I really needed you? Tell me that! Where the hell were you?"

And all because I ventured to suggest that the young man she lived with might not be the best person for her. A poet, he called himself. A scruffy runt with no discernible means of support whose name I can no longer recall.

I should have known better than to allow Yvette to cajole me into going with them to a "poetry slam," as she called it, in a little café down a narrow cobbled street into a small room filled with an audience in its twenties, my daughter's generation crowded at tables, sitting on the floor, leaning against walls—bell-bottoms, platform shoes, fashions of an earlier generation rediscovered as innovation; dreadlocks, afros, headwraps, cultural elements as current fads. Four young men on a tiny stage noise the small room with drumbeats and prosaic performances eliciting enthusiastic applause.

And then my daughter's disheveled dwarf clutching the mike and mumbling his intention to read a "pome" he wrote while sitting on the john (enthusiastic applause) "and it goes a little something like this . . ."

I couldn't take it. I walked out in the middle of a "pome" that ought to have been floating in the sewer along with everything else flushed after "sitting on the john."

Next day when I called Yvette at work before leaving for the airport for my flight back home her answers on the phone were monosyllabic. "I know," I said. "I'm sorry. I shouldnt've walked out."

No response.

Two months later passing through New York en route to Washington I take a cab to the embassy for a brief visit and call my daughter at work. "She doesn't work here anymore," I hear. Another call and I discover that another tenant occupies her apartment.

I learned from Andrea that she'd got a job in another state. That was about three months ago. I just hope she left that little parasite behind.

I return home and a few weeks later I step over the threshold of a house in Spring Gardens and my life begins to unravel.

Now today Isamina is leaving. Her suitcases are already packed.

"I don't feel loved," she said yesterday.

"But I love you," I said.

"You never show it," she replied.

What more can I do? I wondered but did not ask.

The two months since I've resigned have given me ample time for reflection.

Human life is a speck in the span of time, a fleeting, futile waste. I review my life and ask myself, what have I accomplished? For what will I be remembered? My twenty years of public service? The legislation and ministerial orders I introduced? Speeches I've made? No, for those accomplishments are but memories dispersed by rumors that surround me like a malodorous fog.

And Isamina? What will she remember? That in twenty-four years of marriage I've rarely stayed out late at night except when official duties required it of me? Never slept in another woman's bed but always returned to my own? (unlike her own father whom I happen to know has an outside woman he keeps in a house in town and everyone knows including his wife, I'm sure).

Will she remember the labor of love invested in this house of which she's so proud, which is my design right down to the landscaped flower garden? And what of spare evenings and weekends spent adding, renovating, building—the butcher-block table in the kitchen; the jungle gym for a child that never came ("I don't know why you're building that thing! Suppose the child falls and hurts itself?"); the two-car garage that originally was a carport ("Why don't you hire somebody to do that? How d'you think it looks you banging and sawing like some common carpenter?"); the deck where we lazed and listened to the ripple of the river flowing past our backyard; the orchard that bears now throughout the year with mangoes, gooseberries, bananas, plums, guavas?

No. For in her eyes the works of one's own hands are but hobby creations lacking the luster of conspicuous consumption, thus are of less consequence than English chocolates and cut flowers. And imported canned peaches and fruit cocktail do not grow in tropical orchards.

"I can't live like this anymore," she said.

And I agree. I too can't live like this anymore. But even in our agreement we disagree.

On the morning of the day on which this entry is dated, Isamina Belle returned home with provisions purchased for preparing a farewell meal and found her husband hanging from a varnished joist in their bedroom.

MISS ESTHER

[noon]

Over on the side of the village where the land begins its downward slope toward the valley, Sonny-Boy is sitting on a rock in the middle of the yard watching Esther hang clothes on the line, thinking how funny it is that time can flip by so fast and yet leave so much change behind it.

Not long ago he and Esther were two young parents with a little bare-assed boy running around this same yard chasing fowls. Now they are two gray-haired old people about to bury a forty-eight-year-old son who hang himself.

Fowls are pecking in the dust, a cock crows in the distance, the breeze is flapping the clothes on the line and all of a sudden Sonny-Boy can sense the presence of Gladstone close by. But the feeling is different from last night when he put his foot on the floor to get out of his bed to go in the yard to pee and the air was so heavy with the spirit of his son that he changed his mind. Today the spirit is a melancholy and calming presence while Esther is talking around the clothespins in her mouth and asking him, "What kind of place that is over there, eh?"

"What you mean?" he asks her.

She takes the pins out of her mouth. "I mean," she's saying, "what kind of place that is that can turn somebody into something his own mother who carry him for nine months in her belly can't recognize?"

And Sonny-Boy is frowning and thinking, Ain't it just like a woman to think that way? "The place en done nothing to Gladstone," he's saying. "Gladstone wasn't tough enough, that's all. A lot of people does meet it hard but they don't turn mad."

"*You* say he was mad," she's telling him. "But who turn him mad? From what he say it is all-you over there who mad, living in a blooming lunatic asylum and don't know it."

She walks over and sits on the rock beside Sonny-Boy and her voice is a whisper as soft as the wind as she says, "What kind of place it is where people don't even speak to one another? Eh, Harold? Where people don't even say Good morning, good evening, good day? What kind of place it is where somebody can dead and bury and you don't know?" She shakes her head slowly in bewilderment. "They say we poor and backward? But what kind of uncivilized people them is over there? Tell me, Harold. What kinda place that is?"

And she begins talking about the old man that used to sit on a chair in front of the apartment building where Gladstone used to live, a man who always had a pleasant word to say to Gladstone. Say Gladstone remind him of folks down south where he come from —friendly and courteous. All that summer he and Gladstone would talk whenever Gladstone pass by. Then winter come. Winter, where you don't see nobody, Gladstone say, because it so cold that every man jack hustling to work and hurrying back home.

So it en till the next year when it warm up that Gladstone notice his friend en at his usual place in front the building and when he ask the super that is the first time he find out that the man dead and buried months ago—he dead one week and his wife dead a week later, one right after the other—and Gladstone never hear about it, never see no funeral, no wake, nothing.

"Gladstone ever tell you about that?" she's asking Sonny-Boy.

And Sonny-Boy has to shake his head, no. Gladstone never tell him about that. But Gladstone never was one to tell you what was on his mind.

Esther is continuing, asking Sonny-Boy what kind of brute-beast place it is where a man can be lying on the street and people stepping over him like he is a crack in the sidewalk; and where in the midst of so much plenty, people have no food to eat, no place to sleep? Eh? What kind of inhuman place that is?

And she's looking around the yard. "We en got much. But Gladstone woulda never starve here. Never woulda find himself with no roof over his head." And she's saying to Sonny-Boy that she can't even imagine how it would feel to be in a strange place with no food, no shelter, nobody to turn to. "And the way you say it in the letter make it sound like you think it was his fault."

And right away Sonny-Boy is saying, with his voice rising, how Gladstone was stubborn, hard-ears, full up with false pride. "America en no place for false pride! He coulda call!" he's almost shouting. "Think I woulda see him on the street and starving and not help him? He's my son, Esther!"

But Esther is waving her hand as if that isn't the point. "Nobody en blaming you," she's saying. "Everything does happen for a reason."

And she's going on to tell Sonny-Boy how, after Gladstone come back he telling her all kind of 'nancy story—about all the degrees he got (like he en know she know better), the big jobs he had with the United Nations, the federal government, the city, the state. And the stories changing. One minute the last job he had was as a diplomat at the United Nations, next minute it was a university professor. And at first she saying yeah, yeah, to pacify him because although he is her son, you can never tell what somebody with a nervous breakdown would do. One little thing mighta set him off and who knows what he might do? But he's insisting, It's true, Ma, and she's saying, I know, I know.

But then one day big-head Booboo who think he know everything come up to her and telling her how proud she must be of Gladstone, eh Miss Esther? And how proud he is to see a Village boy do so good in Away and come back to share all his experience and make his contribution to the country. And the way Booboo talking she got the feeling Booboo making mock sport at Gladstone and picking her to see if she believe Gladstone incredible stories.

But you know, it is funny how many people really believe what Gladstone say, like they forget the boy come back bushy-haired, red-eyed, and not himself. Which make you wonder about all the people who does come back making all sorts of claims about what they do in Away, how much big shots they is, how much money they making. It make you wonder.

Anyhow, one morning Gladstone get up, bathe, put on shirt-and-tie and say he going to look for a job. That same afternoon he come back home with a big smile on his face and giving her a big hug. He got a job at the community college. "They believe me!" he saying over and over. "They believe me! Can you believe it?" And he's letting loose this big, belly laugh.

That is when she realize nothing wasn't really wrong with Gladstone. The boy was mamaguying everybody.

And that is where he meet that Springer girl—at the community college. And that is why he is a dead man today. Nobody can't tell her different. He shoulda never take up with that girl.

All of a sudden silent tears begin to trickle down her face.

And Sonny-Boy is sitting there with his arms on his knees and inspecting his hands like they are some kind of new discovery, not knowing whether to sit quietly and leave her in peace and let her tears wash away some of her grief or whether to put his arms around her and comfort her. Because even though they lived together for so many years and brought a child into this world, the boychild they were a few hours away from putting into the ground, after thirty years of separation they are strangers again feeling their way toward one another in the dark.

While he's thinking all this he hears her say something about Gladstone not inviting her to his wedding and when he ask her if that is what she said she says, "Yeah. You hear right. Never invite his own mother to his wedding."

And she goes on to say how Gladstone came to her one day when she was down in the valley sowing some corn and stand up over her and say, "Ma, Isamina and I getting married." Just like that.

She didn't know what to say, so she keep right on sowing her corn. What she could say?

As a mother she was glad he was marrying up—Mr. Springer is a big-time architect, and his wife is one of the Greenes that own the plantation and rum refinery up in St. Helen.

But it is one thing to reach; it is another to overreach.

She would've been satisfied to see him marry a schoolteacher or somebody like that from the same background—poor but raised themself through education. But the Springers? If they invite her to their house how she going stop herself from making herself and Gladstone shame? She can't eat with knife and fork. She don't know the proper way to behave in big-shot company like that—doctors, lawyers, politicians, even the prime minister and his wife does go up there.

So she told Gladstone, "If that is what you want, if you really want to get married, go ahead. But—and I don't want to put my mouth on you—remember what the old people always say: the higher the monkey climb the more he does show he backside." And besides, she want to know, why that girl marrying him? Why she en marrying somebody from her own class and background?

Gladstone get in a huff at this and walked away and never say another word to her about the wedding. Never give her an invitation and she never asked—a mother shouldn't have to beg her son to invite her to his wedding; is she who carry him for nine months, not the other way around.

The day he was getting married she walk down to the cathedral bright and early and lay down under a pew up in the balcony (she never know churches had balconies before). That is how she witness Gladstone wedding, curled up under a pew and peeping down at the ceremony. Tears come to her eyes to see her son putting the ring on the girl finger; seeing them walking down the aisle while people looking at the couple and smiling. He looked so nice in his tuxedo suit.

She wait until the church empty before she get up from under the pew and walk out into the sunlight and meet the sexton walking back from closing the big iron main gates.

"Beautiful wedding, eh?" he said.

She nod her head.

"You a friend of the bride or groom?" he asked her.

A lump inside her throat blocked her answer, so she just shook her head and kept walking out the small gate.

Gladstone always was a funny child, keeping things to himself. One day after he come back from Away he says to her all of a sudden, "You know I never carry Gran-gran from the church?" And she's asking him what he mean he never bear Gran-gran.

That is when he tell her how Mr. Springer step in front him and position himself at Gran-gran coffin and wasn't no place for him to hold—the same Mr. Springer Gran-gran en had nothing to do with when she was alive, unlike the other stupid neighbors who called him "Duke," saying he remind them of the Duke of Edinburgh. Gladstone carrying that grudge ever since he was thirteen and she never know. (She decide not to tell Harold the part where Gladstone tell her his father never intervene to tell Mr. Springer that family first, how it was cousin Albert who see what happening and tell him rest his hand on top of the coffin, as a compromise. Telling Harold that, she told me, woulda only get him upset.)

But that was the way Gladstone was. Keeping things to himself and if you didn't dig them out of him you would never know.

Like when he come back from Away. If she didn't sit down with him day after day and pick him about what happen in Away he woulda kept it bottled up inside probably till he explode. Remind her of the time he get a nail jook in his foot as a little boy and she had to take a needle and prick the spot to let out the puss. The night she do that was the first night he sleep and didn't keep her awake with his crying.

Perhaps if she was there to pluck out whatever was paining him this time he woulda be alive today.

ANDREA

By one of those coincidences that remind us of the forces that manipulate people and events like pieces on a giant draughts board, Andrea, the first woman Gabby lived with, arrived in the country the same day he died.

According to Manface the taxi driver, he was only trying to make conversation with Andrea when he asked her, "You know who kill himself today?" and went on to give Andrea the news that the man she'd lived with for three years had hanged himself just a few hours ago, perhaps even as her plane was landing. She stared off in the distance then murmured, "Ain't that something. That son of a bitch. He would do something like that."

That was the last reaction he expected from this woman that set his heart thumping as soon as his eyes clapped on her standing outside the arrival lounge wearing an ankle-length flowered skirt and a blouse tied in a knot at her midriff.

Andrea St. Clair. His buddy Erskine little sister. He didn't recognize her but as soon as she got in his taxi she said, "You're Erskine's friend." And she's snapping her fingers trying to remember his name. He told her. And right away they started talking about old times, mostly about things involving Erskine, which bring back the shock he felt when he got the news one Sunday morning that Erskine smashed his car into a wall the night before. They was buddies from small. And it looked like she was just glad to have somebody to talk about Erskine with. Even after all these years. But after a while he changed the subject. "So how things up in America?"

After he helped her with her suitcases she invite him in "for a little drink . . . okay?" He couldn't keep his eyes off her. He couldn't believe this was little Andrea, now such a fine-looking woman. What a body!

Now here she is sipping a gin and tonic in her mother's house with pale Yankee legs crossed knee over knee, foot behind calf, intertwined like two snakes, and he's curious to know what she knew about Gladstone Belle that would cause her to react the way she did when he tell her Gladstone dead.

At the same time he is also admiring the way her straightened hair cascades shiny black down to her shoulders, resisting even the strong breeze that is rattling the wide-open jalousie windows on their hinges, ruffling his shirt and riffling the pages of the magazines on the center table. What a woman! Like an American model.

"And I saw him just the other day," she's saying.

She lifts her glass of gin and tonic off the center table, takes a long sip and begins to talk—more to herself, it seems, than to him. "Know how I met him?" she says.

And she continues talking almost as if he wasn't there, sipping her drink and saying, "First time I set eyes on Glastone Belle was when Erskine invite him up. He and Erskine were working at the technical college together."

From the minute she walked in the drawing room that Saturday afternoon and set the bottle of rum on the center table and then stooped down to get the glasses out of the cabinet and her dress hiked up halfway up her thighs she could tell Gladstone had his eyes on her the whole day.

So she wasn't surprised when every Saturday after that she would see him walking from the bus stop toward their house where he and Erskine would sit down and drink till they were ready to go wherever it was they went roaming. And every time she had a cause to come in the front room where they were she would feel his eyes on her, though she never paid him no mind.

For the first few weeks he and Erskine would leave the house and she wouldn't see him again till the next Saturday. Where they went she don't know (and she really didn't care). Then one Saturday as they are getting up from the table to leave the house Erskine says in a offhand way, "Andrea, you coming?"

This was a big surprise, her brother inviting her to go somewhere with him and his friends. It had to be Gladstone who put him up to it.

Mind you, she didn't really like Gladstone; but she was curious. He was from town. Different from the boys around here.

"Coming? Coming where?" Though she was looking at her brother as she's asking him this, she could feel Gladstone's eyes on her.

Erskine shrugged. "If you don't feel like it . . ." he began to say.

"I didn't say so," she answered back, and went on to say how she had her housework to do and she had to go around by her friend Dorothy later to help her bake a cake. Besides, Ma wouldn't like it.

Erskine shrugged again and said, "Suit yourself."

But Gladstone butt in with, "Come along. We only going down by the lighthouse. Plus Cynthia coming too."

So after hesitating a little she said, "All right," saying it like she was doing them a big favor.

They took a long walk down to the lighthouse, picking up Erskine's girlfriend Cynthia at her house. When they reached the lighthouse the four of them stood at the edge of the cliff looking down at the waves pounding the rocks. Then they went down a track through the bushes to the beach. She remembers the casaurina trees whistling in the breeze and the leaves making a soft carpet under her feet. Erskine and Cynthia paired off out of sight, leaving her and Gladstone.

Her first impression of Gladstone was that his voice was too soft and girlish. And he didn't even try to kiss her. She remembers thinking that perhaps he didn't like girls.

Whatever they talked about that day couldn't have been about anything important, though they must've talked a lot, walking and sitting on the beach, skipping stones, things like that, because it was near dusk time and the breeze was evening cool as they finally walked back home, Erskine and Cynthia in front, she and Gladstone behind.

The next Saturday when Erskine was ready to leave as usual, Gladstone said, "You go ahead. I'll catch up with you later."

Erskine gave him a long look (friend or no friend, Erskine didn't like anybody messing with his sister). Finally he said, "All right" and left.

She and Gladstone ended up just sitting on the front steps talking. That night and every Saturday after that, Gladstone would catch the last bus back to town, waiting till they heard the bus engine in the distance then kissing her and dashing off in the dark down to the bus stop on the main road.

When she told her mother she was going to live with Gladstone in a rent house in town, her mother surprised her.

"You sure that is what you really want?" her mother asked her.

And when she said yes, all her mother said was, "Well, you's a woman now. Hope you know what you doing."

The first few months were like a fairy tale. All the furniture they had at first was a bed, a wardrobe her mother gave her, and a dinette set. And they were happy with that. In those days all she used to wear in the house was one of his shirts—no panties. He didn't like her wearing them.

But it wasn't long before she began to see a change in him—picking on every little thing, saying things like, "This shirt en press right," or, "You call this split-pea and rice? Look more like soup to me." Things like that.

And she would go in the bedroom and cry to see that she was trying so hard to please him yet he's saying such hurtful things to her. That is when she hit on a plan. Perhaps if they had a child things would be better.

So she started asking him what he think about having a child and at first he's saying no, not yet. But after a while she's noticing he's beginning to soften up. Perhaps a little boy would be a good idea, he's saying. So every now and then when they're cuddling in bed she would raise the question, telling him how she love him so much she want his baby—some men like to hear that, you know. But it was true. She wasn't lying.

Then one night he agreed, saying, "All right." That night he went barebacked.

When it was time for the baby to come she went back home to her mother to have it.

But when she came home with the kid, it was like she brought a whole new set of problems with her. Gladstone couldn't stand to hear a child crying. Especially at night.

When Yvette began to cry he would cuff his pillow and yell his favorite cuss words, "Fa Pete's sake, dammit!" and want to know why she can't keep that blinking child quiet? Asking her if she didn't know he had to have some sleep.

And at first she would get up out of her warm bed, take Yvette out of her crib and do whatever was necessary to silence the child—feed her, change her diaper, or just rock her back to sleep.

And y'know what's hurtful? D'you know? When she got back into bed Gladstone would be fast asleep—fast asleep!—and she would lay awake listening to him snoring. Sonofabitch. Snoring!

One night when Yvette began to yell and scream, she lay still, saying to herself, "This is enough of this shit!" She'd had it, y'know? Had it up to here (and she's raising her palm neck high as she says "here").

So she's lying in the dark with anger building up inside her, waiting for the sonofabitch to tell her to keep the baby quiet.

And boy, as soon as he opened his mouth she let him have it.

"Why you can't get up sometimes?" she asked him. "It is your child too, you know!"

But boy, who told her say that?

"Fa Pete's sake!" he burst out. Then he repeat it. "Fa Pete's sake!" All this time thumping his pillow, *whomp whomp whomp.* "Keep the blooming child quiet, fa Pete's sake!" he's yelling, so damned loud that their neighbors must be hearing them in the middle of the night.

But ain't it funny how your brain works? Ain't it? As vexed and shamed as she was she found herself wondering who the hell was Pete. Fa Pete's sake. Fa Pete's sake. Up to now she don't know why he could never just come right out and curse like a normal human being.

But the sight of him beating his pillow and doing what he called swearing reminded her that he came back from overseas with a nervous breakdown, so she's thinking: perhaps the baby's crying set him off, y'know? And she is alone, she and her child, in the middle of the night with a goddamn crazy man. The child is yelling, the man is crazy, and she's scared out of her cotton-picking mind. Because what if this man kill her and her child?

So she picked up Yvette and held her against her shoulder, trying to shush and pat and bump the poor child to keep her quiet.

Well that night she changed Yvette's diaper and fed her and as she's coming back in the bedroom Gladstone is mumbling into his pillow, something about women that always want children but don't want to mother them.

"Ain't that something?" she asks Manface. "Ain't . . . that . . . something? Then she continues, telling Manface how next thing you know, Gladstone's sleeping and snoring and she's lying next to him crying.

She can't understand men. As long as Yvette wasn't crying Gladstone would be holding her, playing with her, laying her against his shoulder, even dancing her to sleep when her eyelids began to droop. But as soon as she began to cry, hear him: "Andrea! The baby crying." And she would be the one have to feed her or change her.

That was bad enough. But what was even worse was that nothing really changed between them; he was the same old Gladstone, only difference was that instead of showing her affection like she hoped would happen after they got the child, he's giving all his love to the baby—when she wasn't crying, that is.

Up to this point Manface, as he told me later, wasn't too interested in the story Andrea was telling him. What he really was interested in was in scoring with this woman he'd known since she was a girl but had turned into such a *fine* woman. But this part of the story about her getting a child to heal the relationship between her and Gladstone hit a nerve so that he find himself wondering why it is that women always think they can use a baby like glue to patch them and their man together—like his woman Gladys who try the same thing and every time he look at her hatred boiling inside him knowing that when he leave her it would mean he'd be leaving his girlchild too, his flesh and blood.

But as he's thinking this Andrea is continuing, saying how one day Gladstone came in and first thing he say before Good evening or anything was, "When you going get off your big ass and look for work?"

Can you believe it? Can you imagine? There she was: washing clothes, cleaning the house, going to the shop to get something to cook for him when he came home, picking up Yvette every five minutes because all day she's yelling and screaming. She just finished nursing her and putting her to sleep. So finally she's sitting at the table with her legs stretched out, fagged out, resting a little bit before putting on the pot to cook. And in comes Mr. Gladstone telling her to go look for work after he was the one who told her, Don't worry. I'm going take care of you. That Gladstone? She learn a lot from him. Men? Men ain't shit, she's saying.

To make it worse, Gladstone's mother never liked her. The day Gladstone took her and the baby over by his mother, see her: peering at the baby, examining it. Finally she says to her son, "Well, it is everything of you. It is a Belle all right." Like Andrea was trying to put somebody else's jacket on her son.

But she wasn't really surprised because the *first* day Gladstone take her home to see his mother, she stay in the house and heard the old hag saying to Gladstone out in the backyard, "What you see in that girl? What happen? She mother give you something in your food? I know them country people, you know."

Anyway, soon after Gladstone tell her get up and look for work, she got herself a little job at a garment factory.

But things ain't get no better. No sir. She's coming home so tired all she want to do is sleep and Gladstone coming in all hours of the night, sometimes with his breath smelling stink of rum (Yes, the same Gladstone Belle deputy prime minister. You didn't think he was like that in his young days, eh? she saying to Manface). And he's even criticizing the way she's raising the child, talking about, "Listen to you. 'Waw-waw.' The child trying to say 'water' and you talking about waw-waw. No wonder you-all so inarticulate." The same Gladstone Belle that when he entered politics people saying he is such a man of the people. They'd didn't live with him so they don't know no better.

But that day when he criticized the way she was talking to her child, she ain't said a word. Not a damn word. She stopped arguing, yes she did. Stopped crying. And began planning. You got to plan, y'know.

And one day when he came home she meet him with, "Gladstone, my cousin send for me." Just like that. Never let him know a thing all the time she and her cousin writing back and forth and her cousin arranging for her to come up to live with her and her husband in the States.

No. She wait cool till she had her visa and plane ticket and everything. Tossed him away like used toilet paper and ain't looked back since.

And in all the years little Yvette growing up with her mother, before she could see her way to send for her, Gladstone never give her mother one red cent to help raise his daughter. Not one blind cent.

Years after her mother wrote her and tell her how he entered politics, and she's reading about him in the newspaper, she heard on the radio that he was going to address some assembly at the U.N.

She got on the subway and went down to the U.N. and sat at the back of the hall in one of the seats they have for the public and watched him—short and dark, white kerchief in his breast pocket, with a little extra weight showing in his face but looking smart in his double-breasted suit, talking his talk at the microphone—and a feeling rise up inside her, one she didn't expect and couldn't control. You know the kind of feeling a parent does get at prize-giving day? That kind of feeling.

And going back on the subway to her apartment in Brooklyn she remembering her conversation over the phone with Yvette, telling her that her father was here and Yvette saying, "I know."

She didn't tell Yvette she was going to see him. Didn't ask her how she knew her father was here. But after coming from the U.N. she's rocking in her seat with the movement of the train whizzing and rattling through the tunnels beneath the streets of New York and feeling that Yvette should at least see what her father look like now.

When Yvette called later that evening and she told her about going down to see him, there's a pause on the phone, then Yvette is asking her how he looked, if she talked to him. And she's saying, no she didn't talk to him. What would they talk about after all these years? And he looked all right to her. Fatter, perhaps. But after all, he was prospering.

It is only lately that she came to find out that for years, every time Gladstone came to New York on government business he and Yvette would spend time together, going to museums, movies, even Broadway shows. First time it happened, according to Yvette, she was in high school and her father wrote and told her he was coming up on government business and if he could see her.

When she asked Yvette why she hid it all these years and never told her anything, hear what Yvette saying: "I didn't think you would like it. You always hated him." Damn right she wouldn'ta liked it. But she didn't hate him.

She never set eyes on him again after that time at the U.N. Never wanted to. She was only curious to see how he looked now he was a big government minister. That was the only reason she went down there.

Now here she is, home for the first time in umpteen years and what happens? He kills himself the same day she arrives. Ain't that something? Eh? Just like him to do something like that.

Manface notice that by now she's on her fourth or fifth glass of gin and tonic. The woman can drink like a fish.

And she's staring through the window, with her knees still crossed and the breeze ruffling her sleeveless white cotton blouse. And she's telling Manface, "Excuse me" and getting up and leaving the room and when she comes back in he notices her face freshly powdered and a slight redness in her eyes.

"So. Where we going today?" she asking him in that hard, bossy tone that is like a grater rubbing against his nerves. But as he's looking at her he realizing that what he's seeing is only the shell that's covering the woman somewhere underneath.

"Wherever you want to go," he say. After all, he's a taxi driver and she's the customer, and if things turn out the way he expects, soon she'll be more than a customer.

Meanwhile, as Miss St. Clair, Andrea's mother, told me later, she in the back house hearing what her daughter saying and remembering the photo on her dressing table, the photo Andrea send her last year: Andrea, Gladstone, and Yvette posing in front of a fountain with Gladstone in the middle wearing a double-breasted suit with the jacket open and no tie, with his arms around their shoulders, Andrea with one arm around Gladstone waist and leaning forward showing all her teeth and with one heel kick up behind her; Gladstone with a smile on his face, and Yvette staring at her mother with a disapproving frown. Yvette, a big woman now that Miss St. Clair would never recognize as the little girl she raised, except that she is the image of Gladstone—dark, same round face, short. Gladstone couldn't disown her not even with a gun to his head.

But Andrea in there in the front house giving her taxi-driver friend a story that making Miss St. Clair say to herself, Wait a minute. Ent that a picture of Gladstone, Andrea, and Yvette standing together with a fountain in the background that Andrea herself send me?

And even though she know she en crazy, she wiping her hands on her apron and going in her bedroom, picking up the photo off the dressing table and staring at it while in the front room Andrea talking as though she en had nothing to do with Gladstone since all those years ago when she leave him, confirming to Miss St. Clair something she's known for most of her life: the only body you can believe is yourself. And sometimes not even that, because sometimes you find yourself lying without meaning to, without even planning it. That is why whenever anybody come to her with a story all she does do is listen, say uh huh, and nod her head, make them think she is a gullible idiot. Because one thing you can bet on: every story got more sides than a sea egg got prickles.

Something else she been discovering more and more as she get older: trying to discover who a person is is like trodding down all kinds of dead ends in a maze. Every time you think you find the real path you got to turn back and start again. And Andrea in there leading her taxi-driver man down one of her dead ends.

MISS ST. CLAIR

I bring two children into the world and me and Mr. St. Clair, God rest him in his grave, raised them the best way we could.

And when it come time for them to go out on their own, I let them go. I never believe in keeping my children drawing up under me all their life like overgrown infants, so when Andrea come to me and say she moving in with Gladstone and I asked her if she sure she know what she was doing and she say yes, all I tell her was, You's your own woman.

So she move out and begin living with Gladstone.

What I think about Gladstone Belle? I never like the boy. He come from town and think we's country bucks, backward and stupid. Andrea say no, he shy and that is why he don't talk much. Young people? You can't tell them nothing. They think they know everything.

When she come to me few months after she move out and complaining and crying about how Gladstone does talk to her like she is a child, and he en loving to her, I give her one piece of advice. If you en happy, I say, leave. But she en listen to me. Instead of leaving him she end up with a pickney.

I remember when she bring Yvette to me the day before she left for Away—she know I don't like going to the airport. She crying, the child crying, but I en shed a tear till the next day I look up and see a plane high up in the sky and climbing and I wondering if that is the plane Andrea on. Couldn't let the little girl see my tears, though. She woulda start all over again.

Yvette. Two years and nine mornings old the day Andrea bring her to my house and left her. Bright and good company for me, with me by myself in the empty house after Andrea and Erskine move out and Mr. St. Clair passed away.

A handful, though. Running around the place on her little chubby legs pulling at everything her hands could reach, full of questions, full of energy. But good company. A real blessing.

But before you know it, it seem like one morning I wake up and Yvette is nine and passing her exam for high school.

And every letter Andrea write she saying how things so expensive she can hardly save anything and the few cents she save up en enough to send for the child plus she don't have no place decent to bring her to: her apartment small, scarcely big enough for she let alone she and a child. Plus the schools over there bad, bad. The children en learning nothing, she say, and they ungovernable, so Yvette would be better off getting a good foundation over here before she send for her.

And it all sound like excuses to me, like she enjoying life and en want a child weighing her down. Because I figuring, how bad can it be? It is big America, after all. It can't be no worse than over here and Yvette doing good here: healthy, bright, happy. Plus, if she really finding it so hard, why she don't come back then?

But like I say, the child was a real blessing in me old age. Grandma you want a cup of tea? Grandma you want me pick your gray hair? Sitting quiet next to me in church. Reading the Bible for me at night because I couldn't see to read no more. A real blessing.

Her father? Gladstone? I don't like to put my mouth on people, but I always used to say that man going suck salt one day. But I never say that to Yvette. Never turn her against her father. No matter how worthless he was, he was still her father. I figure Yvette had sense and would see for herself.

When Andrea first left he would put couple half-dead dollar bills in Erskine hand, like what he was giving was enough to feed and clothe a child in this day and age.

Then he stop altogether. And how you think the child feeling? Growing up and seeing her father picture in the papers—once he even speak at prize-giving day at her school—but never once coming by the house to say how you doing, to spend time with his own daughter.

Once in a blue moon he picking her up at school and buying ice cream and all kind of foolishness that en good for the child.

But you should see Yvette face whenever she come home after he do that—like she win a grand prize, talking about her daddy this and her daddy that.

Prize-giving day. The same year she left to go with her mother in Away. The child is eleven, happy that morning when she leaving the house. I think I can see her now: her uniform stiff-starch-and-iron, her hair plait nice and with two ribbons at the back, panama hat on her head, her skin shining with coconut oil. And she trying to hold in the smile on her little face. But coming home that afternoon she looking sad with her prize in her hand (a dictionary). Why? Her father en come to his own daughter prize-giving, that's why (although he was there the year before to give a speech—but that was an election year).

All the parents there except hers. I couldn't leave the house to go up at the school for prize-giving—I had my work to do.

That was the kind of father Gladstone Belle was.

How I feel when I hear he hang himself? How I can feel? I is a Christian woman. I don't wish bad on anybody.

Soon as I hear the news I step down at the shop and beg Miss Thorne for a phone call and ring Yvette in Away to tell her that her father dead. At first I thinking the girl en hear me because all I hearing on the line is silence so I have to ask her if she hear what I say.

"Dead?" she saying.

"Yes," I say. "They find him hanging in his house."

And in the silence on the line Miss Thorne looking at me hard even though she know I en the type of person will make a phone call and not pay her for it. I hate begging people for favors, especially somebody like Miss Thorne who married Mr. Thorne and get more out of life than she expect. So even though I going pay for the phone call I hurrying up the conversation to get off the phone. "You coming for the funeral?" I ask Yvette.

But hear what the girl telling me. "No," she say. Her voice so low that I en sure I hear right.

"You en coming?" I ask her.

That is when she telling me she en know if she can get the time off.

Can't get the time off? Is a emergency. Mean they don't give you time off for emergencies over in America? That is what I thinking.

But the words en coming out because all of a sudden cry-water building up behind my eyes. Listening to the silence on the line and hearing Yvette saying how she can't leave her job to come to her own father funeral give me a feeling like I staring into a deep gully between father and daughter that it is too late for either one of them to cross now that Gladstone dead.

Yvette must be hearing me crying because she saying, "Don't cry, Granny. Don't upset yourself. It's not that I don't want to come, Granny."

But I know she only saying this to pacify me.

And I'm thinking that perhaps I shouldn'ta turned her father away when he tried to see her after her mother left for Away. But who perfect, eh? Who perfect?

Every night as God send I does get on my knees and ask for forgiveness for whatever mistakes I make in life. Cause I is only a mortal.

Dear diary,

A child without a father is like a house without a roof and memory is the highway back to the past, a highway strewn with contrition and remorse as I recall infant and childhood years of my daughter Yvette:

> the way she stood in her crib and stared toward the door as I entered the ward where she was recovering from her hernia operation;
>
> the way she felt in my arms when I picked her up;
>
> the way the talcum powder fragrance of her made me a happy father;
>
> the way she stretched out her arms and said "dance" when her eyelids began to droop with sleepiness;
>
> the way I laid her against my shoulder and danced around the room till she grew heavy in my arms;
>
> the way she pulled my ear and sucked her finger until she fell asleep;
>
> the way her breathing was the deep inhale and exhale of baby breath sweet smelling as warm milk;
>
> the way she waited for me by the day-nursery door, knee-high and gazing up;
>
> the way she picked her shoes from all the other infant shoes tossed in a corner pile while Miss Walcott laughed at the amazement on my face and said, "They does do it all the time. They know their own shoes. Don't ask me how";
> the way we sang together as I carried her home from the day nursery on evenings;

the way she tottered as she learned to walk;

the way she seemed always on the verge of falling;

the way she sometimes fell and got right back up;

the way she called me "Gahstun" and my mother fumed, "These children nowadays, calling their parents by their first name like they and their parents is company. I don't know what the world coming to";

the way she screamed and stamped her feet and stared at the cockroach I held with my thumb and index finger;

the way she stopped crying when I said, "See? It's dead. It can't do you nothing";

the way she always said afterward when she saw a dead insect, "See? It can't do you nothing";

the way she sensed her mother's fear of the waves that splashed her legs as her mother held her on her hip;

the way she bawled and stretched her tiny arms to me;

the way I held her on my hip and braced against the waves;

the way she wiped seawater from her face;

the way she no longer was afraid;

the way she giggled when I tickled her ribs;

the way the soles of her feet felt softer than a woman's breast;

the way she threw herself backward while I held her on my knee;

the way she trusted me;
the way my hand flew to her back to catch her and she laughed;

the way my heart pounded and I could not breathe;

the way my throat felt dry and my voice came out as a whisper saying, "Don't you ever do that again";

the way she sat astride my shoulders and held onto my head as horses galloped around the racetrack;

the way she bounced up and down yelling, "Run, horsey!"

the way the only way I knew she'd fallen asleep that day was when I saw her balloon drifting away in the breeze and she said nothing;

the way Miss St. Clair yelled from her front window, "WHAT YOU WANT?" and slammed the window shut;

the way I heard my daughter's voice—"Gahstun! . . . Gahstun!" —inside the house;

the way I, a grown man, walked away and cried;

the way my daughter grew up so fast;

the way she no longer called me "Gahstun," or anything at all;

the way silence stretched between our words;

the way everyone said she was the image of me;

the way she was the image of me;

the way she caught a plane unknown to me, and where she is today I cannot say;

the way I lay on my bed and cried the day I heard she'd left;

the way my mother said, "You miss her, nuh."

the way I remember:
not being there to wipe my daughter's tears;

not being there to scold her when she needed it;

not being there to make her do her homework;

not being there to turn the stupid TV off;

not being there to ask her stupid mother why she sent the stupid idiot box for the child and why couldn't she keep it with her stupid, idiot self in the States;

not being there at the prize-giving day I missed because of work;

not being there to watch and cheer at the interschool athletic meet when she came second in the hundred-meter dash;

not being there. Not being there.

SONNY-BOY

[noon]
Midday. The sun directly overhead and so scorching hot it bleaches the blue from the sky.

And the *palang! palang!* of the school bell disgorges a rush of children from the schoolhouse. Playful voices yelling, screaming, laughing in the schoolyard and here and there a boy in khaki short pants and shirt, a girl in navy blue tunic, white blouse, and panama hat walking or running home for lunch.

And Sonny-Boy, strolling across the village in the hot sun to his son's bungalow, rapping at the front door and waiting, knocking again and waiting before finally hearing footsteps inside the house.

And when Isamina opens the door her eyes are swollen and puffy, the face of a woman who has been crying.

"You never meet me," Sonny-Boy says. He stretches out his arm for a handshake. "I's Gladstone father."

Isamina is staring at him as though she just woke up from a deep sleep. "Yes. Yes," she says at last. "We have a photo of you." She shakes his hand. "Come in," she says. "Come in."

She walks ahead of him toward the dining room where a pile of notebooks are scattered on the table. She clears away a spot in front of one of the chairs. "Excuse the mess," she says. "But I was just looking through Gladstone's diaries. Have a seat. Have a seat."

She flips through one of the notebooks, still standing up.

"Funny," he hears her say. "You think you know somebody, live with them for years, then you discover you never really knew them at all."

As Sonny-Boy tells me later, he is impressed with the proper way she talks.

"Here," she says. "Look at this."

Sonny-Boy takes the book she hands to him. It is open. And he reads:

Dear diary,

New York April. Horns honking; pedestrians bumping, freight trucks fart fumes, stirring gritty, eye-stinging dust amidst noises, harsh voices, while the Menthol fresh breeze caresses, raises dresses as funk rises from my parka, sweatshirt, layered clothes of odd sizes, feet aching, sweating while I need a shave, feel a cigarette crave. And on a bench on the corner, a face behind a newspaper, no emotion behind it, looks up as I ask, "Do you have a minute? . . . To talk a little bit?" He folds his newspaper, gives no answer, stands, moves farther away. No answer.

And Sonny-Boy says, "This belong to Gladstone?" And there's surprise in his voice.

"Yes," Isamina tells him. "All of these," flinging her hand out indicating the notebooks scattered on the table. "His whole life, it looks like. He left them for his daughter. Did you know he has a daughter? Yvette?"

Sonny-Boy is silent. Yes he knows but he doesn't want to say the wrong thing, so he keeps his mouth shut. Gladstone always was secretive but he didn't think he would be so secretive as not to tell his wife about his daughter.

Looking at the diaries strewn on the table in front of him he recalls times in New York when he would come home tired and hungry to see Gabby chewing a pencil and staring into space or scribbling in a notebook. And when he would fuss about coming home and nothing en there to eat, wanting to know if it was too much to ask for Gladstone to at least start the pot till he got home, Gabby would say is homework he doing. Perhaps some of those times he was writing things like this. Is true what Gladstone wife just say: funny how little you can know about people, even your own flesh and blood.

And as he's thinking this Isamina asks him, "Can I get you something to drink?"

"Got any rum in the house?"

She nods. "How do you want it?"

"A little bit of coke. Not much. With some ice."

After emptying his glass for the second time he says, "Just leave the bottle on the table. Save yourself the trouble, heh heh heh."

He pours his third drink and begins to talk, wanting to know why Gladstone didn't call him if he was having trouble. If he want somebody to talk to (and he looked at Isamina saying, "I don't mean no disrespect to you"), why he didn't call him? He was his father, after all. They coulda talk man-to-man. Perhaps if he'd done that and got whatever it was off his chest, perhaps he woulda been alive today. Because problems ain't nothing but obstacles and ain't no obstacle so high you can't get over it. And nothing certainly ain't so bad that you got to take your own life.

But from when he was small Gladstone always was the kind of child that would keep everything to himself. And instead of growing out of it, look like he get worse. Look what happen in New York.

He, Sonny-Boy was living in Florida, true, and Gladstone was up in New York. But what is distance when your son in trouble? If he knew Gladstone was catching hell he woulda jump on the first plane and go and see what happening. Gladstone didn't have to suffer through no hard times. He woulda even take him back to Florida till he catch himself.

"Don't blame yourself, Mr. Belle," Isamina says. "Things happen."

Easy for *her* to say. How could he help blaming himself when is he who send for the boy? He thought he was helping him. But what Esther say to him not long ago is true. America not for everybody. It is a place where good people, just to survive, can put a shell around them so tough that you stop seeing the person you used to know. He, Sonny-Boy, see it happen all the time. But Gladstone never develop that shell and look how it almost kill him. And is his fault for bringing his own son to a city where human decency is as rare as a virgin in a whorehouse, and even when it is there it seem to be buried deep beneath the filth and garbage that surround everybody.

He didn't even recognize Gladstone when he walked out from the airport with a traveling bag over his shoulder, a carton with four bottles of rum in his hand, and a moustache above his lip.

But Gladstone recognized him. "Pa?" he said.

And he stared at this man that was almost as tall as him, so thick-skinned that he know Esther was feeding him like he was the man in the house.

He say, "Gladstone?"

And Gladstone say, "Yes, Pa. It is me. And this for you." And he holding out the carton of rum like he want to hand it over quick before he forget.

Those early days was good days. Good days. Showing Gladstone around, going to places he never went to in all the years he was in New York.

"This is the Empire State Building," he remember saying. And Gladstone staring up at the building, making Sonny-Boy chest swell out because he can bring wonder to his son face just by showing him things that he pass by every day without even noticing.

He remember Gladstone saying, "When you going show me where you work, Pa? I want to see where you work."

But he was embarrassed. Didn't want the boy to know he was only a janitor. Told him he was an office services engineer. That is what they was calling themselves: office services engineer. Because nobody en what they is anymore in America. Everybody is some kind of engineer or technician. Hell. Nobody en even plain stupid no more—they mentally challenged. You know that? That is the new-fashion word: challenged. What a stupidness, eh?

Anyway, he was always giving excuses like, One day when things not so busy, or They don't like you bringing people on the job. Excuses like that.

He couldn't understand why he was embarrassed. After all, it wasn't like he had a big job back home before he left. If he had, he wouldn't have had to leave so he could get the money to send Gladstone to high school.

After a while Gladstone stopped asking and it seemed around that time that distance begin to widen between them, probably because he began to hint to Gladstone that he could do with some help. He knew Gladstone was in college and had to study but perhaps he could get a little part-time job to help out. *He* was working two jobs trying to make ends meet and still save a little something—doing janitor work at night cleaning offices in the city, knocking off at seven o'clock in the morning and going straight to his next job at a gas station in

Queens till four in the afternoon, then going home and sleeping till nine, when he had to get up and get ready for his eleven-to-seven night job.

It was hard.

Meanwhile all Gladstone doing, as far as he could see, is reading books. So he told him one day, "In America you have to get up and get. Nobody don't give you nothing free. They always take something in return, even if it is only your dignity."

And all Gladstone saying is okay, okay. Till one day Gladstone look at him and say, "Look, it is you who send for me to come here and study. And it was you who come over here as soon as I pass for secondary school and left me and my mother there to scramble. Least you can do is help me out now."

What a blow, eh? What a blow. That is one Sonny-Boy didn't expect. It knock the wind out of him so hard he had to sit down. When he catch himself he say real soft, "That is what you think? After all the money I send for school fees, for books, the barrel of clothes and school supplies and food I send every year, you saying I left you and your mother to scramble for yourself? That is the thanks I get? That is what education does do to people? Turn them stiff-necked and ungrateful?"

But it seem that Gladstone had it in his head that Sonny-Boy owe him something so he living in the apartment like he is Lord Byron while Sonny-Boy working his tail off and coming home and cooking food for he and Gladstone like he is Gladstone mother or woman, one of the two—Gladstone say his mother never learn him how to cook.

One day Sonny-Boy couldn't take it no more. "Look, Mr. Big-shot," he say. "Money don't grow on trees over here, you know. You see them people you see going back home spending money and showing off? Well they just like me, working like a mule from the minute they land here. Like now, I working these two jobs just to support the two of we. Time for you to get up off your backside and help out too."

That wasn't too much to ask, eh? But Gladstone bust out with, "Why you send for me, then?"

So now the blood really flying to his head. "Wait a minute!" he bawling. "Wait a gad daim minute! I send for you. Yes. But not for you to live like a king while I slaving to support you! This is America.

Every tub got to sit on its own bottom over here. You think it easy? Eh? You see gold on the streets here? Eh?" He steups his teeth. "You just like these black Americans over here. Lazy. Living off welfare and food stamps and expecting somebody to help them. . . ."

And Gladstone butting in saying, "You know how you sound? Eh? You know how you sound?" And asking him if Francine that live across the hall is a black American. Because if he not mistaken, the last he know she was from back home just like them and ent she living on welfare? Eh? What about that? And he going on to give this lecture about how all kinds of people get welfare and that more whitepeople living on welfare than blackpeople, as if Sonny-Boy concerned about what other people do. Is he own color he care about. But this young generation? You can't tell them nothing. You can't reason with them.

So all Sonny-Boy can do is stare at his own son to see how the boy turn just like these Yankee children—contradicting their elders; talking, talking, talking and not stopping to listen and learn. And all he can say to the boy is, "This is what all this book learning doing for you? Turning you stupid and disrespectful? If that is the case, you better off back home."

That is when he feel his heart pounding so hard he think it going bust in his chest. He inhale, take a deep breath and sit down, and he thinking, look his crosses, this boy only here a few months and already with his American rudeness he giving him heart attack. But he also realizing that this isn't the only time here of late that his heart racing like that.

When he get home from his gas station job, even though he tired as a dog, sometimes it taking him a long time before his heart can settle down enough for him to drop off to sleep.

Not only that, he don't have time for enjoyment anymore. He used to be able to go to a dance every now and then on Saturday nights, even when Gladstone first come over. Now his days off at the gas station job is Tuesday and Wednesday, so he working there Saturdays and Sundays and when he get home he too tired to do anything but sit down in front the TV and doze off.

Couple mornings after that argument is when he collapse in the bathroom and when he wake up he find himself in a hospital breathing out of an oxygen mask and with a tube in his arm and Gladstone standing up next to the bed looking down at him.

First thing Gladstone say after he ask Sonny-Boy how he feel is, "Pa, I have a job."

All Sonny-Boy was able to say was, "Uh huh?" And he thinking, Look at this, eh? He had to nearly dead with a heart attack and end up in a hospital bed for the boy to get off his backside and find work. But he got a good feeling inside him anyway and he resting his hand on Gladstone arm.

When he come out the hospital things was better, with Gladstone holding down a little job at the college library and helping out with the bills. But Sonny-Boy decide that even though the heart attack wasn't serious (the doctor tell him he could live a long healthy life but he had to slow down), he would hold on a little bit till he figure his son could handle himself, then he would move to Florida where his cousin write and tell him things not so fast down there and the cost of living lower.

When he left for Florida, Gladstone had two part-time jobs: the one at the college library plus another one at a bank.

Next time he see his son, the boy sitting on a park bench like he sit down there waiting for his father from the moment he hang up the phone from calling him in Florida.

And Sonny-Boy can scarcely recognize his own son, this young man with bushy hair and fidgety hands but with his clothes clean somehow.

At first he feel himself standing there like he stick to the spot; then he have to control himself from rushing over, shouting out his son name and hugging him. Instead he walk over calm and cool and say, "Gladstone?" real easy.

Gladstone look up, see him, and start crying, tears running down his face and dripping off his chin.

Dear diary,

Here I am, weeks away from my forty-eighth birthday yet in my memory the day my parents got married feels like yesterday when I, a child of no more than about two or three, am being tossed up among the rafters by my father who is looking up at me with his mouth wide open in laughter, his hands open and waiting to catch me while I laugh with the thrill and fear of suspension in midair.

Forty-six years later I still see through the eyes of that two-year-old infant a tarpaulin stretched from poles at each corner of the yard, turning the entire yard into a tent filled with grown-ups eating, drinking, talking, merrymaking.

And my father's gold tooth glistens as he catches me and asks, Enjoying yourself, Brute?

His hands grip me under my armpits while I look down at the floor far below, screaming, kicking, and laughing the same way I yelled and laughed years later on my first roller coaster ride with him, years older and gray-haired, sitting beside me tense and clenching the bar in front of him. And walking home later after the bus ride back I glanced at him breathing heavily from too many years of cigarettes and I say, You know, I had a real good time today.

And without looking at me he says, Me too.

That evening we sat in the apartment watching TV together and I was content in a way I never felt before.

But happiness is as evanescent as a raindrop on a hot stone at midday. Because it wasn't long after this that I stood in a room watching my father lying in his hospital bed with a tube in his nostrils and clear liquid dripping from another tube into his arm.

Not long after that he moved to Florida leaving me alone in a city surrounded by strangers, searching my memory for childhood recollections of him, which was like peering into a darkened room and glimpsing the outline of a man with a golden-toothed smile coming in at night while the lamplight cast flickering shadows on the walls and danced in the corners of the house as I lay on my bedding on the floor; hearing him wake up early on mornings and the sound of his bicycle ticking along the side of the house as he pedaled off for an early-morning sea bath, and seeing him later flinging one leg over the bicycle saddle and riding off to work; watching him walk out through the front door one night while I am doing my homework at the dining table and hearing him say, I am going to have a kick out of life, and hearing Mamuh mutter, Well, I hope life don't give you a stiff, hard kick in your ass.

That was the year I passed the eleven-plus exam for secondary school with a scholarship to go to Wilberforce.

The day the letter came my old man went straight down by the rumshop after work. He got to brag with he friends, Mamuh said. But she could not hide the faint smile on her face. Earlier in the day she couldn't keep the news to herself either, telling Miss Clarke next door, The government paying for everything—school fees, books, uniform, everything.

Pa didn't come in till late that night, drunk and happy, singing and waking up me and my mother. But that night she didn't quarrel, just said, Keep quiet and go to sleep.

Two weeks later another letter came from the Ministry of Education.

To this day I've never seen the letter but I remember my mother opening it with the sound of the postman's bicycle *tickticking* away in the stillness of noonday, and my mother standing next to the morris chair by the front window staring at the letter with her mouth slightly open, then saying after a while, Error? What they mean error? and sitting down in the chair clutching the letter in her lap and staring through the window.

What happen? I asked her.

She stared at me, and it was a long moment before she said, You pass, but not with a scholarship.

Which didn't make sense. The letter from the Ministry of Education saying that I had a scholarship for Wilberforce was right there in the shoe box under the bed with all the other important papers like birth certificates and so forth.

But her eyes were still locked on and mine as she waved this new letter and said, They say they make a mistake.

And right then, at the age of eleven, I learned that folks like us who didn't have connections to influential people would suffer disappointments and face obstacles in life, or as Ma said as she sat staring through the window with the letter in her lap, Boy, if you don't have a godfather in this country, you suck salt. Or as Pa said later that night to Ma, If you stand up under a coconut tree a coconut bound to drop down and bust open your head.

Ma gave him a long, hard stare and then burst out, Harold, what stupidness you talking, eh? This is the boy future we talking about. Why you always got to be talking gibberish? What wrong with you?

But nothing was wrong with Pa. He couldn't help himself. He was a man thrust by circumstance into a role he wasn't prepared to maintain.

I still remember the night, one of many nights when rum made his head light and his tongue heavy, when Pa made a statement so heavy, so profound, that his rum friends opened their eyes wide and their mouths fell open in astonishment. At least that's the way the story was told when it started to spread the next day.

To this day everybody has a different version of what Pa said that night, which means that no one really remembers. But Miss Clarke, our next-door neighbor, came to the house bright and early the next day and told my mother, Sonny-Boy is a prophet.

And Ma stared at her. A prophet? she said.

Yes, Miss Clarke said. Like in the Bible.

In the Bible?

Which caused Miss Clarke to ask Ma, What happen to you? You's a echo? Then she began to tell the story of what happened at the rumshop the night before.

That evening before Pa could get in the door Ma asked him, What this about people saying you's a prophet?

So now it is Pa's turn to look puzzled and say, Prophet? What you mean prophet?

It wasn't long before people began to come knocking at the front door, sometimes as soon as he got home from work, before he even had a chance to eat, asking for all kinds of advice. It is like all of a sudden

Pa had turned into an obeah man with people saying things like:

—Yvonne acting funny, like she got another man. What I should do? and;

—I like this fella that does work for the waterworks company, but all I try to catch his attention, he en paying me no mind. What you think?

People coming from far and near, and Ma grumbling and asking Pa why he don't charge them. He's the only body she know does give away free advice. And Pa saying how God give him a gift to help people and how she expect him to charge them? If people want to give donations that is one thing, but he can't charge. And Ma saying low so that only I can hear, Is one thing to be kind, is another thing to be stupid. But that comment doesn't reach Pa's ears, otherwise wise man or no wise man her ass would've been in trouble.

And the whole thing reaching national proportions when Dear Suzy who used to give advice to people every day in the newspaper began ending her columns with a warning to her "Dear readers" not to seek the advice of barefoot charlatans who only want to take their money. And the woman who does housework for her, who happen to live in the Village, coming to Pa and saying how Dear Suzy going to obeah man for him because Pa taking away her business. And Pa's only response is to shake his head and say, Poor woman, which really impressed the woman who brought the news and she's telling people that Pa really is a holy man who, in her words, "have no fear of man nor beast." Which is a big joke to Ma who knows better.

It is around that time that I came to learn another lesson: when people say they want advice, what they really mean is they want you to confirm whatever it is that they already decided. Or at the very least they want you to tilt them in the direction they already were intending to go.

And it seems that Pa learned the same lesson after Gladys came to him with this question: Sammy en doing so good in school. You think you can help him?

To which Pa replied, I can't work miracles, adding that he knew Sammy since the boy was a baby in diapers and to the best of his knowledge her son always had a hard head and in his opinion she should try to get the boy apprenticed to somebody to learn some kind of trade because Sammy never going to be a scholar. The boy just not academically inclined, Pa saying.

You see, Pa had got into the habit of telling people whatever was on his mind, like he thought that whatever gave him the gift of wisdom would also shield him from the wrath of people when he told them what they didn't want to hear.

Gladys started raising her voice, wanting to know what kind of prophet you is, eh? Telling me to send my boy to learn a trade? Why you don't send that little, bony boy of yours to learn a trade, eh? Why you don't do that? And she's looking me up and down with scorn while she's saying this.

That hurt my feelings.

But Pa was calm, replying how he never tell nobody he is no prophet. That is something they put on him. And if she not satisfied with his advice, then she should do like Dear Suzy and go see Papa Sam the obeah man who going tell her some mumbo jumbo and take her money.

Gladys flounced out of the house. Next thing you know, she is spreading a rumor that every night when Pa got drunk he would always come knocking at the side of her house whispering and begging her to let him in. But she is a Christian-minded woman, so she always tell him to go home to Miss Esther and stop bothering her. He should be ashamed of himself. Prophet? He en no prophet. If people stupid enough to believe that, well that is their business but she know better.

As soon as Ma heard this, she stopped speaking to Pa, sulking around the house and talking to him through me, saying things like, Tell your father his food ready, or Tell your father to pick up some fish when he coming in from work this evening.

And Gladys's next-door neighbor, Mildred, is telling people what a lying hypocrite Gladys is, calling herself a Christian, when some nights she can stay over in her house and hear Gladys moaning and carrying on. And it en Sammy's father that causing her to carry on so, because everybody know Sammy father left her and living with another woman. Mildred figuring she doing Pa a favor by calling Gladys a hypocrite, but she's only making things worse.

After that, Pa stopped giving blunt advice and instead began answering people in baffling, head-scratching parables. So, grown people would come up to me after they talked to my father, asking me questions like, What your father mean by so-and-so, or what he mean by this-and-that?

But if they couldn't understand my father, how could they expect me to? I was only a boy; they were grown. But of course I couldn't say any of this because in those days children couldn't talk back to adults (not like nowadays), so I would just stare at them or shrug, which would only get them vexed and cause them to suck their teeth and fling off their arms and walk away muttering about how I just as stupidy as my jackass father.

Well, needless to say, the flow of people coming for advice began to trickle, although it never really stopped. Once in a while somebody would come to see him as a last resort.

But the parables never stopped. Sometimes he would be sitting quietly and all of a sudden, out of nowhere, he would let loose a parable.

So the night when Ma told him about the letter that said I didn't have a scholarship, his proverb about a coconut busting your head was the last straw.

That was the first time I could remember Ma raising her voice in the house. But I suppose the frustration that had been building up from having to listen to Pa's stupid parables, plus the shock of shattered expectations were too much to bear, so she let loose.

These stupid sayings of yours got people looking at me funny! You know that?! People laughing behind my back when they see me, or else they feeling sorry for me and Gladstone—you can see it in their face. You en know you is a big joke?! she asked him. You en care you making your whole family a laughing stock?!

All the while I'm sitting at the dining table expecting Pa to defend his sayings either with another of his parables (as he had a habit of doing) or by telling Ma shut up, woman, what you know. But instead he stared at the tablecloth as if there was something there that only he could see.

Finally a long sigh whooshed out of him and his shoulders slumped even more. What they expect we to do, uh? he said.

A beetle pinging against the lampshade gave the silence in the house the heaviness of molasses. Crickets chirped in the bushes outside. Frogs croaked.

Pa gazed at the letter in his hand. First they tell we the boy got a scholarship. Now look at this. Eh? Look at this. What they expect we to do?

And that night for the first time I saw what defeat looks like on the face of an adult.

Ma gazed at Pa for a long time then sighed. God will find a way, she said.

To which my father replied, Well he better hurry up. The school term soon begin.

Hush, Ma said right away. Don't talk like that. And she's glancing over her shoulder like she expects God to strike Pa dead.

But the slump of her shoulders says she doesn't really have much more faith than Pa does.

I never found out where Pa got the money to pay my school fees and buy textbooks, nor where he got the money to take me into town and buy a cricket bat for me after I came second in class that school year.

Even now the smell of linseed oil always triggers the memory of Pa and me walking out of the store with the midday hot sun beating down, me holding the cricket bat, and Pa looking down at me and saying, You got to cure it with linseed oil.

If my life can be told in chapters, that day marked the beginning of the end of one chapter, the one that ended with Pa shaking my hand man-to-man in the airport building and walking toward a plane that took him to Away, a place I couldn't even imagine and only later got an idea about through reading books I borrowed from the public library.

For weeks after Pa left I would find myself listening for him to come home from work, and several times I heard his bicycle bang against the side of the house. But those are the kinds of illusions that loneliness can create.

Many nights I would lie in bed listening for him to come singing and stumbling home, waking up Ma when he came in the back door saying, ESTHER! I HOME! THE BOSS HAS ARRIVED! and then coming over to where I was sleeping on the floor and saying, Sleeping, Brute? and Ma stirring in bed and mumbling, How many times I tell you don't call the boy no Brute. And keep quiet, for God's sake. People trying to sleep.

And sometimes Pa would take his food from the larder and warm it up (Rum drinking made him ravenous. I know. The same thing happens to me), and we would eat at the table with the kerosene lamp flickering before us.

Once when our cricket team was playing down in Australia Pa and I sat every single night next to the radio up to three, four o'clock in the dead of night listening to cricket commentary and eating salt herring and biscuits.

But all of that stopped the day Mr. Gaskins's old Morris Minor came bumping down the road to take the three of us to the airport.

When we reached the airport, Pa and Mr. Gaskins each carried a suitcase into the terminal building, with the weight of each suitcase bending their bodies sideways.

Ma and I watched from afar as Pa showed the woman at the counter his papers. It was as if Ma was already putting distance between herself and Pa so that when he really left the shock wouldn't be so great.

After Pa checked in we stood in the middle of the terminal—Ma in her good beige dress with white lace trim around the neck, broad-brim straw hat and shining black pocketbook, Pa in his only dark-gray suit with the two-button jacket and dark-brown felt hat cocked at an angle. It looked to me like he was outgrowing his suit, which didn't make sense because grown-ups don't grow. Mr. Gaskins wore a long-sleeved white shirt with the sleeves rolled up to his elbow.

With all the talking that was going on and the aroma of food, the only difference between the airport and the market was the voice coming over a loudspeaker every now and then.

". . . flight number 461 now boarding . . ."

That is my plane, Pa said.

And the noise in the airport almost drowned out Ma's voice reminding Pa of the two dozen flying fish she fried that morning and wrapped in plastic and newspaper and packed in the suitcase. Those will hold you for a little while, she said. What you don't want right away you can freeze.

Pa said, All right, all right. He didn't say it but you could tell he was thinking he was a big man who didn't need nobody telling him how to take care of two dozen fish.

Then Ma said, Write as soon as you get there.

Soon's I get pay I going send something, Pa said.

Get yourself settle first, Ma said. Don't worry about we.

Pa pulled on his cigarette and at that moment he looked like a movie star with his hat cocked at an angle and his shirt opened at the neck under his jacket.

He stamped the cigarette butt under his foot and hugged Ma. She stared over his shoulder with water brimming in her eyes.

Then he stuck out his hand and looked me full in my eyes. You in charge now, Brute, he said.

We shook hands, man-to-man, with me looking him full in his face and with my lips pressed together knowing that if I opened my mouth to speak I would cry, which I couldn't do because men don't cry.

We watched Pa walk toward the door with his travel agency bag over one shoulder and a carton of rum like a valise in one hand.

Come, Ma said.

So I didn't learn until years later that he stopped at the top of the airplane steps and searched for us among the crowd behind the guard rail on the roof of the airport building, and even though he didn't see us he waved, not knowing that we were already in Mr. Gaskins's car headed back home with Mr. Gaskins making conversation to lighten up Ma's spirits.

He soon come back, Mr. Gaskins said. Soon as he make enough money he going come right back to you and Gabby here. Look at me, he said. I work like a slave in the London Transport. But you think I was going stay over there? No sir. That en no place for human beings to live, far more die. But if I didn't do that, if I didn't go away, you think I woulda had this little motorcar to help me make a few little extra cents? Things going work out, he said.

That night I lay on the floor and heard Ma crying softly. And it brought to mind another night when Ma and I were sleeping and Pa came in, drunk as usual. For some reason he and Ma started shouting and next thing I know, *PAKS!* He delivered a slap to Ma's face. Ma held her face. The house was silent. Then she uncoiled and began windmilling her hands, hitting him every which way and yelling, You come in here with your drunk self and hit me? Eh? In front your son? That the kind of example you setting? And Pa hitting her back, but not with any force. After a while he walked back out of the house and Ma lay in bed sniffling into her pillow the same way she was crying that night after we came back from the airport.

It was the first of many such nights.

FUNERAL DAY

Two o'clock and the *gong! gong!* of the grandfather clock in Isamina's sitting room is a fading echo when she hears a knock at the front door and the thought comes to her that it couldn't be the car from the funeral home. They weren't supposed to pick her up till three o'clock.

As she told me later, she really wasn't in any mood for visitors just hours before her husband's funeral, so it was with reluctance that she got up to answer the knocking at the door and who did she see as soon as she opened the door? Henri the undertaker's assistant dressed in his charcoal-gray trousers, black jacket, and top hat bowing and saying, "Good afternoon, Madam."

Sunlight glinted on the hearse parked in front of her house. Nothing is as sobering as a black hearse still and silent at your front door on a sunny afternoon.

Henri tiptoed and peered over her shoulder and said, "Ah. The sitting room. It is not ready yet?" Receiving no answer he said, "May I?" and eased politely by her standing in the doorway and right away began moving furniture away from the center of the room—the center table, the two mahogany chairs—placing everything next to the piano over in the corner. All the while she's still standing in the doorway wondering what in blazes is going on.

When he got to the sofa she heard him mutter, "I can't move this by myself, oui."

So he strode over to one of the front windows and leaned out. Just so happened that Seymour the rummy was passing at the same time.

"Hey! Garçon! Garçon!" Henri shouted out. And when Seymour looked over his shoulder Henri added, "Can you spare a minute?"

Normally Seymour would have asked Henri who he talking to or let Henri know his name en Garçon before continuing on about his business. But as Seymour admitted later, the only reason he stopped was because he was curious to see what inside Gladstone Belle's house looked like, to see how bigshots does live.

(When I told my mother this she said, "See? Men just as malicious as women," to which I made the mistake of correcting her with, "The word en malicious, Mumah. You mean nosy," with her firing right back at me, wanting to know since when I get so Yankeefied I talking about "nosy." And what difference it make anyway? "You always missing the point," she said.)

Which point was well taken, of course, because it was pure nosiness or maliciousness, whatever you want to call it, that caused Seymour to turn back and go into Gladstone Belle's house to help Henri lift the heavy sofa and put it against the wall. "Nearly give me goadies," he said later. ("Woulda serve him right," my mother said. As if wishing a hernia on a man is a light matter.)

Henri thanked Seymour, looked around the room while wiping his hands together as though washing them, then he eased past Isamina again (still standing at the door) and returned with a coffin carriage which he expanded concertina-like and set in the center of the sitting room.

Just then a big, black, American car stopped behind the hearse and out stepped the undertaker and his son Jeffrey.

Henri asked Seymour, who was still eyeballing everything in the house, if he wouldn't mind giving them a hand, please.

So Henri and Seymour and the two Simpsons carried the coffin into the house and laid it on its stand. Henri thanked Seymour again, who said "Don't mention it" and walked out of the house, still gazing around.

By now Isamina had her voice back. "What's going on here?" she asked Mr. Simpson.

Mr. Simpson looked puzzled. "I don't understand," he said.

"My husband. Why did you bring him here?" Isamina wanted to know.

Mr. Simpson begins to wring his hands and hunch his shoulders, looking really uncomfortable. "I was told there was a change of plans," he says.

"By whom?" Isamina wants to know.

"Miss Esther. She, uh . . . she said there was a change of plans. I assumed . . . I assumed you all agreed. I, uuhm, didn't think to question it, the mother of the deceased and all that."

"And I am the wife of the deceased," Isamina says. "You never thought to call me?" Her face is a mask of fury and restraint.

And Mr. Simpson feels helpless as he sees, advancing like a storm cloud on the horizon, a family bassa bassa over funeral arrangements.

At three o'clock on the dot Miss Esther and Sonny-Boy draw up to the house in Mr. Gaskins's little old Morris Minor. The car is as old as the pyramids but Mr. Gaskins keeps the body shining and the engine purring.

As everybody came to find out later, Miss Esther went to her son's funeral in Mr. Gaskins's little old car because she told Mr. Simpson the undertaker flat out that she wasn't driving in no big, black car looking like the hearse her son was in, so Mr. Simpson had no choice but to agree to pay Mr. Gaskins's taxi fare.

Mr. Simpson meanwhile is still trying to pacify Isamina (young Jeffrey Simpson and Henri are outside leaning against the hearse) when Miss Esther marches into the house with Sonny-Boy tagging behind her looking as if he and Miss Esther just had a quarrel and he's trying to be careful not to do or say anything to start her up again.

As soon as Isamina's eyes clap on her mother-in-law she says, "You ordered this?"

"Order what?" Miss Esther wants to know.

"This," she says, pointing to the coffin. "To have Gladstone brought here."

"This is where he live, ent it?" Miss Esther says. "This is where he must leave from."

Meanwhile Mr. Simpson the undertaker is keeping an anxious eye on Miss Esther peering into the open coffin with an expression on her face that says she isn't too satisfied with the job he did with her son.

Sonny-Boy isn't saying a word, just standing around looking as though he wishes he was invisible.

According to what Mr. Simpson told people later, the next thing he heard is Isamina Belle saying, "Why must you always interfere? Why couldn't you ever just leave us the hell alone?"

Mr. Simpson looked around and saw on Isamina's face what he later called "an expression of someone two steps away from the precipice of lunacy." Mr. Simpson talks like that sometimes.

But either Miss Esther didn't see what Mr. Simpson saw or she didn't care, because she looked her daughter-in-law up and down and said, "Us? Us? Gladstone is my son and you talk 'bout interfere? I en interfere enough. If I'd interfered more Gladstone would be alive today."

Who told Miss Esther to say that? Isamina charged at the old woman screaming, "What d'you mean by that? You . . . You! Get the *hell* out of my house! This minute!"

Which everyone agrees was an inappropriate thing to say under the circumstances.

But Miss Esther stood her ground. "You house?" she's saying. "You house? This is Gladstone house. This is my son house. Tell him, Harold." And with that she's turning to Sonny-Boy who, by the look on his face, is thinking that he don't want to get mixed up in no woman-business.

"Well? Open your mouth and say something," Miss Esther is saying to Harold. "Don't stand up there like a idiot, like somebody thief your tongue."

Well, as man, Sonny-Boy has to defend his dignity in front of Mr. Simpson, so he tells Miss Esther, "You should be shame of yourself behaving like this at your son funeral." And he looks from her to Isamina. "Both of you."

Miss Esther is looking him up and down with scorn. "Well well," she's saying. "Look at this. Mr. Stupidy got a voice, eh? Mr. Good-for-nothing can talk after all. Mr. All-he-can-think-about-is woman telling me how to behave. You?" she says, "I spurn you."

Like Mr. Simpson later said, this last expression was like a loud fart in the midst of high-class company—totally unexpected, bringing the verbal battle to a temporary halt as everyone's eyes are fixed on Miss Esther as if they're wondering where she learn such an expression.

Meanwhile Henri and the undertaker's son who were outside leaning against the hearse puffing their cigarettes are back inside the house after hearing the voices raised in argument and have joined Isamina and Mr. Simpson in staring in dumbstruck silence as years of grievance come spilling out of Miss Esther with her son lying less than three feet away in his coffin with his arms at his sides and his eyes closed.

"This worthless man left me and Gabby and never show his face again. Pick up with some worthless woman over in America and en had nothing more to do with me and Gladstone, his only son—as far as I know.

"Every night he coming home stinking of rum like he was at Thorne rumshop all night when I could tell he was with some woman—like big-bottom Delores that live down the trainline. Still live down there to this day in the old house her mother dead and left for her." And she faces Isamina and Mr. Simpson.

Everybody is shuffling in embarrassment but Miss Esther is going on with, "Ask him what he used to be doing coming from her house all hours of the night. Uh? Ask him. And ask him why me and Carlotta-who-used-to-sell-sweets-in-the-bus-stand roll on the ground one day. I'll tell you why. Because she had the brass to tell me I got the ring but she got the man, that's why. Think I forget that?

"I minding my business walking to the market when I hear some big-mouth woman saying, 'Carlotta! Look your friend!'

"And another voice asking, 'Who?'

"And the first woman answering softer but still loud enough for me to hear, 'Sonny wife.'

"At first I en paying no mind, because I already hear the gossip about how he got this woman that does sell sweets near the market and I figure no sense raising my blood pressure unless I got proof. Gossip is like the wind—you can't stop it from blowing. So I keep my head straight, minding my business, not wanting to bring myself down to the level of these gutter rats, when the next thing I hear is this long steups, she sucking her teeth and saying how I might got the name and the ring but she got the man.

"Next thing I know we rolling on the ground and a crowd walling we in so that we bumping against people legs till a man say, 'All right. All right. Stop this.' And hands grabbing me, and Carlotta struggling with the little bow-leg man that holding her and she saying, 'Lemme go! Lemme go! So help me I go kill she today!' and the man telling she that if is any killing it look like I doing it.

"I is a wife but I en no damn bride. So I tell this one here (glancing at Sonny-Boy with deep scorn) that if I ever catch him with another woman I going kill him stone cold and cut out his seeds.

"So I saying all that to say," And she's looking straight in Sonny-Boy's face now, "don't you *ever* be so foolish as to tell me how to behave, a old hard-back woman like me, or so help me I will put you six feet down right next to my son lying over there."

Mr. Simpson is sighing as if relieved to get the point of this whole story. Henri and Jeffrey Simpson, on the other hand, have anticipation on their faces like they're hoping for more entertainment from Miss Esther.

Meanwhile a crowd has appeared out of nowhere and is looking in through the door and windows, staring at the spectacle of church-going Miss Esther letting loose this tirade against Sonny-Boy.

Isamina is so shocked that she's forgotten all about the quarrel she and her mother-in-law were just having. She grabs Miss Esther's arm and says, "You want to sit down? Want a cup of tea?"

Some people swear to this day that they saw a smile on Gabby's face lying there in the coffin. But I for one take that with a smidgen of salt. As we all know, people will embellish if you give them the chance.

Whatever the case, events soon spiraled out of control.

First, Isamina's parents arrived in their new chauffeur-driven car.

But, and everyone present agrees on this, as soon as Mr. and Mrs. Springer stepped in the door Gladstone's coffin began rocking, at first an almost imperceptible *thump! . . . thump!,* then gathering momentum, going *BUMP! BUMP!* on its carriage.

Right away Mr. Simpson the undertaker rushes over and grabs a handle on each side of the foot of the coffin to steady it but is tossed to one side like a rag doll, teetering on one leg, holding on with one hand.

So he grabs the handles again with both hands then bends down and embraces the coffin, looks around at the men in the room and begins bawling, "Help me, nuh?! Help me with this!"

But everybody—men and women alike—begin backing off.

Meanwhile Isamina is staring dumbfounded at the spectacle of her dead husband defying the laws of nature just as his in-laws step over the threshold of his house and her brain is a vacuum, sucked empty of all comprehension of what her eyes are seeing.

But as time went by during the days after the funeral and as she thought about it, she began to wonder, absurd as it may seem, if perhaps her husband was making a final sign of displeasure toward her parents with whom he never got along. What other explanation could there be?

ISAMINA

According to Isamina, the first time she saw Gladstone she was in the cafeteria at lunchtime when she noticed this man sitting a few tables away looking like the loneliest man in the world, eating sandwiches out of a greasy paper bag and drinking what appeared to be cocoa from a quart bottle.

Up to now she doesn't know what drew her attention to him this particular day, except perhaps a certain forlornness about him. (Actually, according to Gladstone's diary entry for that day, that was the day before he suggested to Andrea that she get off her fat ass and find a job).

He certainly wasn't the kind of man she'd been attracted to before—dark, obviously common class. But for some reason she found herself staring at this man who was obviously from way up in the country, new to town and new to the job. Who else but a country buck would bring his lunch from home in a bottle and a greasy paper bag?

He must have felt her staring, because he turned his head and their eyes met briefly before she quickly looked away.

When she got back from lunch she was surprised to hear from her secretary that the man that she'd seen in the cafeteria (A) wasn't from the country as she'd thought and (B) was the new reference librarian who'd been there for months.

"Country?" Monica said, in that brusque way of speaking that she had. "He live not too far down the road. With a woman."

As if she was concerned whether he lived with a woman or not. He could have *three* wives. He wasn't her type. Monica was too presumptuous.

But she didn't say any of this to Monica. The less said the better. Monica had a tendency to be familiar and she always had to remind her, as subtly as she could of course, that their relationship was that of secretary and administrative assistant.

Every day at lunch after that she would see the new librarian in the cafeteria but she would sit so that she faced away from him, though she could feel his presence, feel his eyes boring into her.

So it didn't surprise her when a few days after she first noticed him she's walking from the main building after work when she hears footsteps hurrying behind her and a soft voice saying, "Administrative assistants always walk so fast?"

She knew who the voice belonged to though she'd never heard it before.

And as he came abreast of her she cut her eye at him and said, "Pardon me?"

What people say is really true. You can't judge a book by its cover. Gladstone turned out to be nice and gentlemanly with a sense of humor that had her laughing at almost everything he said. How people change, eh? How people change.

That weekend they went to the cinema. And every day after that would find them having lunch together, sometimes in the cafeteria, often sitting under a tree in the yard, something she'd never done before.

One day Gladstone looked in her face and said, "You really don't remember me, uh?"

Remember him? From where? What a funny thing to say.

That was when she discovered that this man that she felt herself drawing closer to every day, contrary to all expectations and previous experience, was the same Belle who was in her brother Sammy's class in school, the boy they dropped off in the Village a few times until her mother came flying out of the house one afternoon as soon as she and Sammy got out of the car, telling them loud enough for Oswald the chauffeur to hear, "Let this be the last time I look down this hill and see that boy getting out of this car, you hear me?"

That memory from years ago caused her to say with a laugh, "Well, well, well. Fancy that. This is a small world, eh?"

Instead of laughing along with her as she expected (they were children back then, after all), he stared at her with a face so inscrutable that a warning pinged inside her head. But life is full of signals we ignore and remember later and say I shoulda.

The second little signal was when she invited him home for dinner.

Dinnertime for her family was a time for catching up with what went on during the day. A what-happened-in-school-today time. And, how's the new servant girl working out? You think you going to get that contract? And so on. Eating and chatter. That was her family at dinner time.

But that night with Gladstone sitting at the dinner table was unusually quiet. For one thing, Gladstone only spoke when spoken to and then only in short sentences. Mummy was unusually silent. Dad kept trying to pull Gladstone out of his shell.

After Gladstone left Dad asked her, "Peaches, you really serious about this boy?"

She nodded yes.

"Seems like a nice fella," he said.

But from Mummy: "Where'd you get him from?" A question she didn't feel obliged to answer.

A few weeks later when she invited him to dinner again one of the questions Daddy asked him when they were having a drink before dinner was, "So. What do you plan to do with yourself, young fella?"

"Do with myself?" Gladstone asked him.

"Yes. You know. Careerwise."

"Oh," Gladstone said. "Maybe get into politics. Or law. Maybe medicine."

She remembers her Dad saying, "Hm," or something noncommittal like that and staring off into space.

Later at dinner, to her great surprise, he asked Gladstone how would he like to work with the prime minister. A question straight out of the blue.

She could tell from the way her Mummy stared at her Dad as if she thought he'd just lost his mind that this wasn't something they'd discussed.

Meanwhile Gladstone was the only one who didn't seem to be affected. She remembers him giving her father a steady stare before saying, "That would be nice." He nodded his head slowly, adding, "Yeah. That would be good."

Daddy said, "I could arrange it, you know."

Without looking up from cutting his meat with his knife and fork Gladstone shrugged. To her, Gladstone was obviously trying to be cool and casual. This was a mistake. Daddy liked to impress people with his political connections as one of the founding members of the PLP, so from the slight frown on his face she could tell he wasn't pleased that Gladstone didn't seem to be impressed.

Nevertheless he was a man of his word.

A couple weeks later when Gladstone told her he was handing in his two-weeks notice of resignation and would soon begin working in the prime minister's office she wasn't surprised because one night when she and her father were sitting in the veranda Daddy asked her, "You sure you serious about this boy?" When she said yes he just stared down at the lights in the village below and after a long silence said, "Well, at least he look like a bright boy which is more than I can say for some of them fellas always coming around here. I like him."

She never knew he didn't approve of her boyfriends.

Their wedding about three years later was a grand affair—colored lights strung across her parents' backyard; a five-piece band playing live music; more food than even the yardful of guests could cram down, as hard as they tried.

And while her father toasted his "new son and rising star in the party" with his glass upraised, her eyes and her brother Sammy's locked across the room as Sammy raised his glass and sent her a wry smile acknowledging the irony of their father toasting as his son-in-law the same boy their mother'd forbidden them from associating with all those childhood years ago. Life is like a jigsaw puzzle sometimes. You never know how and where the pieces will fit.

But talk about puzzles? A little over a year after their wedding, Isamina goes on to say, Gladstone came home one day and said he was thinking of running for a seat in parliament. True, he'd told her father he was interested in politics but she figured he'd only said it to please him.

So there she was in the weeks leading up to the elections, sitting next to him every night driving to political meetings where she was always astonished to see the transformation that would come over him as soon as he stepped up to a microphone.

It was like he became a different person, not the shy, quiet Gladstone she knew but a fiery, thoughtful orator generating tumultuous enthusiasm in people her father called stupid people who didn't care who led them as long as they could get babies and have a good time every now and then.

In the car driving toward the meeting he would be silent and pensive, gripping the steering wheel and staring at the road ahead. And he always seemed out of place sitting on the platform with the other politicians, looking like a rough country man who somehow found himself in the midst of this party of sophisticated lawyers, doctors, and university professors; dark, short, and stocky with the beginnings of a paunch; sitting with his legs open rather than crossed like the other men; peering at his fingers, the floor; glancing at the crowd every now and then.

But then his turn would come and he would stride to the microphone. And right before her eyes he would change, his voice becoming mellifluous and soothing, less high-pitched than usual; he would stand erect, his eyes scanning the crowd as he spoke. And how he spoke: slowly, deliberately, presenting his points clearly and precisely. A surgical performance, the newspaper said once.

And the crowd would be silent. No heckling, no interruption, waiting till the end to let loose.

One night a man rushed up on the platform and grabbed him around his waist and tried to hoist him up while the other politicians sitting on their chairs up on the platform are staring in alarm, not knowing if this man is some kind of madman or, which is the same thing in their minds, a supporter of the opposition party.

When the man found he couldn't lift up Gladstone he raised Gladstone's hand in the air and pushing his face right up to the microphone bawled out, "This is the next prime minister! Eh? EH? Hip hip!"

And the crowd is shouting back, "HOORAY!"

And it is clear by the look on Roachford's face that he isn't too happy about what's going on but, prime minister and politician that he is, he is clapping along with the crowd.

The night Gladstone won his seat her father held a victory celebration. All the party supporters seemed to be there, their cars parked in the yard and alongside the road leading down the hill past the Village where Gladstone grew up and where, by the way, she and Gladstone now lived.

And she watched her husband standing in the middle of her parents' living room, stocky, hair trimmed close to his skull, a slim moustache above his top lip, teeth small and even like a young child's and sparkling against the blackness of his skin. Handsome. But something about him stirred a slight unease inside her.

The supporters are all smiling at Gladstone with their glasses raised as her father toasts "the biggest victory of all. The victory of one of our own Village boys."

And somebody shouts, "Speech! . . . Speech!"

And Gladstone grins, raises his glass and with his eyes focused on hers says, "To obstacles overcome, to hills climbed, to victories won."

Some of the guests look uncomfortable for a brief moment. They all raise their glasses and say, "Hear, hear." And something in his expression causes the unease she felt earlier while looking at him to grow. But in the euphoria of the moment the feeling soon fades.

Later when she is entering the kitchen to get drinks and ice for the guests she overhears her father saying to her mother, "You hear that little cocksucker? 'To obstacles overcome. To hills climbed.' You hear him?"

And Mummy is saying, "What you expect? I tell you from the beginning. Didn't I tell you I didn't want him in this family? But you wouldn't listen. A nice boy, you said. Putting in word for him and getting him a job. The boy is Village riff-raff. Always will be common class." She sees Isamina and clamps her mouth shut and immediately busies herself doing some trifling task.

Both of them watched her in silence as she entered the kitchen, with her pretending she hadn't overheard and they pretending they hadn't said anything. Really, she didn't know what the fuss was about.

Over the years, the only time her mother set foot in their house was the day Gladstone died. Her father would drop by sometimes. He and Gladstone seemed to get along fairly well.

So why did Gladstone's coffin begin to rock as soon as her parents entered the door on the day of his funeral? Perhaps it was an earth tremor, or perhaps the dead do have a way of making their presence felt. What d'you think? she's asking me.

But I could offer no opinion, only shrug, for from the morning of Gladstone's death when I witnessed things my rational mind could not explain I'd begun to feel as though the world around me had become a less solid and certain place.

Back at the house, Mr. Simpson the undertaker is still wrestling with the rocking coffin and pleading, "Help, in the name of God. Help me with this."

But the men in the room are staring at him as though thinking that a disturbed duppy is the undertaker's problem to control, not theirs, which causes Mr. Simpson to shed some of his usual decorum and bawl, "All-you stop standing up there and come help me out, nuh! Henri! Jeffrey!"

But neither Henri nor Jeffrey are anywhere to be seen and their absence is only increasing Mr. Simpson's desperation and making the men in the room more resolved not to lift even a little finger to help him, because they didn't fail to notice that Henri and Mr. Simpson's son made themselves scarce as soon as the coffin started rocking. First Henri, backing toward the door then easing outside as quick as a scalded cat. Then the undertaker's son doing the same thing and joining Henri outside where Henri is puffing on a cigarette like it is the last one in the world and waving his arm and telling the undertaker's son, "From this morning I tell him, oui. I tell him M'sieu Belle sit up in his coffin right in front my two eyes but he don't believe me. *Now* he see for himself, oui. *Now* he see."

So the men in the house see this and are thinking, if Henri getting paid to help the undertaker and Jeffrey is the undertaker son and *they* make themselves scarce, why should they get themselves involved in duppy business?

Meanwhile in the midst of the commotion, Isamina's brother Sammy is standing in the doorway with his eyes fastened on the bucking coffin of his brother-in-law while the undertaker with his voice cracking in desperation is shouting, "JESUS GOD, SOMEBODY COME AND HELP ME, NUH?"

SAMMY SPRINGER

One day weeks after the funeral, Sammy Springer and I are sitting in rattan chairs on the veranda of the Colony House Hotel. Sammy Springer is wearing bathing trunks, has a towel draped around his neck and is sipping what looks like a rum and coke.

An old white woman with tanned, blotched, leathery skin, deep collarbones and shriveled arms and thighs, is reclining in a plastic and aluminum chair next to Sammy, neither moving nor speaking, dead behind her sunglasses for all I knew.

And Sammy is telling me how he never really got close to his brother-in-law but he can remember the first time Belle and his sister met. You might say he introduced them.

She was about nine, in her St. Catherine's Girls School uniform, sitting in the backseat of the car with Oswald the chauffeur in front at the wheel, and he and Belle and a yard full of school boys are pouring out through the gates after the three o'clock school bell just rang.

He hopped in the front seat next to Oswald and said something like, This is Belle. He live in the Village.

Belle scotched himself in the corner away from Isamina in the backseat, looking through the car window all the way home.

When Oswald slowed down to turn into the Village where Belle lived Belle said, "You can drop me here." They could barely hear him, his voice was so soft.

Oswald glanced over his shoulder and told Belle he could drop him right home.

But Belle said, "No. No. I can walk the rest."

So they stopped on the tar road running past the Village up to their house. Belle got out.

Every evening it was the same: Belle drawing up in the corner of the backseat not saying a word, and getting out on the tar road and walking into the Village.

Then one morning he saw Belle on the main road walking to school and he leaned forward to his old man sitting in the front seat next to Oswald and said, "Look, Dad. That boy in my class." But his old man ignored him, staring straight ahead without answering.

Sammy looked at Isamina but she only shrugged her shoulders.

That same afternoon as soon as he and Isamina got out of the car their mother was in the driveway waiting, apparently so that Oswald the chauffeur could hear when she said she didn't want to see that boy driving in this car with you and your sister, d'you hear me?

The next afternoon while they were driving home Isamina asked him, "What you tell him?"

"Who?"

"Belle."

"I tell him we have music lessons."

From where he was sitting in the backseat next to Isamina he could see Oswald's eyes meeting his in the rearview mirror.

So most days they would pass Belle walking to and from school.

But Gladstone Belle was a strange man. After he married Isamina, all the many times he visited the old folks' house, for parties, family occasions, sometimes just dropping by with Isamina, he and Sammy would talk but they would never mention their school days. It was as though they never happened.

And while they were talking about politics, sports, the kinds of things men talked about, Sammy's conscience often would be nagged by his memories. But Belle never said a word about their school days, not to him, and as far as he knew, not to Isamina.

Gladstone Belle was a strange fella. He, Sammy, could never figure him out.

THE P.M. ARRIVES

[3:45 P.M.]
Back at the funeral house, the coffin has quieted down and the prime minister's white Mercedes with the nation's flag flapping on its bonnet is pulling up behind Mr. Gaskins's old Morris Minor. And out of the official car steps Prime Minister Roachford: white suit, white shirt, white tie, white shoes, white wife wearing a white dress, white gloves, and white, broad, floppy-brimmed white hat.

By now the house is almost filled with mourners, most of whom are irritable at having been to the funeral home to find only the secretary there telling them that the duppy—well, actually she called him the deceased—was at his residence, which cause some of them to grumble and complain about being turned around like blinking idiots and, if you keeping the funeral at the house, say you keeping the funeral at the house. Don't make people go to the wrong place like idiots. We's big people, they're saying, not little children.

To make the situation worse, those who are now arriving are hearing the news about the spectacle of the rebellious coffin and feeling cheated because later when they tell people about what they saw with their own two eyes, so help me god, they will know within their hearts that they actually got their information secondhand.

In the midst of all this discontent Prime Minister Roachford steps into the house and Miss Gittens, Cynthia Gittens mother, comes flying at him like a furious sitting hen. "Murderer!" she's bawling. "You blasted, stinking murderer!"

Nobody saw when Miss Gittens arrived, so a moment lapses before anyone can react. But then as if by signal men rush to restrain her while women's voices go "Shhh!" and the prime minister is adjusting the knot of his tie as though his collar all of a sudden is choking him.

And Isamina strides up to him very ladylike and says almost in a whisper, "You have some nerve to come here," which causes those close enough to hear her to wonder what she means.

At the same time someone whispers, "Look. Look." Eyes turn in the direction where a woman in a mauve dress and black hat is pointing. And later everyone swears they saw Gladstone Belle turn his face to look at the prime minister, but his eyes remained duppy closed.

Needless to say, speculation begins to rage rampant through the room. And as we all know, speculation is the mother of rumor.

INTERLUDE

As people are converging from all points of the village and news spreads that unusual things are happening at Gladstone Belle's house, I am probably the only one unaware of the bacchanal and excitement because I am at home engrossed in his diaries, feeling a little bit like a grave robber poring over the private possessions of the dead but refusing to allow the whisper of my conscience to kill my curiosity, telling myself that, after all, it wasn't as if I went out of my way to procure the man's private thoughts and experiences.

I've often wondered what prompted Sonny-Boy to hand over his son's private personal items to me, what made him come by earlier in the day with a handful of notebooks saying, "Gladstone left these for his daughter, but I don't know where she is and I can't bear to keep them. You's a schoolteacher. You will know what to do with them."

At the time I shrugged it off as just one of the perils of being the only schoolteacher in a community: people come to you with all sorts of requests—to write their wills; to read letters from relatives overseas; to explain official documents they can't make head nor tails of, So tell me what they say, eh? You understand these things; to read the newspaper to them and, as in this case, to do something with their sons' diaries.

It wasn't until I learned later of Sonny-Boy's failing health did I combine this with the death of his only son and Miss Esther's accumulating years and conclude that perhaps in some way Sonny-Boy was seeking immortality for his son, if not himself, through his son's journals. We all do that in some form or other.

But on the day of Gladstone Belle's funeral it was curiosity that drove me, curiosity aroused by what I later called *The New York Diaries.*

THE NEW YORK DIARIES: selected excerpts

"Julio"
by Gladstone Belle

Gimme a light
Julio said today
I bummed a cigarette
But tonight he screams
in gasoline dreams
waking
my eyes of fear and fury
to see onlookers
each in his dispassionate shell
watching
youths yell "Fucking bums
go to hell!"
as subway rats race
from Julio's flame
fleeing
from this inhuman game.

Scuffling in the dark, a man's voice whispering, "Empty his pockets. I check his bundle already."

I pretend sleep and peep through the slits of my eyelids. A bulky man in a bulky winter coat sitting astride the chest of the half-mad, long-haired Indian ("I'm Oneida," he told me once) in the cot next to mine, and the bulky hatless man in the bulky winter coat has one hand clamped over the Indian's mouth and nose while a long-blade knife glistens in the moonlight like the whites of the eyes of the victim who is staring, straining, trying to heave the winter coat man off his chest.

Meanwhile a shorter, muscular companion inside a camouflage army jacket empties the pockets of a pair of pants. "Nothing here," he says.

The eyes of the men on the cot lock in a stare and the only sound I hear is the *thump, thump* as my heart races. Then, in a flash the slash of a knife across the Indian's throat. His eyes widen; he bucks and bumps and twitches and shudders and *thump, thump* goes his hands against the mattress while a gurgle bubbles from the slash in his throat, then . . . silence.

And the room reeks raw with blood and echoes with my heartbeat, *thumpthumpthumpthump* a drum inside my chest so filled with fear I cannot breathe.

A voice inside my head says, RUN! BAWL FOR MURDER! HOLLER FOR HELP! and the bulky man in the bulky winter coat stares at me while his short companion gawks at the dead man's face and says, "Oh Jesus Christ, man. Jesus Christ" as the bulky man wipes his knife across the dead man's chest (Yo-ho-ho and a bottle of rum) and slips it in the pocket of his bulky winter coat then swings his leg and dismounts and bends down over my cot and peers at my face. His breath has the sweetness of chewing gum.

But I am dead asleep, dead . . . asleep, snoring louder than a dozen drunks with sinus.

And through the slits of my eyes I watch the murderers walk away.

And I remain frozen, shivering, fetal with fright, too scared to shift from the piss-damp spot on my bed, afraid two murderers may still be lurking in the shadows; too scared to turn my gaze away from the dead man in the dark.

And daylight is a million hours away. Sixty million minutes, 3,600 seconds before the room lightens and the butcher-shop blood-odor that has long become familiar to my nose draws a cry of discovery, a "Hey! . . . Oh shit! . . . Hey!" of a man's gravelly growl that causes another sleepier voice to cut in with, "Aw, shut the fuck up, will ya? Whassa matter with you?"

"This motherfucker's dead!" the first voice says. "Jesus! This motherfucker's fucking dead!"

Pandemonium erupts. Voices.

"What?"

"Who is it?"

"Shit!"

"Move! Lemme see!"

"See what? Fuck you! This ain't no fucking TV show!"

"No shit, you stupid asshole! Move lemme see."

And I wait till footsteps surround my cot before I stretch, open my eyes and sit and go, "What the . . ."

"You ain't seen nothing?" a man asks me. Wonder is in his voice, the awe of death.

"You didn't hear nothing?" the policeman asks me later, familiar with death. He tells us not to leave the city.

"That's a big fucking joke," a big, bearded white man wearing a blue ski cap says. "Where the fuck they think we're going? To Hawaii, for Christ's sake?"

Everybody laughs. An exhalation of fear more than the evidence of mirth.

Sitting in my apartment in Brooklyn, cross-legged on the green-and-yellow floor cushion when suddenly I hear the sound of furniture pelting below and Elsie's voice like smoke filtering through the floor clear as day shouting, "Why you don't get your ass out my apartment and look for a fucking job . . ."

A man's voice rumbling, ". . . tell you a'ready ah cyan find no work . . . think it easy?" words echoing my predicament—me with a bachelor's degree magna cum laude trudging the streets of this city for almost a year responding to letters of enthusiasm pungent as a whore's perfume; appointments; interviews.

Yesterday: warmth frozen from a welcoming smile the moment I appear in the doorway; the stride around the desk, one hand held out for my handshake, the other holding a raceless resume; the "Have a seat, please," shuffling of papers; same questions; same rehearsed responses rendered seated erect with a slight forward earnest lean; a charade, a treadmill jog that ends with "I'll get back to you" or "We'll keep your name on file," all heard before. All for a fucking city job no experience required.

So I step from the building onto a sunlit sidewalk in a city of passersby whose eyes and mine never meet, an uncivil city dressed in the emperor's invisible clothes of Broadway shows, museums, and high-priced restaurants.

(One of several undated poems. Chronological order unknown.)

"Black"
by Gladstone Belle

I am,
incidentally,
black.
A . . .
who happens to be
black.

Fancy that.

Immigrated from my country
escaping
tyranny,
seeking opportunity
just like
"the larger society."
Just happen to be
black.

Is that a fact?
What
about loyalty, community, cultural identity?

What?
Professional integrity!
That's the key
because

I am not,
Just happen to be,
parenthetically,
black.

Say
what?

Walking from the subway station, feet aching after trekking between interviews, I notice as I approach my apartment building an extra pile of trash on the sidewalk.

But as I reach closer I recognize what's left of my belongings: two pots and a frying pan; forks and spoons (knives gone); notebooks; file-holders; textbooks. No clothes, no bed, no floor cushions, no dinette set. No stereo.

Clement, the Trinidadian super, is standing alongside one of the two columns at the entrance to the building and says as soon as he sees me, "I try, Professor. I tell them, Leave the man things in the lobby, oui, so I can keep an eye on them. But you know how it is with these people. Mr. Goldberg want back his apartment. What I can do, eh? Sorry."

But I don't blame Clement. Clement is good people, trying his best to keep the tenants comfortable, which is a hard thing to do when all the owners want to do is to collect rent. Calling me Professor. Asking, "Hey, Professor. Find a work yet?" And I'm embarrassed always having to say, "No, man. Not yet" while he replies, "Maybe tomorrow, oui."

Clement's heart attack a few months ago melted all remaining fat off his already lean body. Now his eyes and cheeks are sunken holes as he tells me about buying a home in Florida.

Perhaps he'll meet my father and they'll be friends.

But it's three weeks now that I've been living on the streets. Wonder how Clement is doing?

People think you get used to not having a bath, no change of clothes. But as Julio once said, "Only the crazies don't give a shit. They don't even know who the fuck is seeing them."

But who knows, eh? Who knows?

Because once I tried to start a conversation with one of the men the government released from the asylum because, they said, he wasn't a danger to the public. Of course, one night I saw one of those men who wasn't a danger to the public grab Martha who used to be a schoolteacher in Jersey around the waist, hoist her layers of grimy clothing, jackknife her like she was a barbie doll and ram his penis up her ass (at least that's what she said later) while Martha is yelling and struggling as the two of them fall to the ground and the man is ramming and grunting like a mating bull while everybody else seems frozen—standing, lying, huddling under the bridge—staring at the pumping ass of the man lying on Martha who is spread-eagled face down on the ground while car wheels *thumpthumpthump* on the bridge overhead. And the man whom government officials say was not a danger to the public gives one last grunt and shudder then stands and walks away with his limp penis dangling from his fly while Martha remains prostrate and spread-eagled with her clothes bunched above her buttocks as another crazy man paces back and forth muttering, "You all are CHICKENSHIT! Fucking CHICKENSHIT! If you were not all so goddamned CHICKENSHIT! CHICKENSHIT! . . . I could've pressed the goddamned button . . . pressed the button and ZAPPED his fucking ass. NUKED his fucking ass, goddamnit." Nobody knows if he's talking about the incident that just occurred or if perhaps he thinks he's the president of the United States, because he's pumping his fist in the air and yelling, "JUST GIVE ME THE WORD, GODDAMMIT!"

And I'm gazing at him and wondering if perhaps he really was president. Once.

Where was I? Oh yes. I walked up to this fella who not too long ago had been released from a single-room-occupancy hotel/halfway house, but before I could open my mouth to say a word the man yelled, "IS THAT YOUR FINAL WORD ON THE MATTER?"

Who knows what goes on in a crazy man's mind? Perhaps their unwashed odor drives them crazier.

Needless to say, I left him alone.

Today a whiteboy with long, dirty, brown hair and a beard, wearing clean overalls and pulling a shopping cart begins muttering, "Nigger-niggerniggernigger" as soon as he reaches abreast of me.

And all I recall is watching as the boy staggers back against the wall holding his nose with a stream of blood coursing down his moustache and beard.

I continue walking and hear a young woman's voice asking behind me, "What happened?" even as the rumbling engine of a passing truck drowns his reply.

A hand grabs my shoulder; I attempt to shrug it off.

"Hey, buddy. I said hold it!" A growl from a small man making himself big by deepening his voice (one gets to know these things).

I stop. But I do not need to turn around. It is a cop. I know it. But at the same time I'm thinking, this is the first human touch I've felt in all my months of homeless wandering.

But today is my lucky day. They bring me to the precinct in the squad car but don't arrest me. The black cop (my African American brother) who sat in the passenger seat beside the white cop who drove said when we got to the precinct, "Muhfucking monkey chaser here kicked his buddy's ass. Hippie-looking motherfucker. You shoulda seen 'em." Everyone in the room laughs. All homeless people are pals, you see.

A young black female cop offers me a cup of coffee.

Just called Pa collect in Florida.

"You on welfare?" the landlord said and my eyes fixed on his old man's stare. But at least I have a lease for another year, so my mouth said "No" as I wished him dead and my pen scratched paper with a rhythm that said "nigger," "schvartze," two sides of the same flipping coin, only difference is who's making the call.

All of a sudden the apartment became silent and I knew I had crossed a line. But I was too young and stubborn to back down. Besides, it is hard to know where the line is when your father is not the hearty man with the gold-toothed smile that you looked forward to firing liquor with, to being man-to-man with in New York. Instead you're sharing an apartment with an old man with gray hair who comes home every evening, tosses his hat on the chair and falls asleep on the couch after fixing dinner and snores in front of the color TV.

Streets littered with broken glass and trash. Garbage overflowing on the sidewalk. Is this New York?

Children yelling, playing in water that gushes from a fire hydrant. Water wasting. Water washing debris into gutters. This can't be New York, where streets are clean and paved with gold and folks dress in Sunday clothes like in the movies, I was told.

No. This is New York where roaches run ubiquitous as mosquitoes in rainy season and mice scurry across living room floors as if their names are typed on the lease, a place where neighbors pass you in the hall not even looking you in the face much less to say a simple, civil “good morning,” “good evening,” or “good day”? Yes. This . . . is . . . New York.

. . . office services engineer is a fancy name for janitor . . .

This was all I had time to read before a mind told me to check my watch. Almost four o’clock, time for the funeral to leave for the church.

I made a final check in the mirror before hastening to the door hoping to make it to the funeral home in time to share a ride to the church with someone.

But as soon as I opened my front door I noticed for the first time the line of cars parked along both sides of the road and the onlookers and mourners assembled in the road and flowing in and out of Gladstone’s house.

By the time the clock in the parliament building tower struck four, things had settled down enough for Mr. Simpson to begin closing up the coffin.

As he is screwing the final fastener the loud braying of a jackass breaks the silence, causing everyone to rush to the windows to see what this new confusion is about.

And right before their eyes is the spectacle of Peg-leg Pollard wearing a swizzle-tail coat and top hat sitting catercorner on his donkey cart with his peg leg jutting off straight in front of him as usual, except that today the wooden leg isn't exposed but is swathed in black cloth. The whole cart is draped in black.

"Now what the hell is this?" Isamina is asking.

Which is the same question on everybody's mind as they all look at the undertaker for an answer, placing Mr. Simpson in yet another predicament where he finds himself wringing his hands and stammering something about a letter and a donkey cart and man of the people and "Yuh-you mean you didn't know about this either?"

"Know about what?" Isamina Belle wants to know. "What are you talking about?"

Which causes Mr. Simpson to hem and haw and uhh and ahh and mop his forehead and look terribly distressed.

The day after the funeral he comes by to apologize to the widow, explaining that day-before-yesterday, the day before the funeral, the prime minister called him personally. He's in his office when the phone rings and his secretary whispers behind her hand, "It's the prime minister."

He picks up his phone and Roachford starts in right away saying how he wants his former deputy prime minister carried to his final resting place in a donkey cart as befitting a man of the people.

Hearing this, all Mr. Simpson can do is sit there with the phone against his ear, speechless with his mind spinning. A jackass cart? What the prime minister think? That Gladstone Belle was Jesus or something? But of course he couldn't say any of that. You don't want to cross the prime minister if you have any sense.

So all he said was, "Yes, sir."

Then after he hung up the phone he rested his head in his hands, pondering his fate—an ordinary undertaker going about his business and suddenly being caught in the carnival of politics. And what the hell is he going to tell the family of the deceased when a donkey cart shows up instead of a hearse, eh? What he going tell them? Furthermore, where the France he going get a donkey cart from and make the whole thing look presentable and not like the stupid spectacle he's sure it's going to be?

And he finished his explanation to Isamina Belle hoping that Missis Belle wasn't offended but he hopes she understands the jam he was in.

Thus was his explanation to the widow on the day after the funeral.

But on the day of the funeral all he can do is wring his hands in distress, caught as he is between a widow's wrath and the reputation of a prime minister who is rumored to be as ruthless as a cobra, while the eyes of everyone in the house are shifting between him and the widow, expecting her to erupt in volcanic fury.

But to everyone's surprise, including the undertaker's, Isamina Belle simply throws her hands in the air, strides over to the window and says with her back to the room, "Go ahead. Do what you want."

Later Isamina admitted that the fear in Mr. Simpson's eyes hinted to her the predicament he was in. A donkey cart for a hearse. This was the kind of gimmickry one could expect from Anthony Roachford, the kind of circus spectacle that had kept him in power all these years. She didn't want to get the little undertaker in trouble. At any rate, mental exhaustion had begun to wear her down.

Miss Esther on the other hand begins to stride toward her daughter-in-law and opens her mouth to speak. But collapses in a faint.

So now it is more confusion, with one woman holding smelling salts under Miss Esther's nose, another one fanning her, Sonny-Boy looking on bewildered and everybody crowding around.

So it was that Marva Goddard, who'd known Gladstone Belle ever since working with him back when he was just an assistant to the P.M., drove up just in time to see the bearers place the coffin onto a black-draped donkey cart.

And the jackass, having no understanding of the solemn nature of the occasion, is unleashing a loud stream of piss, which is a big joke to the village children watching on.

But Marva Goddard has her eyes on Isamina Belle descending the steps in her black dress and veil and can't help but be impressed by the dignified bearing of this tall, stately woman who, according to Gladstone himself, had gone through such turbulent times in their marriage.

The funeral procession starts off, crawling so slowly behind the donkey cart that Marva wonders if she wouldn't be better off parking her car and walking. But she sighs and figures what the hell, and creeps along in low gear like everybody else while her thoughts wander, recalling the night Gladstone Belle confided in her about his marriage in the bar at the Golden Sands Hotel on one of those "retreats," as the P.M. called them, where every six months or so he and his cabinet and their aides would spend a weekend at a hotel or somebody's remote estate feting at the taxpayers' expense.

She'd just slipped out of a committee meeting where almost everyone sat around in swim trunks and bathing suits planning for the upcoming elections.

Outside on the terrace a steel band was playing yellow-bird calypsos for the tourists and at the reception desk one of them wearing shorts, sandals, and Hawaiian shirt was complaining about low water pressure.

Gladstone Belle, with his tie loosened and his shirtsleeves rolled up, was sitting at the bar.

And as the bartender set her drink down and turned away she said, "Didn't see you at the meeting."

He shrugged, then tossed back his drink and began playing with his empty glass.

"You all right?" she asked him.

For a while he just stared at the glass he held in his hands without answering. Then he said, "My wife wants a divorce."

Dear diary,

Sooner or later, everyone feels the need to confide. And so last night I made a fool of myself, with steel pan music wafting in from the terrace, liquor in my head and a drink in my hand and Marva sitting on a stool beside me. Now in the sober light of day I feel silly, vulnerable, but relieved. . . .

He began what turned out to be a long confession that night by jumping in at the deep end, no dipping his toes in the water first, no innocuous details leading up to the big confession. It was as though he was continuing aloud a stream of thought that was in progress before she joined him at the bar.

His relationship with Isamina was rocky from the very beginning, he told her. Right from the giddy-up. A man's supposed to come first with his woman, right? That's only natural, isn't it? But you think that was the case? No sirree. Take, for example, the year they met. Isamina was supposed to spend Christmas with him at his mother's house. They agreed. Everything was set.

But on Christmas Eve he's up at her house helping her decorate the Christmas tree and he's discussing what time he would come the next day and pick her up, telling her what his mother was cooking up when he left home, how nice the house was smelling and what a good time she, Isamina, was going to have. But then he begins to notice that he's the only one talking and she isn't saying a word.

Finally he asked her, What happen? and that's when she said, I changed my mind.

Can you imagine that? Changed her mind.

He was furious, wanting to know what she mean she changed her mind—at the last minute?

And she's snapping back at him saying how her family is very important to her and does he expect her to hurt her family's feelings by not spending Christmas with them?

Right at that moment her mother marches into the room with a smug smile on her face as if she'd been listening before entering the room.

By New Year's day his anger had subsided and he proposed. Isamina accepted. That must've wiped the smile off the old bitch's face, eh? He didn't have any illusions. He knew the old hag didn't want him in her family.

(And the thought occurs to Marva: why would he want her for a mother-in-law, then? Especially seeing that Isamina seemed to be so tied to her family. But then she remembers something she'd come to learn herself: the "L" in love most often represents lunacy, not logic.)

Meanwhile Gladstone is still talking about how jealous and insecure he was of Isamina's earlier boyfriends, even though she was constantly telling him, You don't have to be insecure. I don't want anybody but you.

Easy for her to say, eh? Easy for her to say. And he raises his empty glass and hollers, Hey bartender, another one of the same. And whatever the lady is drinking.

And when the drinks arrive he continues, telling Marva how he didn't know how they survived those first two years to get married. But they did. Although they had a couple of real close calls. Like the time she invited him up to her parents' house to a party, a bank-holiday fete and he showed up wearing jeans and shoes without socks. He thought he was sophisticatedly casual, you know? But not to Isamina. Oh no. Not her. The first thing she says even before he can put his foot in the door is, "*What* are you wearing?"

He looked down at his clothes in puzzlement and asked her, "What d'you mean?"

She pointed to his jeans (which were a new pair of jeans, by the way). "That," she said, and pointed down at his feet. "And why are you not wearing any socks! Christ!"

He shrugged. He didn't see the problem. He thought he looked pretty cool.

She let him in, turned her back and walked away and refused to speak to him.

Her brother Sammy came over and chatted for a while. Her father asked him if he didn't drink and when he said yes, Mr. Springer said, "Well, get yourself a drink, man. Help yourself. You en a stranger" and slapped him on his shoulder and rejoined his guests.

But to Isamina it was as if he didn't exist or was some insignificant servant hovering around.

He was so embarrassed that finally he slipped out and walked back down the hill and went home, expecting her to follow him saying how sorry she was, that she wasn't trying to change him. All that stuff. But he walked down that hill by himself and stayed at home the rest of the day.

Next day at work she ignored him. Didn't meet him at the library and have lunch with him in the cafeteria as usual.

That evening when he saw her leaving he hurried to catch her and began begging, telling her he was sorry; he should've been more sensitive to her feelings and tried to make a good impression and he wouldn't do it again, and on and on. But she's walking with her head in the air, not saying a word while he's carrying on like that, making a big fool of himself.

But things eased back to normal, though for weeks after she would bring up the subject, asking him why he had to show up at her parents' party in jeans and no socks when he knew she wouldn't like it, asking him, "Why'd you do that, Gladstone?" And he always had to be telling her how sorry he was and he would never do it again.

But they had good times too: going to the movies; picnics; quiet evenings sitting on her parents' veranda sometimes noting the moon's slow passage across the sky, sometimes on moonless nights when the stars would seem like reflections of the village lights below or vice versa; days at the beach embracing and kissing while the waves tried to knock them off balance, lying on the sand, once even pushing her bathing suit aside and penetrating her standing waist-deep in the water.

(This latter revelation makes Marva uncomfortable. By now the slur in his speech has thickened and he's talking to her like she is one of his male friends.)

When they got married . . . Oh. That's another thing. She wanted a big elaborate wedding. But he put his foot down. No big wedding, he said. Just a small church ceremony with close family and friends. He was expecting a big fight. But you know what? When he told her no big wedding, bracing for a big argument, all she said was, All right. Now, that almost knocked him over. Women, eh?

So they had a small wedding. One thing he always regret, though: his mother wasn't there. Didn't want anything to do with it. Told him herself. Didn't like Isamina—that Springer girl, she called her. You making a big mistake, she said. So she refused to come to the wedding.

First few years of the marriage were pretty good. Pretty darn good. Although they did have their quarrels from time to time—like any couple. And it wasn't long before the sex became boring, her just lying there, same thing every time. Sometimes he had to push her legs open.

(Now Marva is really embarrassed, an unwilling listener to intimate details she'd rather not hear, uncomfortable not least of all because she wouldn't want anybody knowing something like this about her.)

But Gladstone keeps right on, saying that he was young and in love then and naive enough to think that things would get better. Now he's older and wiser, he says.

(And as he says this he fixes on Marva a long stare while the sound of cocktail conversation and steel band music drifts in from the patio.)

Anyway, when the baby miscarried his marriage became like a go-cart careening downhill. So what d'you do when things get out of control? You step off, that's what. So that's when he and Debra began to step out, get it? Ha ha.

(And Marva's twiddling with her glass and looking at Gladstone and saying to herself, Hahaha. What's so funny? While a faraway look suffuses Gladstone's face as he explains to her that Debra was his first girlfriend that came back into his life. He'd never forgotten her. . . . Marva interrupts him with, "Why're you telling me all of this, Gladstone?" which causes him to ponder the question, but only for a moment before he shrugs and tells her, "I don't know . . . I don't know." And it occurs to her that these confessions of his probably are like pus being vented from a festering sore, because he simply continues.)

About a year ago when he began to quarrel with Isamina for scratching the car she burst out all of a sudden, "I'm tired of you treating me like SHIT!"

That is when she started this long talk about how all these years she was the submissive wife, burying her own personality, living her life according to what he wanted, losing her self-esteem—she'd even given up her job, a job she liked, because he said so. But no more. She wasn't taking his shit any more. She's a big woman and she'll be damned if she's going to continue letting him treat her like shit.

He felt as if he'd just slammed into a wall in the dark.

But she continued, saying how she did the best she could to be a good wife to him, but no matter how hard she tried it was never good enough and sometimes she thinks he wanted a servant, not a wife. Many days she felt so depressed she felt like killing herself. Because she's a good woman, and he's taking her for granted.

Then she dropped the bomb, saying, This isn't working out, Gladstone. I'm not happy. I need a divorce.

A divorce! The bottom dropped out of his guts. It was true that every so often he would do something that would cause her to blow up—but not on purpose (like forgetting her birthday or anniversary) and she would rehash old grievances from the earliest times of their relationship and, as man, he would be belligerent at first, not backing down, not admitting he was wrong but would always end up apologizing and they would make up until next time the same thing would happen and so on.

Sometimes in those earlier quarrels he would holler, Well, do what you want to do! and pretend to be hard and unflinching, and she would back off from the ultimate step, saying something like, Gladstone, you've got to change your ways. I can't take this any longer.

But this time was different. This time she mentioned divorce.

For the next few days they were strangers in a house seasoned with silence. At first he used the tactic that had always worked before: waiting for her to give in first. Then it occurred to him that something was different. He felt a coldness in her that wasn't there before. That is when he broke down and said he was sorry and even gave in to something he'd been fighting her over for a long time. Look, you've been wanting to open a boutique for a long time now, he said. I think it is a good idea. He would put in a word for her at the bank to help her secure a loan.

Biggest mistake he ever made.

As soon as she opened the boutique in town she became a different person, talking about wanting her space! What kind of nonsense was that?

So he asked her where she got that kind of talk from, TV? You're watching too much American TV shows, he told her. Those shows should be banned. The country didn't need that kind of crap, fa Pete's sake. Those blooming hacks and lackeys who ran the station had no initiative or imagination. That was the problem.

And what's she saying to this? "Go ahead! Ban them! Fire everybody at the station!" she's telling him, saying how he never takes her seriously. Never thinks she can think for herself or have ideas of her own.

He didn't fire the personnel, but the very next day he issued an order as minister of education banning all foreign TV shows which, as everyone knows, caused a big uproar among the population, with normally decent middle-class people—civil servants, teachers, even a lawyer once—hurling the vilest cuss words at him in public. He couldn't walk or drive anywhere in peace without people wishing the worst kinds of calamities on him and his family and all his heirs and successors. People can be spiteful, eh? And the uproar only ended after the P.M. rescinded the order and almost sacked him from the cabinet. You're singlehandedly eroding the popularity of the whole party, you know that?! A.R. said—A.R. was his nickname for Anthony Roachford.

(And while Marva is listening to him and recalling the controversy, it occurs to her that a substantial number of the world's major upheavals probably grew from similar domestic quarrels and fits of pique.)

But of course she doubts Gladstone appreciates this irony because he's rolling right on, talking about how not too long ago he had the flu and his wife never asked him how he felt, never brought him a hot cup of lime tea like before. Nothing.

His marriage feels like it's sliding down a steep, slippery slope, he says.

Yes. He had his faults. The way he was raised, the man was in charge of the household. So perhaps he was a little dogmatic in the beginning, wanting things done exactly his way. But over the years he'd begun to change. He really changed from the man Isamina married twenty-odd years ago. But, women? Huh. It looked like the more he tried to change the more change she wanted. She didn't appreciate his effort.

Over the past few weeks he tried everything, even crying like a baby, fa Pete's sake. Asking her to reconsider, to let them try one more time, promising to try even harder to make it work.

But what did she do? Answered him as if she was talking to an infant, telling him, I know you've changed, Gladstone. You're much better than you used to be. But the problem is, I don't think you know how to love. I feel so lonely sometimes. You're cold. We always have these arguments, then you change for a while. But then you go right back to the same cold, moody person you are inside. I'm tired, Gladstone. Just tired.

(Marva couldn't help but feel sympathy for her colleague sitting with his elbows on the bar, holding his drink and with tears in his voice as he released his pain.)

But then, just like a man, he spoiled it all by saying, Women. We men think we're tough and women are soft and emotional. But it's the other way around. Women can be the most hard-hearted creatures in the world, shedding a few crocodile tears and going on with their lives, leaving the poor man to drink, cry, and turn stupid.

(How typical, Marva thought. How typical for him to feel sorry for himself and not see what he put his poor wife through all these years.)

So when he turned to her and asked her what she thought he should do, she took a long time before finally asking him if he'd ever talked to his wife the way he was talking to her now. Do you ever tell her the way you feel? she asked him.

And she read his answer in the way he stared at her without replying.

Later that night when he knocked on her door she let him in. He wasn't the only one who needed the reassurance of someone else's company.

But lying in the dark afterward with him snoring beside her, she wondered whether it was worth it. When she woke up in the morning he was gone and the next time she saw him was at Sunday brunch where he pulled her aside and said, "That conversation we had? Keep it between you and me, eh?" and winked. They all drove home that afternoon, but not before the two of them agreed to meet for drinks after work the following day.

But the following day he called her at work, telling her to meet him instead at Windy Crest, a bayhouse in the country.

She held the receiver to her ear, wondering what the hell she was getting herself into. She'd been attracted to him almost from the day she began working at the ministry but he was married and wasn't known to step out on his wife. What happened in her room Saturday night was not something she'd been planning to repeat.

"Marva?" she heard him say on the phone.

And she snapped herself out of her thoughts and answered, "Yes, I'm here."

"Well?"

What did she have to lose? It was secret. They were adults. What the hell? So she said okay and that evening after a twenty-minute drive from the city she turned into a gateless front yard of sandy earth rutted with car wheel tracks and bordered with hibiscus and crotons. A signboard on two poles at the side of the steps leading up to the veranda of the wooden house raised on stilts read in carved lettering, Sandy Crest.

She walked around to the back of the house onto the beach across which stretched a jetty running from the deck of the house and into the water.

That evening, like refugees seeking familiar faces amid the devastation of war they clung to one another, with Gladstone's marriage like quicksand under his feet and her own relationship smashed by her discovery of a letter written to her boyfriend from some woman in Canada making final arrangements for her boyfriend's plane flight and their subsequent life of bliss in her apartment in Toronto ("I can't wait to see you," the letter said, "to feel your sweet kisses and caresses. To feel the touch of your hand on my buttocks . . ."), a letter that gave her the strength to face the deceitful, low-life so-and-so as soon as he walked in the door a couple weeks ago and tell him to leave her place. Pack his things and leave. She didn't ever want to see his deceitful, two-timing face again.

The last time she and Gladstone met at the bayhouse it was a full-moon night. And as they lay on the jetty still warm from the sun that had not long set it seemed to Marva that just as a natural forest fire, though destroying old trees, can be the catalyst for new and vital growth, so had the disintegration of Gladstone's marriage made him a more sensitive man and attentive lover who, as on that last night, feathered her face, ears, neck, breasts, stomach, navel, and inner thighs with caresses as soft as petals, left damp tracks on her skin as his tongue trailed over her body, and when he penetrated her she could not help but moan, writhe and yell his name while waves crashed and exploded in plumes of spray on the rocks nearby and wave-tops swished beneath them and died foaming deaths on the beach.

But even as they caressed and whispered in the aftermath, and as the winds grew chilly and she gathered the two pieces of her discarded bikini and wrapped herself in the blanket they'd been lying on and trotted to the car, she felt somehow that this was just an interlude and Gladstone would be seeking reconciliation with his wife.

The softness in his voice when he spoke Isamina's name and the faraway focus of his gaze told Marva that he didn't believe what she in her intuition knew: his marriage was over.

Now here she was driving slowly in first gear behind the man she'd always admired and finally enjoyed as a lover, while the boyfriend she always thought she'd live a happy life with was leaving the country to live with some slut in Toronto. Life is something, eh? Life is something.

THEOPHILUS BASCOMBE

Meanwhile, it's 4:30 and the slow-moving funeral procession has just reached the main road where Theophilus Bascombe, or T.B. as everyone nicknamed him since childhood (to his annoyance), is leaning on the parapet of his two-story house looking down at the jackass plodding along with its head bobbing and he's saying under his breath, "Look at this blooming ignorance, uh? Look what this country come to. A jackass carrying a kiss-me-ass coffin."

Behind him in the living room his wife is calling, "Theophilus! Gladstone funeral coming yet? Tell me when it reach!"

And Theophilus is muttering under his breath, "Gladstone Belle can kiss the crack of my big black ass." But aloud he says in his deep voice, "Yes. Come. It's here." And he adds a sarcastic, "Hurry up. You don't want to miss it." Which of course he knows she isn't in any danger of doing, as slowly as the procession is moving.

So his wife is rushing out onto the upstairs gallery and looking down at the funeral procession crawling along behind the coffin on the jackass cart and she's saying, "There's a thing, nuh. In the midst of life you're in death. Such a nice, nice man. And so young. You never know when the Lord going take you."

And Theophilus is thinking to himself, Nice man my ass. All that boy ever was, was an ambitious, selfish little cocksucker that would step on anybody to reach what he want.

He, Theophilus Bascombe, was working at government headquarters for twenty-three years—twenty-three long years!—and never reach no further than senior clerk when that knotty-hair little half-mad lunatic as black as coal come in one day as assistant to the prime minister. Assistant! He, Theophilus Bascombe, working at government headquarters for twenty-three years and just like that this half-mad boy that turn crazy because the university work was too much for him come in with seniority over men who'd been there for years, and just because he's screwing Springer daughter. Everybody know that.

Everybody know it is Mr. Springer that pull strings and get a make-up job for his future son-in-law. Out of thin air they create a job for this boy that went to university in America and had to come back empty-handed (and empty-headed) because his brain couldn't take the studying. Talking about he had a nervous breakdown. Ha! Nervous breakdown my ass. The boy couldn't make the grade.

There never was a prime minister's assistant before. Never was such a position. Not in colonial times. Not since independence. Never. Now all of a sudden this flipping boy that ought to be in the blasted madhouse come into this new post the prime minister create. And what he doing? Running around behind the prime minister wiping his ass, that's what.

All of a sudden Mr. Roachford can't talk to anybody direct anymore, nor nobody can't talk to him direct. Not even his ministers. What a stupidness, eh? It is like Mr. Roachford en prime minister no more but some kind of king you got to speak to through an intermediary—Gladstone Belle.

It is, Belle this, Belle that. "Belle call Pettiford at the ministry and tell him I want to see him after lunch." And when the minister of agriculture calls back it is Gladstone Belle he talking to. And from what Theophilus can gather from the telephone conversation, minding his own business of course, is that Mr. Pettiford wants to know if one-thirty is all right. And Gladstone Belle going into Mr. Roachford's office and coming back out and saying on the phone, "Yes. One-thirty is fine." Yes. Imagine that. Not even "Yes, Mr. Minister" or "Yes, Mr. Pettiford." Just yes. Couple weeks and the position gone to the boy head.

And everybody taking it. But not he, Theophilus Bascombe. No sir. So it wasn't a month before he and this young, forced-ripe nincompoop tangled.

He accustomed to taking his monthly reports directly in to the prime minister, or leaving them with Cynthia his secretary if the P.M. is busy. But the same month Belle started working he's telling Theophilus, "Here. I'll take them."

And Theophilus is saying, "No. These are for the prime minister."

Hear Belle: "I know. I'll take them."

So Theophilus decide to stand his ground. "No," he said. "I always hand them directly to the P.M. or leave them with Cynthia here."

All this time Cynthia's filing her nails with an expression on her face that shows she's enjoying this power struggle that's brewing right there in front of her.

But Belle surprised him, the little prick.

"Okay," Belle said. "Have it your way." In his prissy little girlish voice.

And he Theophilus marched right in to Mr. Roachford's office with the report in his hand.

But the P.M. took one look at the report and asked him, "Belle out there?"

"Yes, suh."

"Well, leave it with him." Mr. Roachford waved his arm in a dismissive way. "And in future leave all reports with Belle," he said.

So he had to crawl back outside with his tail between his legs like a mangy dog and hand the report to this Belle, this flipping boy that was running around in short pants probably with his ass at the door when he, Theophilus Bascombe, was working right here at government headquarters. Twenty-three years! Twenty-three frigging years and look what thanks you get.

Well, from that day on he en had nothing to say to Belle other than what was necessary to do his job.

He see Belle run for a seat and win it. He see him head all kinds of ministries over the years and be envoy to this and ambassador of that. And people acting like he is the second coming. But he, Theophilus Bascombe, know better.

So Gladstone Belle? Gladstone Belle can kiss the crack of his big, black behind. And he hope he get a grave next to a big-dicky duppy faggot who will lambaste his ass till eternity come to an end. That is what he deserve.

Because when he heard the talk about Gladstone Belle being involved with the disappearances and murders, and about him raping that young girl in the village, he, Theophilus, wasn't surprised.

The day after two little boys found Cynthia Gittens dead in the cart road on Somerset Plantation years ago, the talk whizzy-whizzying around the office was that before she left work that evening she and the P.M. were having a heated discussion. The last words somebody heard her saying coming from Mr. Roachford's office were, "I'm disappointed in you, sir." Cynthia accustomed to catching the bus to go home but that day the P.M.'s chauffeur pick her up in front the building. The last anybody see of her alive is her getting into the prime minister's white limousine.

Theophilus never tell this to a soul except his wife, but he was putting on his hat and looking out his office window up on the third floor and look down and see Gladstone Belle sitting in the front next to the driver when Cynthia got in the car. He knows it was Gladstone Belle because when he heard the talk and remembered the jet black arm and elbow hanging out the car window and part of a face, he put two and two together. It had to be Gladstone Belle. Who else it could be? Belle was the P.M.'s right-hand man. He and the chauffeur kill that girl as sure as his name is Theophilus Uranus Bascombe.

Of course his stupid wife is asking him, "How you know it was Gladstone Belle? You say you only see his arm and part of his face. It could've been any dark-skinned man . . . or woman even. I don't think you should accuse the poor boy like that. Don't let anybody hear you, nuh, because you know how it is with you. You does put two and two together and get six, then turn it upside down and get nine. That is how rumors does start."

Well, he didn't say anything but the rumors started anyway. People aren't stupid—like his stupid wife.

And as for the thing about the girl up in the Village, Gladstone Belle with those big, red eyes of his always looked wicked to him and unstable. He wouldn't have trusted him near his daughter. So *that* story didn't come to him as any surprise.

So Theophilus Bascombe is looking down from his second-story veranda watching as a wreath slides from on top of the coffin and lands at the side of the road and a hunchbacked man hobbling along beside the donkey cart stops and bends to pick up the wreath. Nobody is helping the hunchback as he is straining to straighten himself up with the wreath in his hand, and by the time he manages to continue walking the donkey cart and coffin are several paces ahead.

Theophilus Bascombe hears his wife say beside him with a tear in her voice, "Look at that, nuh T.B.? Even the cripples love him. Remind me of Jesus."

And this causing Theophilus Bascombe's head to feel as though it's going to explode with fury. Plus he *hates* it when she calls him T.B. And she knows it. So he can't help himself. He shouts out, "Jesus! Woman, you need a dose of salts to clear that shit out of your head, you know that? And how many times I have to tell you don't call me T.B.?"

He lets go one long steups, sucking his teeth loud and long.

THE HUNCHBACK

When the hunchback heard the news that Gladstone Belle had just killed himself he leaned against the parliament building gate with badfeels—nauseated, dizzy, emptiness in the pit of his stomach—as though he had missed breakfast that morning, his eyes fastened on the backs of the two women who'd just passed him, one of them saying, "You hear they just find Gladstone Belle hanging in his house this morning?" and the other one asking, "You mean Gladstone Belle the minister?" and the first woman answering, "The same one." And the hunchback wanting to run after them to ask the first woman if what she was saying was true. But he couldn't run, not only because of his infirmity but because he was so stunned that all he could do was stand there amidst the noise of traffic and passing people, feeling such a mixture of disbelief and loss that he found himself hobbling away from in front of the gate of the parliament building toward the bus stand to catch a bus for home. And in the bus stand all people talking about is how Gladstone Belle kill himself. Gladstone Belle hang himself in his house.

When he got home he made himself a tot of hot cocoa and sat in his back door in a daze. Gladstone Belle was one of the few people who ever treated him like a normal human being.

The first time he saw Mr. Belle up close was the first day of parliament after Mr. Belle won his seat for the first time. He's standing by the parliament gate where he usually does beg his alms every day, but this time a crowd of people is standing with him watching the bigwigs walking into the parliament building yard, the parliamentarians in their ceremonial black robes, other dignitaries in suits, the women in full-length dresses and hats.

Tell the truth, Gladstone Belle looked a little out of place to the hunchback: short, pitch-black, stocky, like a country buck among this company of doctors, lawyers, businessmen, and one business-woman—a hotel owner.

Every day when parliament was meeting, the hunchback would speak to all the politicians as they passed him standing by the gate. None of them ever stopped to speak much less to put anything in his tin.

But one day Gladstone Belle stopped when the hunchback said, "Morning, sir."

Gladstone Belle answered, "Morning," then asked him, "How long you been doing this?"

"What?" the hunchback asked him.

"This. Standing out here."

"Oh. Couple years now," the hunchback said. And found himself talking about how he'd had a job at a tailor shop making pants but the owner of the shop had to let him go after the customers started to complain he was too slow. Mr. Rice didn't want to let him go because he knew what the situation was: the hunchback was a good tailor but sometimes his arms would ache so bad he had to leave work early or sometimes couldn't come in at all; sometimes sitting in one place all day would make his whole body one big ache. Plus, people see a hunchback and it is like they think his deformity is a contagion. They en coming too close to him; most times they not talking to him but to Mr. Rice. And you could see distaste and fascination in their expressions, the way their eyes not staying on him for long but being drawn back anyway.

So Mr. Rice say, "I going have to let you go. Things getting a little slow." Then his voice raising with false enthusiasm, "But when things begin to pick up I'll call you back."

The hunchback understood. Business is business. So ever since then he's been out here by the parliament building gate every day with his cup begging, which was hard at first. Still is. It's hard to beg people. Even when they stop and drop something in his cup he know it's not out of concern for him as a human being but out of pity, or what some people call charity. And pity, charity, whatever you want to call it, is like castor oil—hard to swallow. Although he notice some people take to it like it is nourishment.

And Mr. Belle chuckling and saying, "That is a good one. I must remember that."

And the hunchback telling him, "Glad you like it. You can use it if you want. Call it my contribution to the country."

This sweeten Mr. Belle too. He chuckling some more.

And the hunchback going on to say that most times when he see some big-shot man reach into his pocket or some high-class woman reach into her purse and drop money into his tin he realize they're probably doing their good deed for that day, or that week, maybe even that year. With people like that he takes a different attitude, telling himself to enjoy the privilege of watching something rare—money going from the rich to the poor.

Mr. Belle throwing back his head and laughing, hahaha, at this one too. And the hunchback feeling like a real comedian, an unusual feeling—nobody don't laugh at what he say; nobody don't talk to him. And it's occurring to him how much he's yapping on about things he never discussed with a soul except his mother who is dead and gone years now, things like how people forget his name—Simeon Joseph—and only call him by the nickname that attached to him as permanent as his hump ever since childhood: Camel.

One day Mr. Belle greeted him as usual with, "How you doing, Simeon?"

"Like a one-legged man in a ass-kicking contest," he answered back.

It was an election year, and a few nights later at a political meeting Mr. Belle used the same phrase to describe the opposition party. So next thing you know the whole country making big joke of the opposition People's Democratic Party (or People's Doctors' Party, as everybody called them), saying that the party is like a one-legged man in a ass-kicking contest—they can't win. Even the newspaper get on the bandwagon. Well, to make a long story short, the PLP won that elections by the biggest landslide in history and everybody saying that is Mr. Belle aphorism (as the newspaper call it) that do the trick. The hunchback had to shake his head when he read this, because if anybody had come up to him and tell him he had a aphorism he woulda get nervous and gone straight to the hospital.

Anyway, whatever it is they choose to call it, he didn't mind Mr. Belle getting the credit for it because the day the government was being sworn in Mr. Belle come up to him and give him a brand new wristwatch (a user's fee, Mr. Belle called it). And as the years pass by, every once in a while, even after Mr. Belle rise to head one ministry after another—health and recreation, tourism, education—even as a big minister he would stop and ask the hunchback, "Feel like firing one?" and they would cross the street (the hunchback hopping-and-dropping next to Mr. Belle) heading for Ben's Bar at the corner across from the parliament building. And they would sit at a table on the veranda upstairs, looking down at the people passing by and old-talking, where sometimes Mr. Belle would hint at some of the hard times he had in America, never giving specifics though, just saying things like, "You never realize how easy it is to lose your dignity, your very humanity, till bad fortune hits you," then staring off into space. Of course the hunchback wanted to prod him to find out more but he would have been out of place.

And when they were leaving the shop Mr. Belle would slip a bill or two in his hand.

So what you think people say about seeing them together? All kinds of stories flying from one mouth to the other. One story is that he does get women for Mr. Belle. Imagine that? He can't even get a woman for himself. Another one is that he is Mr. Belle outside brother on his father side. But you can't mind people. People will talk, so let them talk.

Now Mr. Belle making his final journey and he, the hunchback, holding his wreath as if Mr. Belle slipped it on the ground and asked him personally to hold it for him.

Until a policeman comes up to him and barks at him, "WHAT YOU DOING WITH THAT? HERE! GIVE IT TO ME!" and snatches the wreath and lays it on the coffin where it promptly slides back off.

And each time the policeman puts the wreath back on the coffin it slides off again until finally he shoves it back into the hunchback's hands saying, "Here! You hold it!" like it was his idea in the first place, and marches back up to the head of the procession leaving the hunchback hobbling along, keeping pace with the plodding donkey cart.

EDDIE WHITE MICE

At four o'clock that day, Eddie White Mice, the albino, knocked off at the jewelry store where he works and pedaled his bicycle straight for the cathedral to get a last look at Gladstone Belle, or at least his funeral procession.

When he reached the church around half past four, he found a big crowd already outside the cathedral gates and lining both sides of the street as far as he could see, waiting for the funeral procession. And more people still coming.

Eddie come to pay his respects partly because he owe his job to Gladstone Belle and as he's looking around at the droves of people around him he gets the feeling that though some of these people just here out of curiosity as usual (funerals are an entertaining spectacle for some people), most of them come to pay their respects to a man that was a rarity in politics—a man of decency and principle.

Eddie knew Gladstone from when they were back in the Village growing up together, although Eddie is a couple years older than Gladstone so they weren't friends. In fact as far as Eddie can remember, Gladstone didn't have no friends in the Village. As long as Eddie knew him Gladstone (or Gabby as they called him) would always keep to himself. You would see him walking to and from school in the week and the library on Saturdays, minding his business.

One of the clearest memories that Eddie recall is how Gladstone used to make kites and sell them around Easter time. Good, pretty kites too. Said he learned himself. Nobody didn't teach him. Fellas figured he was telling lies, but who don't tell a few lies every now and then? So that wasn't no big thing. What surprised them, though, was how spiteful and competitive he was. It was like Gabby always believed he had to be the best and would do anything to stay on top. His kite had to be the highest one in the sky. And to make sure of that he would string razor blades on his kite tail.

First time it happened, everybody flying their kite, spinning them in whirlies, diving them, enjoying themselves. And Gladstone kite, a singing angel, flying high by itself, droning like a giant bumblebee.

All of a sudden a kite that was just up there doing a jig near Gabby's singing angel, for no apparent reason begin flapping and floating in the wind like a merry bird that just suffered a fatal heart.

And the owner of the kite bawling, "Hey! What happen?" but the fellas only shrugging their shoulders while they watching the kite sailing away, figuring it serve him right for buying cheap cord that can't take the force of the wind.

But soon after that the same thing happen again to somebody else. Another kite that was flying just below Gladstone's singing angel floating listless and dead.

Suspicions rising now.

"You have razor on your tail!" the owner of the second dead kite yelling.

But Gladstone looking at him with his eyes wide open with innocence and saying no, not he.

But fellas spacing away leaving Gabby standing alone.

At the end of the day fellas notice that he waiting back like he want to make sure he is the last one to haul in his kite. Fellas really suspicious now.

Next day is like World War II with razor blades slashing and slicing and kites dying like birds downwind of the chemical factory, flapping and floating away lifeless in the wind, Gabby's singing angel among them.

Gabby never fly kite on the pasture in the Village again. Next Easter he up on the hill near the Springer house where none of the other boys liked to go because the rumor was that Springer had a gun and would shoot anybody who came near his premises.

But when Mr. Springer didn't do anything to Gabby, that made him even less popular. Fellas dropping remarks whenever he passed by.

One particular fella, Turkey, always would shout out something like, "Hey! High school boy!" as if that was a big insult, the same Turkey that end up diving for coins the tourists pelt overboard. One day a shopkeeper step out in his yard to get a barrel of salt meat he had stored out there and see Turkey head pushing through a hole in his paling. Turkey trying to thief the man salt meat. The shopkeeper pick up a piece of two-by-four and land it against Turkey head. Ever since then all Turkey good for is to go around begging people for little odds and ends of work. He's all right as long as he make his regular visits to the madhouse to get his medicine.

The funny thing is, if Gladstone had mixed up with them back then they would've lost respect for him, a high school boy mixing with them. You can't please people. And that is what Eddie admired about Gladstone: he kept to himself and didn't care what people said.

The first time Eddie saw Gladstone after he left the country to go to live with his father in America was when he, Eddie, was in New York. He's watching the people crossing the street at the corner of Broadway and Thirty-Fourth Street in New York, marveling how they reminded him of a line of ants when all of a sudden a familiar-looking figure catch his eye and he find himself staring long and hard at a man that looked like Gabby standing at the corner wearing an old parka, pants that was too big for him and old army boots. But it couldn't be Gabby. For one thing, this man had a beard.

But finally his brain had to admit what his eyes were telling it, that it was Gabby standing there looking like one of the homeless people that Eddie was so surprised to see in a rich city like New York. He turned and began walking back in the direction from where he was coming, not wanting to embarrass Gabby by letting him know he'd seen him.

And he never told a soul. For one thing, nobody would believe him. He never even mentioned it to his cousin who had enticed him to come up to New York only for Eddie to discover that the apartment his cousin was bragging about when he came home for vacation was so tiny the bedroom could barely hold a single bed so Eddie had to sleep on the sofa. Not only that. He enticed Eddie to come and join him, saying he had a taxi company and was looking for somebody to help him run it, a business partner. "I prefer to keep the business in the family," he said.

But Eddie got there only to find out that the big taxi company was two old green taxi cabs his cousin bought from a man that wasn't making no money with his cabs but give Eddie cousin the story that he was retiring to Florida. The taxis always breaking down and his cousin always under them saying he fixing them. And the man still living in the same place but when Eddie cousin went over by his house to complain the man saying a deal is a deal, business is business, and the taxis is Eddie cousin problem now, ha ha ha.

So for three whole months Eddie's driving taxi, even though he didn't know the roads ("Use the map I give you, man," his cousin saying). And every week not a cent. ("I en make no money this week. Next week. You don't know how it is with the bills, man," his cousin saying. "In this country they does kill you with bills.")

So is a good thing Eddie'd had the presence of mind to buy a return ticket to safeguard himself.

So the day Eddie saw Gladstone was a few days before he was due to go back home and he was strolling around sightseeing for the first time because his cheap-ass cousin's idea of showing him around New York was to say to him on the few times they were on the subway, "This is Grand Central Station," or "This is Thirty-Fourth Street where the Empire State Building is," like Eddie, number one, couldn't read the signs for himself and two, had x-ray eyes and could see the Empire State Building from where they were sitting in the train down below the ground.

After a while the memory of Gladstone in ragged clothes in New York was so surreal that Eddie began to doubt that it was Gladstone he really saw. Could have been somebody that looked just like Gladstone. Once or twice he had a dream where he, Eddie, was the one in ragged clothes roaming and homeless in New York. And he would wake up sweating and panicked, then glad that he was able to come back home.

Not long after Eddie got back Gladstone came back too. But whereas Eddie knocking about the place sucking salt and can't find no work, in two twos Gabby get a job at the technical college, mad as he was.

Next thing Eddie heard, Gabby and the Springer girl getting married, then Gabby running for a seat in parliament and winning it. And it occur to him that what he observe about America while he was there is also true for this country: it take a lunatic to run a lunatic asylum.

One Saturday not long after Gladstone won his seat in parliament Eddie is sitting on the bridge by the culvert smoking a cigarette when he sees Gladstone approaching him.

Gladstone walks up to him and says, "What's happening, Eddie?"

Eddie flicked his cigarette butt behind him into the muddy bed of the stream that was empty at that time of the year because of dry season.

"I cool, man," Eddie says.

And right away Gabby starts a conversation talking about how excited he is about being in parliament, all the ideas he has, and on and on he going, although Eddie never opened his mouth to say a single word to encourage him.

Just when Eddie is about to slide down off the culvert and excuse himself and ease away from Gabby who isn't only a lunatic but now a prattling politician as well, Gladstone stops talking and looks Eddie straight in the eye and says, "Thanks."

This stops Eddie short. "For what?" he says.

"You know. Back in New York," Gladstone says.

Eddie's getting ready to ask Gladstone what he talking about but the seriousness in Gabby's eyes confirm what he'd come to doubt as time passed by: that it really was Gabby that he saw that day looking raggedy and homeless.

"Thanks, man," Gladstone says again.

What could Eddie do? He shrugged his shoulders, because what he did wasn't no big thing. He wasn't the kind of man to get satisfaction out of another man's misery.

A few days later Gladstone stopped his car next to Eddie liming on the bridge and leaned across in his seat and said, "Come around by my office tomorrow."

Next day when Eddie showed up at Gladstone's office at the government building Gladstone came out to meet him when the secretary told him Eddie was out there. And in his office he gave Eddie a letter. "Take this to DeSouza," he said.

Next day Eddie had a job at DeSouza's Jewelry where he's been working ever since.

No matter what people may say about Gabby, and whatever faults he might have, to Eddie, Gladstone is a man, an all-right fella. And he, Edward John, come to pay his last respects. And who don't have faults?

Right then the parliament building clock begins gonging for five o'clock and Eddie hears a voice in the crowd holler out, "He coming! The funeral coming!"

And every pair of eyes look up the road to see the police escort of two motorcycle policemen cresting the little hill and coming toward the cathedral.

Everybody's expecting the hearse to appear next, but what they see cause almost every mouth to drop open: Peg-leg Pollard sitting cater-corner on his donkey cart, dressed in a top hat and swizzle-tail coat and black pants with one leg rolled up as usual but this time the bare wooden stump poked off at an angle is wrapped in black cloth; the donkey plodding slowly toward the crowd with its head bowed and bobbing, pulling the cart also draped in black, with a coffin laid on top of it.

For a moment nobody utters a word. Then everybody begins talking at the same time, wanting to know if they seeing right, if that is Gladstone Belle coffin on top of Peg-leg Pollard donkey cart, and oh Lord the world must be coming to an end; I never see nothing so in all me born days.

The excitement is so much for one hawker who left her tray and run all the way from the market just to see Mr. Belle for the last time that she collapse and somebody passing a vial of smelling salts under her nose and she shaking her head and heaving herself up and standing on shaky legs with her eyes open wide and the woman next to her can barely hear her murmuring over and over again, "Look at my crosses. Look at my crosses" while close to them a man that not too long come back from picking fruit in Away saying in a freshwater Yankee accent, "D'yuh b'lieve this? Man. D'yuh b'lieve this?"

But sudden so the mood of the crowd swing like hurricane winds after the passing of the eye. One minute everybody is dumbstruck, next minute laughter is like a chain of fireworks crackling through the crowd, with women cackling and men going "Hunh hunh hunh" after their brains absorb the spectacle their eyes see a moment ago.

But not everybody is laughing.

RALPH CADOGAN

Ralph Cadogan who used to work with Gladstone Belle back when he was minister of labor is standing in the crowd and saying to himself, "What a tragedy. What a blasted tragedy." And he's wondering whose idea it was to place the former deputy prime minister in a position to be a subject of such ridicule, a man who commanded respect with his sternness and discipline.

Ralph remembers one morning when the clerks in the office were skylarking, talking, reading their newspapers while members of the public were at the counter waiting for service.

"Look at that!" a woman waiting at the counter said.

Ralph looked up from behind his newspaper, startled.

Usually the public was sullen and silent, waiting until the clerks felt like it was time to start working.

But this woman was different. "Half past eight!" she's saying. "Half past eight and they reading newspaper and skylarking. And look at she." And she's pointing at Marcia Cadogan ambling in to work. "Traipsing in like she going to a excursion."

And Marcia is looking around and behind her to see who the woman is talking about.

"They does treat we like we don't pay taxes," a man muttered.

Who told him to say that? His support only seemed to boost the woman's courage. She raised her voice. "Where the minister?" she bawled out. "Where he is?"

Usually Gladstone Belle came in at around nine o'clock and, according to his secretary, worked sometimes till way past six. But this morning he was in his office, unknown to everyone.

He must have heard the commotion and came out of his office in his shirt-and-tie and suspenders, with his sleeves rolled halfway up his forearms.

"What's the problem here?" he asked.

The woman looked him up and down. "Who you?"

"I'm the minister," Belle told her. "What can I do for you?"

"What you can do for me," the woman said, "is get these lazy, good-for-nothing parasites here to get up off their big, fat backsides and serve the public. Is we taxes that paying all-you, you know."

Gladstone Belle politely told the woman to excuse him, then beckoned with his finger for the staff to follow him to the staff room.

That day his office became the most efficient government office in the whole country when all of the clerks realized that civil servant jobs weren't lifetime sinecures like they'd all thought.

The following week when parliament met, Gladstone Belle stood up and unleashed a speech lambasting the lazy, insolent, downright uncouth "army of occupation" that lives off the sweat and labor of the hardworking people they treat with such contempt, and finished the speech by introducing legislation giving ministers and other heads of department the right to dismiss unproductive civil servants on the spot, but also allowing the right of appeal to the high court to prevent, he said, "this legislation being used as a political weapon by this or future governments." Even senior civil servants could be "retired."

When Ralph and the others in the office heard this they realized that Belle had bluffed them the week before. But it was too late. He couldn't fire them then but now he could.

And in rumshops, barbershops, in the market, on the streets, in homes, the whole country let loose a collective yell of approval when the speech was broadcast, so much so that the passengers on a tourist ship anchored in the bay grumbled about not being informed of what they believed to be a massively attended sporting event or celebration taking place on shore.

One day in parliament he lambasted one of the members of his own party, calling the honorable member from St. Augustine a flea, a tick, a pimple on the ass of humanity, a chiseler, a lazy nincompoop who was a leech on the backs of the working man.

Apparently one of the man's constituents met Gladstone Belle one day and complained that the people in St. Augustine had been asking for the longest time for the government to run water to the district and every time the honorable member of parliament was running for election he would promise but upward to now they still have to bring water from the river miles away. Gladstone Belle investigated and found that the constituent was telling the truth. That is when he lit into the honorable member's backside in front of the whole country.

Gladstone Belle made a lot of enemies. But in Ralph's opinion Gladstone Belle was the only government minister he'd ever known in all his years as a civil servant who was honorable not only in title but in character, a real man who should have been buried in a state funeral, not hauled through the streets on a donkey cart with people pointing and laughing.

And as if to underscore Ralph's assessment, the donkey, which by now has reached the cathedral gates, begins braying, peeing again and easing its bowels out of pure nervousness at the sight of the large crowd of curious onlookers. So a whole new wave of laughter rolls from the crowd, with one woman asking Peg-leg Pollard why he didn't take his donkey to the toilet before he left home so the donkey wouldn't make him shame in public.

The bearers unload the coffin from the donkey cart and carry it slowly through the cathedral gates toward the church while the crowd standing on both sides of the pathway look on mostly in silence as the wind rustles the leaves of the trees and wood doves coo in branches overhanging the gravestones of those long dead.

MILLIE

The setting sun seems to be resting on the roof of the parliament building before sliding out of sight for the night, the evening breeze a soothing balm, and inside the cathedral angelic choirboy voices surf waves of organ music that roll over the congregation's funereal singing.

The hymn ends, the congregation sits in a silence so total that even the occasional discreet cough and a shifting restless backside are noisy intrusions on the sing-song ecclesiastical drawl of the foreign bishop's eulogy.

All of a sudden, a woman's loud, wailing "Waaaaaaaaauuuuuuu-uhhhh!" floats through the cathedral's open stained glass windows out to the quiet of the churchyard.

And among the crowd standing in the churchyard, eyes meet and there is silence, the silence before questions, comments, and speculation erupt and collide in the evening air, people wanting to know who that? Who bawling out in the people cathedral like they in some little Holy Ghost Baptist church? Must be somebody that never been inside a place like that before. Somebody that en know how to behave in the cathedral where whitepeople and big-shot blackpeople does worship. En accustom to stained glass windows, high ceilings, statues, and paintings of whitepeople in robes. Never see a foreign bishop. Got to be somebody like that.

And inside the church every head turns to see a round-faced woman wearing a broad-rimmed black hat with a veil sprawled back in the pew with her eyes closed and her bosom heaving while the woman next to her lifts the veil and fans her face with a folding fan.

And all around the church people whisper, wanting to know who that.

And among some the word spreads that it's Millie. Millie who used to sell sweets and nuts at the side of the main road. Millie who, as she always says, too old now to be lugging a tray all the way down to the main road just to make a few half-dead cents so she does bake a few coconut breads and sell from her front window at home. Millie who, as the bishop began his eulogy, cast her thoughts back to when Gladstone Belle used to be a little boy in short pants walking every day to Wilberforce Secondary School.

Every day she would give him a small paper bag of roast nuts or maybe a sugarcake to take with him to school and he would say, "Thanks, Miss Millie." A bright little boy. A mannerly little boy that never forgot to speak to her every time he passed her sitting behind her tray. It was always, "Good morning, Miss Millie" or "Good evening, Miss Millie." A nice boy. Miss Esther raised him right.

Every Sunday morning Miss Esther would pass by, taking him to the pentecostal church with her, and Millie would always ask Miss Esther to pray for her and Miss Esther would answer back, Yes, Millie. But you should come to church one of these days too, you know. And Millie would always tell her, Yes. One of these days. Not meaning it because Sundays were her best days for selling sweets—God would understand that. But she never tell Miss Esther this because she come to realize that the god she believe in got more compassion and understanding (and more sense of humor) than Christians, who don't know how to take things easy sometimes. Miss Esther was a good woman, though.

But Sonny-Boy? Well, that is a different story. Sonny-Boy was always a worthless, good-for-nothing man who liked his grog and his women. One night in a weak moment she let him sweet talk her into inviting him into her house. That night when Sonny-Boy got inside her, years and years of no man in her bed since her Mr. Branker passed away caused her to nearly break down the old bed—she couldn't help herself. And when she and Sonny-Boy lying next to one another catching their breath and cooling down, she feeling so shame because her hollering and carrying on musta reach her next-door neighbors' ears.

But good thing for her, as she realized later, the sounds of her voice screaming and her bed thumping inside her house was no competition for the wind, claps of thunder, and sheets of rain outside. God does work in mysterious ways, eh?

But after that night she would fight her feelings every time Sonny-Boy beg her, only giving in once in a while when her human will wasn't strong enough to fight the urges that would build up inside her. And when she would be under Sonny-Boy bawling "Oh God!" and Sonny-Boy, man that he is, would think it was because of him, only she would know that was only part of it, the other part would be her reminding God to have the understanding to forgive her human weakness. And he always did, never bringing pain nor pestilence upon her (God is a good god), keeping her healthy so she could make a living and be content. That good-for-nothing Sonny-Boy, sitting two seats in front her now next to Miss Esther. Still looking good in his old age.

But Gladstone, lying there in the coffin now, grew up to be a fine boy even after Sonny-Boy left to go overseas and left him and his mother in that old house catching hell by themselves.

When Gladstone came back from Away and enter politics she was so proud of him she was first in line to vote down at the elementary school election morning.

And she never regret it. Because Gladstone Belle was like a diamond in a bucket of human waste. A gentleman in the midst of a bunch of thieves and liars who promise the world right up to election day then sit down in parliament and get fat off of poor people.

Just a couple months ago, after long months of fighting herself over it, she asked him if he could do anything to have the government help her with her house. Her old house want repairing bad and she en able to fix it and she fraid one day it will fall down on her head. It took her a long time to get up the courage to ask him that.

Soon after she approached him with her problem a government lorry draw up in front her house with lumber and workmen. That must have been one of the last things Gladstone Belle do before he resigned from government.

Now he's gone, lying at the front of the church in a coffin while the bishop up there in the pulpit calling him a true son of the soil.

It was then that she heard a wail coming from inside her like vomit she couldn't hold back.

MARIE ANTOINETTE

When heads turned to see who was cow bawling like that in the people cathedral, Marie Antoinette LaSalle from Martinique, who is generally believed to have the ability to communicate with spirits (her real name, for those who really know her, is Martha Skeete: Maisy Skeete's daughter from Shrewsbury Village), swears she saw the following scene from where she was sitting at the back of the church.

Two old women, one short, stout, and dark with her head wrapped with a white cloth, the other medium height and copper-skinned with her gray hair styled in a bun, glided up the aisle about six inches off the ground and stopped by Gladstone's coffin.

Old Mr. Holder, a war veteran who's been carrying a grievance about not being buried in the cathedral's graveyard with full military honors, popped up out of the floor and joined the two women hovering by the coffin.

"What you doing here?" the dark woman asked him.

"Same as you," Mr. Holder said.

"What you mean same as me?" the dark woman answered back. "He en you family."

"All of we is family," Mr. Holder said. "Especially when we dead." And with that he turns with a mischievous grin on his face and looks right at Millie.

And it was at that very instant that Millie bawled out and almost frightened the piss out of those sitting near her, causing them to jump off their seats like jacks-in-the-box, at which point Mr. Holder leapt high in the air, jackknifed, took a header and dove back down through the cathedral floor, with the two women hovering by the coffin shaking their heads and the copper-skinned one steupsing her teeth and saying, "Always showing off. I hope he dive straight down to hell."

At which point Mr. Holder's head bobbed above the floor and he said, "I heard that."

And the two women chorused together, "So what?"

Which caused Mr. Holder to look from one woman to the other with a disgusted expression and say, "Women" then sink out of sight beneath the floor.

Meanwhile Gladstone Belle is sitting upright in his coffin and blinking his eyes as if he just woke up from sleeping and looking around and wanting to know, What happen, uh? What happen? And his two grandmothers are telling him that it is only Mr. Holder showing off as usual. And his mother's mother, the short dark one, is telling him to lie back down and rest himself; he don't want to give anybody in the church bad vibes. And the other grandmother is asking her where she learned an expression like that—bad vibes—then turning to Gladstone and admonishing him for dying in the house on the spot of land she left for him, saying, "I left that property for you to live on, not to dead on."

And Gladstone is looking at her and saying, "How could I help it?"

And the shorter grandmother is telling the taller one how she's irrational because she know Gladstone didn't have no choice in the matter. To besides, this en the time for argument. Hold your quarreling for later, she saying. We have a lot of time for that. This is a solemn occasion. We shouldn't be spoiling it with useless bickering.

And the tall one retorting, "Bickering? Who bickering?"

And Gladstone looking from one to the other as the discussion between his grandmothers is growing heated with the two of them chest-to-chest and poking their hands in one another's face while the bishop is looking down at the deceased lying in the coffin with his eyes closed and assuring the congregation that Gladstone Belle is resting in the arms of God.

Which is causing Marie Antoinette LaSalle to snicker behind her hand while the woman sitting next to her is muttering under her breath, "Damn godless heathen."

So goes the account of Marie Antoinette LaSalle to some, Martha Skeete to others.

AT THE GRAVESITE

The funeral service continued without further mortal interruption. But just as the bishop descended from the pulpit to lead the coffin down the aisle, a thunderclap boomed directly overhead, lightning flashed, and torrential rain began to slash in through the open windows and batter the tree leaves in the graveyard, showering the church steps, drenching the onlookers in the churchyard and scattering them in all directions hustling for whatever shelter they could find, soaking the gravestones and the earth and creating a waterfall that whooshed from the drainpipe of the church.

The bishop stopped in the doorway with his Bible clasped to his chest with the wind whipping his cassock around his ankles.

The sexton rushed up to him with an umbrella; the mourners in the church watched the bishop lean toward the sexton and say something they couldn't hear above the drumming of the raindrops and the whistling wind, something that caused the sexton to hurry back into an alcove and return with a raincoat which he helped the bishop put on.

An old man leaning on his cane at the end of a pew near the front of the church was heard to suck his teeth and mutter, "Why he wearing raincoat. God can't protect he? What about we?" which struck those nearby who heard him as a particularly blasphemous thing to say and caused his granddaughter to tug his arm and hiss, "Grandaddy!"

Meanwhile the bishop is glancing up at the sky, which is a blanket of dark gray, and beckoning for the bearers to follow him as he steps out into the deluge.

But the bearers all hesitate, looking at one another as if asking, What you think? Think we should follow him out in this rain? Some shrug. One man even steps away from the coffin and takes a seat at the end of the pew nearest the door and gazes out at the downfall with doleful eyes.

But Sonny-Boy grips a handle of his son's coffin and says, "Come." The sitting man gets up and they all lift the coffin off its carriage and step out into the torrent while the choirboys in their white robes, who had never stopped singing, march into the lashing rain like onward Christian soldiers and their high-pitched singing voices drift back to the congregation in the church sounding like a chorus of drowning cats in a storm at sea.

People swear they never saw rain like that before except in a hurricane. Slashing sheets of water that stung their skins and soaked their clothes to their bodies, whipping winds that had women clinging to their hats with one hand and trying to hold down their dresses with the other while the men hunched and turned up their jacket collars and everyone slogged behind the undertaker, the bishop, the choirboys, the coffin and its bearers.

When they reached the grave the mound surrounding it had turned to sludge that sucked the feet of the bearers struggling to place the coffin on the planks laid across the hole.

Then the rain stopped. As suddenly as it had started.

And as the sky became clear blue again with birds chirping and cooing in trees, the odor of the earth began to rise to everyone's nostrils as happens after sudden hot-day rainfalls, though not the fecund aroma that usually pleases the senses but a moldy stench that reminded the mourners that they were in duppy territory, after all.

And prime minister Roachford with his all-white attire and all-white wife is standing nearby on the paved path waiting until the two grave diggers bring wooden planks which they lay from the path to the grave so that Roachford and his wife can join the mourners at graveside.

Once there was a time when Roachford was young and popular and people would see it as his due that their prime minister shouldn't get his white shoes dirty. But those times are long gone.

So as Roachford and his wife step like tightrope walkers along the planks toward the graveside a man is heard to mutter that he don't know why them planks don't shift and capsize Roachford big, fat ass, he and that bony wife of his.

And a woman's voice is heard to chime in in agreement, "Deed."

Meanwhile the evening breeze is cool, barely ruffling the tree leaves. The sun now is a red, fiery ball hovering above the cemetery wall, the choirboys' voices trill in the duppy quiet of the churchyard against the hum of traffic and voices in the streets of the city, and Gladstone Augustus Belle is finally about to be laid to his rest.

But just as the bishop opens his Bible and is about to speak, across the graveyard comes a young woman sprinting and weaving among the gravestones.

All heads turn to watch this young woman in her calf-length denim skirt, black boots, cream T-shirt-looking blouse and with a black handbag clutched in her fist hurdling over graves in a rush toward the graveside funeral of Gladstone Augustus Belle.

"Who that?" a voice among the mourners is heard to say.

Andrea and Miss St. Clair can't believe their eyes. It's Yvette, their Yvette, the last person on this earth they expect to see today.

And for the first time public tears trickle down the cheeks of Andrea St. Clair, the mother of Gladstone Belle's first and only daughter (officially, that is), while everyone except the two St. Clair women are wondering who this young woman is who en even wearing decent funeral clothes.

Perhaps it would satisfy people's thirst for the dramatic to say that the funeral of Gladstone Augustus Belle erupted into a cataclysm of emotion and memorable incidents. But this wasn't the case.

Of course you had the usual: Miss Esther throwing her hands in the air and wailing and bawling, "Leh me go with him! Oh God, my son!"; Sonny-Boy clenching his jaws and standing with his arms straight down at his sides and leaving the women to restrain and console Miss Esther, figuring that women like these kinds of dramatics; Isamina Belle the widow dabbing her eyes with her handkerchief and sniffling ladylike while Debra, the old girlfriend, is wiping her eyes and honking into a kerchief while Carl hugs her shoulders.

And, according to Marie Antoinette LaSalle, Carl's dead grandfather is shaking his head and saying how Carl is a bewitched ass and a disgrace to the Bostick name and Carl's grandmother is contradicting her husband right there and saying how Carl is a sensitive, loving young man and, what wrong with that, eh? Tell me, Ignatius Bostick.

What wrong with that? And the grandfather sucking his teeth and saying how Carl is a blinking idiot who too soft with women and let a little pussy turn his head—the boy stupidy, that's what he is. Stupidy. And Carl's grandmother pushing up her mouth at this and refusing to speak to her husband long after the living people left the graveyard.

And Miss St. Clair and her daughter Andrea are hugging Yvette and trying to console the weeping young woman. Tears are coursing down Andrea's face, tears which she said later, "Sneak up on me like a thief in the night." And Manface the taxi driver is standing a little ways off from the mourners with his hands x-ed in front of him as though he's protecting his balls from attack, while he has a not-too-pleased expression on his face because bringing Andrea and her mother to the funeral meant losing paying passengers and he en even sure he going get anything for it because all Andrea doing is telling him take her this place and take her that place and letting him kiss her now and then but keeping her legs closed tight as a safe. He losing money and en even getting no pim. If the fellas ever know about this he would be the biggest laughing stock.

And Millie begins one big bawling again, keeping the most noise at the graveside, cow-bellowing, "Waaauugh!" and collapsing back onto the man behind her who's having a hard time keeping his balance supporting this hefty woman who he don't even know.

A mild problem did develop, though. So much rainwater had fallen into the grave in that brief downpour that it was half-filled, so that when the time came for the coffin to be lowered all of the bearers' eyes turned toward the undertaker and the one closest to him said, "What you think?"

The undertaker considered for a moment before saying, "Let him down," which seemed like a sacrilegious thing to do, not to mention the distinct probability that the coffin would float. So everybody around the grave is eyeing one another.

The bearers, in an okay-if-you-say-so manner, attach the canvas straps to the coffin, all except Sonny-Boy who says, "Wait!"

But Miss Esther touches his arm and says, "It's all right. He always liked water. Couldn't keep him from the sea when he was little."

Sonny-Boy looks at her like she is a blinking idiot, but he attaches his strap with a disgusted expression on his face and they lower the coffin into the grave while Miss Esther sobs behind the kerchief she's holding to her mouth and the bearers gaze down upon the floating coffin.

"Release the straps," the undertaker said.

They flick their wrists, unhooking the straps, and watch as Gladstone Belle sinks slowly to his rest below the surface of the muddy water.

Marie Antoinette LaSalle said later that the only reason why the coffin didn't float is because the two grandmothers sat on it and sank out of sight below the water with their grandson.

Meanwhile the bishop, who has reached the part where he is supposed to say dust-to-dust, ashes-to-ashes, gazes down at the mud with disgust before finally bending and scooping a handful of ooze and dribbling it, *plop! plop!,* onto the muddy water in the grave while Yvette the daughter stands next to her mother screaming, "Daddy! Daddy!" in such heart-rending bereavement that every woman's eyes overflow with tears and women's crying ripple in the air while the men all appear ready to lend consoling shoulders but are restrained only by the looks in their women's tear-filled but warning eyes.

Everyone agrees it was a good funeral.

THE PRIME MINISTER

His wife sitting beside him, quiet, hands in lap.

Slight, almost imperceptible bounce as the car follows its police escort—two motorcycle policemen—out of the cathedral gate. Windows rolled up, tinted, sealing street noises out, locking quiet in so that police sirens are mosquito whines as the car glides past traffic that pulls aside to give the prime minister's car the right of way.

Funerals. Depressing reminders of human mortality, your own inevitable end drawing closer. Increasingly funerals are those of friends, acquaintances, colleagues your own age. Like Gladstone.

Funny how death can mitigate enmity, dissipate ill feelings if only temporarily. Not that he ever felt ill will toward Gladstone. He raised the boy from nothing right up to deputy prime minister, trusting his judgment, his honesty, his loyalty.

Look how time flies, eh? Feels like yesterday when he, Anthony Roachford, came back home from university overseas decades ago with a degree in his hand, ideas filling his head, intentions to change things. Young and foolish. Full of enthusiasm. But you learn. Boy, do you learn.

People talk, but what do they know of the compromises that have to be made? It's easy to criticize. But what do they know of the choices faced? The threats and contingent "aid" from northern "powers?" How can they know about the inducements of power that shimmer before your eyes and distort your vision and can warp your blasted soul if you're not careful? He's seen it happen to the best-intentioned men. And women.

Returning home full of fire and zeal, champion of the man in the street, the masses, only to discover eventually that the masses are nothing but sheep and politics is the playground of the mediocre seeking power.

So there were times he felt like a colossus towering above the scrabbling lilliputians in his party but needing to have a few bright lights around him to counterbalance the burden of incompetents riding the PLP train to power. Hence Gladstone. Cabinet minister right from his first election. General right-hand man over the years. Handled every portfolio except finance. That was his, Anthony Roachford's, domain.

Too much of a tight ass sometimes, though. Thought he was the only man in the world with principles. But every man has his price. Give him an ambassadorship, let him cool off a little, enjoy the perks that accompany overseas assignments, then recall him back to the fold.

The Preacher, some of the fellas called him, laughing but not really laughing. Straight arrow, they said. Made enemies. Mostly because with his intelligence and personality he shone brightest in the party. But he knew how to handle Gladstone, knew his weakness for high living and prestige.

But lately he began acting strange, persistent. Asking questions, making insinuations bordering on accusations. But you've got to remember, the boy has a history of mental illness. Unstable.

Accepted his resignation but hoped he'd straighten himself out and come back.

Now he's gone. Hard to believe.

He remembers. Less than a year after he hired Gladstone as his assistant and a few weeks before he announced the date for the next elections, Gladstone in his office saying, I'm thinking of running against Sebastian. What d'you think?

What the hell could he think? The boy was a good assistant, true. But people didn't call the party the People's Lawyers' Party for nothing (no matter how much he stressed in his speeches, People's *Labor* Party). The opposition would make mincemeat of this youngster in the campaign. The whole country would hear how he dropped out of college because of a nervous breakdown, or worse (given the opposition's penchant for fabrication).

But one thing he's proud of: his political instinct. He gave Gladstone the okay and what happened? Gladstone won hands down. The only decision he had to make was which portfolio to give his young new colleague. (Funny how he's always thought of Gladstone as young though he was only five years his junior. The oldest person in the whole party was only thirty-five. Those were the days, eh? The young turks, they were called.)

Minister of Sports and Recreation, that was the first portfolio he gave Gladstone. An easy one. Low visibility, low budget. Give him a chance to get some experience, learn some of the ins and outs of government, of being in the cabinet.

Low visibility? Right away Gladstone embarked on a fitness crusade, heh heh heh. Jogging to work. In shorts, T-shirt, and sneakers. What a sight. Heh heh heh. People laughing. This was long before jogging became popular like it is now. What a sight. And a government minister at that.

I have to lead by example, Gladstone told him.

Meanwhile the other members in the party are saying, See what I tell you? That boy is a damn madman.

Perhaps. But five years later, by the time the next elections came around, Gladstone was almost as popular as he was, especially among the youth. Why? Because of things like persuading a department store to donate sports equipment to some villages, showing up at the smallest pastures in the most remote country villages to watch cricket and football games then firing a few drinks with the men at the rumshop afterward and driving off half-inebriated. Basic politics. A vote-getter right up to the most recent elections.

Rumors? What rumors? Let me state categorically that Gladstone resigned, and it was an amicable agreement, one that I came to with great reluctance, I must say.

Why did he resign? Why does anybody resign? He wanted to do other things. I tried to talk him out of it. But in the end it was his decision. And as a friend I had to respect that decision, much as I regretted it. But such is life. Anyway, I'm afraid this is all the time I have to spare. Other pressing matters to attend to, you do understand.

They say God protects infants and fools. Perhaps. But when the time came for divine intervention no one protected this fool from the police van at the door, detention, and eventual release into a pariah's solitude.

Curiosity kills.

Or as Yvette, Gladstone's daughter, said when I visited her at her grandmother's house up in the country the day after the funeral, "My personal feelings are none of your damn business," although she did allow me to hold on to her father's personal papers "till you're finished with them, seeing that you have them already," perhaps out of respect for her grandfather sitting across from me and who had given them to me in the first place.

III

THE WIDOW

On a morning when torrential showers began to pour just before daybreak, keeping everybody indoors as heavy rain always does, I found myself leaving my mother's warm house ("Look, where you going in all this rain, nuh?" she's asking me), tramping through puddles, sloshing through mud, bracing against wind that whipped my raincoat and lashed my face with stinging raindrops, heading toward Isamina's house where I rapped on the door which Isamina opened almost immediately dressed only in her robe and apparently unmindful of neighbors' prying eyes that one could sense behind the curtain of morning rain.

And as the wind whistled through the seams of Isamina's bedroom window and rain rivulets coursed down the windowpanes, I witnessed how powerful and perverse an aphrodisiac loss and grief can be (or so I construed it) as Isamina clutched and scratched, moaned and screamed above the sounds of the rainstorm, grimaced and thrashed her head on the pillow and rumpled the sheets with thrusts and gyrations.

But even as our hands slipped on our sweaty skins and the *thump-thumpthump* of the mattress rhythmically accompanied the gush and gurgle of rainwater flowing from the ridging gutter, a tear began to trickle from her closed eyelids and she murmured, "Oh God, I shouldn't be doing this. I shouldn't be doing this," sobbing as she said it. But even as she's uttering the words her thrusts become increasingly insistent, her breathing guttural and rasping, her hands clutching with passionate urgency, her cries loud and echoing among the rafters.

Later as I lay with one hand resting on her buttocks still slick with sweat, listening to the patter of the rain on the roof, the thought occurred to me that the rafters at which I was staring and which had just echoed with Isamina's cries were the same ones that had supported the rope that Gabby swung from while choking, kicking, and shitting his life away, taking his own life just weeks ago.

Or did he?

Booboo, who said he saw Henri boarding the schooner to go back home, says when he asked Henri where he was going, Henri began babbling about M'sieu Belle sitting up in his coffin and saying that nobody know the truth, and something about a bump on M'sieu Belle head and people not understanding what M'sieu Belle trying to tell them. Duppy don't start talking and bucking in their coffin for no reason, oui. That don't happen.

However Booboo and I both agreed that perhaps being around dead people too long had nudged Henri toward the edge of insanity and witnessing Gladstone Belle's bucking coffin was the final shove that sent him over the precipice.

But then I recalled Miss Esther mentioning a suspicious bump she saw on the back of her son's head and saying, "Gladstone en the kind of boy would kill himself. If he had so much troubles that he couldn't stand living, how come he never talk to me about it?" To which Sonny-Boy said, "Wake up and smell the coffee, Esther. Expect the boy to come running to you with his problems like a child?" a sentiment with which I inwardly agreed.

Whatever the case, the fact remains that there I was lying in Gladstone's bed next to Isamina whose skin was still slick with sweat, still sucking in gasping breaths and recovering from a bout of passionate sex. Which all goes to show how much like quicksand (or shit, for that matter) circumstances can be—you never know what you're stepping into until you find yourself deep in it.

When Isamina and I met, about a year before she became a widow, her marriage already was a rusty bucket whose bottom was not far from dropping out.

One day I called in sick and was lying on the beach listening to the swish of the waves lapping ashore when the faint aroma of perfume teased my senses.

I looked around and there was Isamina Belle wearing sunshades and a white bathing suit spreading a beach towel then sitting with her arms clasped around her knees and staring out to sea.

She must have felt me staring because she turned to look in my direction. I waved. Her return wave seemed more a polite acknowledgment than a friendly greeting, so to this day I don't know where I got the courage from to get up and walk over.

I'd known Isamina Springer from childhood, seeing her and her family driving by either to or from their house up on the hill above the Village.

The only time I could remember any of the Springers ever coming down to the Village was once when their satellite dish sailed on hurricane winds and crashed like a flying saucer in the middle of the pasture. After the storm, Mr. Springer and two men came in a truck and picked up the twisted dish while Isamina and her brother sat in the cab of the truck looking on. I was little then.

When she married Gabby and moved into the Village to live in the house Gabby had built on the land his grandmother left for him, most people, and I for one, expected a rude and standoffish neighbor. But over the years she remained polite, though aloof. She would speak pleasantly enough, hello, good morning, but never went beyond that.

So I can't say what got into me that day on the beach.

It was the middle of the week, the beach almost deserted except for a few boys playing in the waves a little ways off, probably playing truant from school.

"Hello," I said.

She looked up at me standing in front of her. "Hello," she said, with her big eyes looking into mine and her face bearing a friendly smile. So I'm trying to be cool though my heart is thumping and my knees are so liquefied that my legs no longer feel like flesh and bone but wobbly rubber. "Mind if I join you?" I managed to say.

She shrugged and made a gesture with her hand that I translated as, If you want to siddown, siddown. This is a public beach. Which of course she would never say, refined as she was in her speech (although she does slip occasionally when angry or excited), as I came to learn that day as she and I became lost in conversation.

Before we knew it the sun was hovering over the horizon and shadows stretched across the sand.

"My. Look how time has flown," she said and stood up and began folding her beach towel. "Gladstone must be home by now." After she gathered all of her things she said, "Well, it's been nice talking to you."

I managed to mumble something like, "Same here" and we said our good-byes, me hopping onto my bicycle and riding home, she driving off in her little red sports car.

Next day she was there again. And so was I after having called in sick the second day running, figuring that as a competent and conscientious, but hardly indispensable schoolteacher, I might as well put my accumulated sick days to good use.

Ever since childhood I've found that people tend to trust me with their most intimate secrets. Perhaps I've been endowed with a gift of empathy, or as my mother said once, "I don't know why people always telling you their business. They think you care 'bout them but they don't know no better otherwise they would keep their business to themselves." But then another time she says, "Why you don't start charging? You would make a lot of money." But whatever my gift may be, it's a two-edged sword because after people lay their burdens on my shoulders resentment often follows what they perhaps perceive as their weakness and my strength.

But none of this was on my mind when on our second meeting Isamina began to unburden on me the anguish she felt about the state her marriage was in: she and Gladstone weren't getting along, she said; she felt so lonely sometimes because her husband didn't talk to her anymore—too wrapped up in his work, too wrapped up in himself; mind you, she said, he always was like that but he was getting worse, so much so that sometimes she got so depressed she felt like killing herself, having no one to talk to, nobody to turn to.

"I feel so lonely," she said.

And there on the beach kneeling before her with my buttocks resting on my heels, she no longer was the Springer girl I'd known or Gladstone Belle's wife but an attractive woman sitting on the beach with her arms clasped around her legs and her chin on her knees.

I looked around, saw no one in sight, and as the waves swished ashore only feet away and the sun's heat warmed my shoulders I savored the softness of her skin against my lips and inhaled the aroma of her breath.

And so it began.

Over the months we would meet at secluded beaches or I'd catch a bus to some remote rural region where she would be waiting in her little red car and we would lie on a blanket beneath shaded trees, on a precipice high above pounding surf, in a lonely cart road between fields of canes, once even in the balcony of a theater on a warm afternoon in a distant town.

And as the weeks went by and we became increasingly brazen I would visit her on nights when Gladstone was away and her cries would echo in the closed house.

But even in the midst of all this bliss I knew my joy was only temporary, least of all because for one thing here I was, a mere elementary schoolteacher born, bred, and raised in the village, now intimate friends with the girl I knew as Isamina Springer, now Isamina Belle: wife of the deputy prime minister; daughter of an architect well known in social and political circles; born into a family that on her mother's side owned a plantation/sugar factory/rum distillery allegedly bequeathed generations ago to the offspring of a slave-owner/slave liaison; member of a class that takes its privileges for granted—the privilege of attending the right schools; the privilege of knowing people who have connections; the privilege of her family name.

And who ever heard about my family's name, Skeete? Just the sound of it is like a blooming joke. Skeete. My father a man who labored in a cement factory till he coughed blood all over his pajamas in a hospital bed and died; my mother a shop attendant till the owner sold his shops and opened a supermarket, putting her out of a job with two weeks pay to sustain her for the remainder of her life.

But as I said this was the least reason of all. Because another factor had begun to insinuate itself within our relationship as with each buried emotion and memory divulged in the weakness of her grief came a growing and noticeable detachment. Eyes that once were pools of warmth now regarded me with growing detachment and I became increasingly aware that I was merely a salve used to ease the pain of her broken marriage, a band-aid no longer needed and about to be discarded.

And so I wondered if perhaps hidden behind all the unspoken words was the truth that her marriage had foundered on her husband's awareness that he too had served a similar purpose, perhaps as the personification of some social rebellion of hers, even though eventually he had clawed his way up to stand beside her on her rung of the social ladder.

But who knows? I might be wrong. Because the only evidence I had that Gladstone Belle ever pondered on such things was the following poem, which I may have misconstrued entirely.

"Evergreen"
by Gladstone Belle

Towering umbrella
dark-green canopy
filtering sunrays through
whispering leaves
sunspots sparkling
on smooth-barked branches
that bend
or break and
fall to dry earth,
tentacle roots
and mushroom shoots or
duppy parasols.

Ancestral giant
in sun and rain
sharing the pain
and joys of
growing boys their
tree house toys of
flystick, guttaperk
from supple or fork-fingered limbs
amputated.

Dead giant
erased from landscape leveled
for lying lawyers, uncivil servants
gucci girls and
bentley boys'
adult toys
imported.

That morning lying next to her, skin touching skin, I asked with dryness in my mouth and trepidation in my chest, "What about us, Isamina?"

My heart thumped for each second she delayed her answer.

Then finally she said, "I don't know."

And lying there in the bed with the staccato patter of the raindrops making music on the roof and the wind easing a slight chill into the bedroom, with our skins still touching, I felt a chasm deep and dark separating us, a divide over which I dared not leap for fear of plunging into the deepest abyss.

SONNY-BOY & ESTHER

It's a week after the funeral of Gladstone Augustus Belle and Sonny-Boy and Miss Esther are sitting at the dining table with the lamp flickering and sputtering in the draft that is sneaking into the house, escaping from the high winds gusting outside.

Over the past couple days Miss Esther has begun to notice a gradual change occurring in Sonny-Boy.

When they got back home from the funeral dusk was settling. They changed out of their good clothes and Miss Esther asked Sonny-Boy, "You want some tea?"

They sat sipping their hot cocoa with the silence of the house heavy around them.

When Sonny-Boy finished he got up and said, "I going down by the shop. I'll be back later." As he explained when he got back, he couldn't stand the silence in the house and she hadn't wanted a wake. So that night he walked down to the rumshop to fire a few grogs with the fellas—his way of trying to forget his grief for a little while.

When he came in she was still up and he was in a more talkative mood so they sat and talked rambling talk about nothing in particular. Village gossip, mostly. Anything to stave off the bereavement that was like wild dogs howling at their minds.

Next night was the same, and the next, till she began to feel comfortable with him again, almost like before he left all those years ago.

So that whole week she would wait up for him at night, pretending to be staying up late because of something she had to do—a dress to sew; a sock to darn; rice to pick—or acting as if she fell asleep in the chair and woke up when she heard him coming in the door.

And every night it was the same thing: him asking her, "You up?" and she making excuse like, "Oh, I was just hemming this old dress" or "I was here reading the Bible and dropped fast asleep."

And they would sit, she in her rocking chair, he in a chair at the dining table, talking, their voices humming and calming in the night.

But now almost two weeks have gone by and Sonny-Boy will be leaving in two days. And over the past few nights it is as if he ran out of words to say and she would find herself doing most of the talking: about who living with who; whose little boy is a vagabond that en going turn out to nothing; and you remember so-and-so who used to live such-and-such a place? And in the silence in between she would feel him staring at her as she rocked in her chair. Like tonight.

But tonight she can't push back no more the thought that she's been having to fight harder and harder to lock in the back of her mind: only two days to go before he leave again, this time for good. The only reason he came back was for their son's funeral. And he en coming back again because he en the type to come home for vacation. He didn't do it when he was young and strong so she know he won't be doing it now in his old age.

When he left the first time, the understanding was that he would only go and make some money and come back once Gladstone was through school. But one day she realized all of a sudden that ten years had gone by and he had sent for Gladstone to join him and she might never set eyes on either one of them again (he'd asked her to come up along with Gladstone, but she never had any feeling to go Away so she said no, she would stay and hold onto the property till they came back).

It is one thing not to have anybody when you're young and strong. You can get by with your friends and by keeping yourself occupied. But then one day it hit you that your friends down to a few—most of them move away or dead. So you stop going to funerals because the constant grief and depression is too much to bear, not to mention the evidence of your own mortality. And it is only you waking up in your house every morning with not a chick nor child to work for or care for or keep your company, and you find yourself eating by yourself and sleeping by yourself and getting old in a empty house and a empty bed. And it en no fun because everybody need somebody to be comfortable with in their old age.

And the last few days with Sonny-Boy really make her realize what a difference it is to have somebody to share your evening years with.

But soon she going be alone again. It would've been better if he'd never come back at all.

A few days ago she was sitting in her rocking chair staring at her fowls pecking in the yard when she heard him come up behind her and she asked him without turning around, "You not going down by the shop today?"

He said no, he feel like staying home. Then after a pause he ask her, "What you think about coming back to America with me, Ess?"

She waited a little bit before answering, not because she had to think about the answer but because she didn't want to answer too quick and give him the feeling that he was the reason why she was refusing.

Finally she said, "I too old to be going anywhere now, Harold. To besides, you know I never fancy going Away, not before Gladstone went, and even less since he come back and tell me how it is over there. That en no place especially for a old woman like me."

And she can hear the irritation in his voice when he saying, "You not old. You only *think* you old. And you *acting* old. At your age people now starting to enjoy life."

"That is some people," she saying. And she want to tell him he old too but decide not to, because she notice how touchy he is about that subject. Second day he come back and he in the yard bathing, she make a little joke with him about the gray hair on his chest making him look like a old billy goat and he snap at her, telling her about she en no young yam either and about how he in better shape than men half his age. As if that was the point.

Although one morning after she left the bedroom she hear something rattling and peep in the bedroom and see him taking pills out of three vials and cupping them in his hand and then going at the back window with a cup of water and slipping the pills in his mouth and pretending to be gargling, like he think he can hide anything from her in her own house.

Away en good for him either, it seem.

All of a sudden as all this going through her mind she hear him say, "You know Ess, getting old in America en easy."

And she was getting ready to snap back with some joke about how she thought he wasn't old, that he was fitter than men half his age.

But the seriousness in his voice stop her and all she said was, "Yes?" waiting to hear him say, perhaps, that when he go back he going settle his business and come back home.

She want to ask him, why you don't come back here and live comfortable? He en got chick nor child to support. Why he killing himself in that place? Why he don't come home?

Because she can see how much he enjoy going down by the shop and sitting down on a bench with Gilbert and the rest of men, idling and drinking and arguing politics and cricket and playing dominoes. And when he come home his food ready and his clothes stiff-starch-and-iron and he and she talking easy like old friends. They even loving up again, something she never think would ever happen to her again, and something he *say* he never do all the years he was in Away (she know him better than to believe this but she let it pass).

But it en her place to tell him all of this. He might think she trying to tell him what to do and do the exact opposite.

And Sonny-Boy looking at her rocking back and forth in that old rocking chair like she en got a care in the world and he thinking that she so settled in her ways and comfortable in what she keep calling her "old age" that here he is throwing out a hint and almost begging her if he can come back home and what she doing, eh? What she doing? Rocking away like she couldn't care if he live or die.

Boy, ain't it funny? Ain't it gad daim funny? When he first come back and the place looked so gad daim small he was saying he could never come back here to live. But over the past week and a half he find himself easing back into life around here. Although the fellas still treating him like he is a visitor and not one of them. But that will pass, he figure.

But Esther? He can't understand her. One minute they're comfortable with one another, fitting one another like a pair of old shoes and it is almost as if twenty-odd years didn't pass between them, next minute she like she is now: like she don't care if he stay or leave, if he live or die.

A few days later when Miss Esther got back home from taking Sonny-Boy to the airport, she sat down in her rocking chair and felt the tears welling up warm behind her eyes and trickling down her cheeks. For days she could feel the water building up behind her eyes.

Now alone in her house the dam breaking and she wiping her eyes with the hem of her dress.

And as the plane began climbing after takeoff Sonny-Boy gazed through the window at the housetops, roads and greenery of a land he knew he would never see again. He could understand why Esther didn't want him back. After all these years she was comfortable. The last couple weeks they spent together was like a vacation. But vacations must come to an end. She didn't want a man in her house, even if it was the only man she lived with and that helped her bring their son into the world. She was accustomed to living by herself and she didn't want him coming back and changing it.

Just then through the plane window he saw the town below and he looked hard to see if he could make out the cathedral graveyard where his son was buried, but he couldn't.

A few weeks later I received a letter from him. And from what I knew of Sonny-Boy from the few conversations I'd had with him I realized how difficult it must have been for him to put his personal thoughts and feelings in a letter. Just writing the letter in itself must have been difficult. Sonny-Boy was not what people would call an educated man.

"Dear teacher," the letter began,

"I hope this letter find you as it left me. How are you? I hope your mother is hearty . . ." and so on, right up to his final thoughts as his plane climbed and gave him his final view of his country.

Miss Esther wept when she read the letter she received from his lawyer that read, "Dear Mrs. Belle, I regret to inform you . . ." etc., etc.

He had left everything for her in his will and the lawyer would be "forwarding the proceeds" as soon as matters were "expedited."

But she didn't need money. With her little piece of land and the little old-age pension she was getting from the government she could manage. She wouldn't suffer. What she really wanted was what she had the few days he was there in their house: him walking around the place sometimes with no shirt on, so that she had to be constantly telling him put on a shirt so he don't catch a cold; him drinking his cocoa first thing in the morning and eating the bakes she fry, saying how he en had bakes since he been to America; him coming home at night sometimes half-drunk but sitting down in a chair at the dining table and talking till both of them start to nod off while the lamp casting flickering shadows on the house walls and everything outside gone asleep except for some mangy stray dog barking in the night.

She en know what he went back for. That en no place for anybody to live. And it en no place for anybody to die either, to be buried among strangers and not close to your family where you belong. She'll never be able to visit his grave every now and then and keep it clear of weeds and talk to him in the silence of the graveyard. She'll never be able to cut flowers from her flower garden and carry for him to smell.

So what she have to look forward to now for the rest of her life? A lonely life with no husband nor child. That en no way to live your last days.

A week later Miss Esther was dead.

Her next-door neighbor, Miss Babb, noticing that a whole day went by with Miss Esther's windows closed, then waking up the next morning and seeing Miss Esther's house still closed up, decided to go over and try to see if she could get in to see if something was wrong.

First she knocked. No answer.

After pulling and tugging she managed to get the door opened.

When she walked in the bedroom first thing she saw was Miss Esther lying in her bed with her clothes on, no nightgown, her arms folded, her Bible on her chest.

The same day the Village is buzzing with the news that Miss Esther dropped dead, the front-page headline of the newspaper is blaring, MAN SLAIN IN POLICE SHOOTOUT. According to the article, police sources revealed that one Sylvester Brown, alias Peewee, opened fire on the police when they came to his house to arrest him for the murder of former minister of education, Gladstone Augustus Belle. Police returned fire and Sylvester "Peewee" Brown was slain in the ensuing gun battle.

When I read the article and remarked to my mother that it looked like Gabby hadn't committed suicide after all and what a shame it was that Miss Esther didn't live to find this out, my mother looked at me as though she was privy to some information that was barred to a mere mortal like me and she said in that cryptic tone she sometimes uses, "She know what happen. She and Sonny-Boy know."

I shrugged.

The day after Peewee was dispatched to hell in the shootout, the commissioner of police called a press conference to announce that, contrary to certain rumors that had begun to circulate, the former deputy prime minister's killing was an individual act of violence apparently resulting from an attempt at burglary.

This struck everybody as strange. Hanging was an odd way of silencing somebody who caught you breaking into their house. Shooting, yes. Stabbing, yes. But hanging? Didn't make sense.

So the police commissioner's press conference only stoked people's curiosity and fueled more rumors.

But in the end, no one knows why Peewee killed the former deputy prime minister, or if in fact he did. Probably never will because, as Sergeant Straker said when I asked him if he believed the official Peewee story, "I en no storybook detective and life en no Hollywood movie. And is soon time for me to retire with my pension. If I was you I would keep my questions to myself."

So, as I began this story by saying, everyone had an opinion ranging from the reasonable to the ridiculous.

Time, however, has a way of dulling people's interest. So as the weeks and months passed, Gladstone Belle faded into the background of people's memories. But such is human life: a comet blazing briefly, no matter how bright its glow, then vanishing.

So, soon Gladstone will remain alive only in the memories of his daughter and his wife, a daughter who returned to America less than a week after his funeral and a wife who had packed her things to leave on the same day he died, a daughter who told me the day after the funeral, "My life and my relationship with my father is none of your damn business" and wanting to know how the hell did I get hold of her father's personal papers (which he'd left for her) and why was I peeking into the privacy of her father's life and other people's too.

"This was your grandfather's idea," I said, bending the truth a little, embellishing on the conversation Sonny-Boy and I had when he gave me his son's journals.

After hesitating a while she finally said, "Well, if he gave you permission, I won't go against his wishes. But they're mine. Make sure you send them to me as soon as you're finished with them." I agreed.

And I have finished. And perhaps at least Gladstone will not only be an evanescent memory but one eternalized by words of recollection garnered from family and acquaintances, his own words culled from his journals and poems, as well as words of mine of rare license to flavor the tale and fill censored voids.

Rest in peace, Gladstone Augustus Belle.